THE CAMDEN KILLER

JACQUELINE BEARD

Vinci Books

vinci-books.com

Published by Vinci Books Ltd in 2024

1

Copyright © Jacqueline Beard 2024

The author has asserted their moral right to be identified as the author of this work in accordance with the Copyright, Designs and Patents Act 1988. This work is a work of fiction. Names, characters, places and incidents are the product of the author's imagination or are used fictitiously. Any resemblance to actual persons, living or dead, places and incidents is entirely coincidental.

All rights reserved. No part of this publication may be copied, reproduced, distributed, stored in any retrieval system, or transmitted in any form or by any means, including photocopying, recording, or other electronic or mechanical methods, nor used as a source for any form of machine learning including AI datasets, without the prior written permission of the publisher.

The publisher and the author have made every effort to obtain permissions for any third party material used in this book and to comply with copyright law. Any queries in this respect should be brought to the attention of the publisher and any omissions will be corrected in future editions.

A CIP catalogue record for this book is available from the British Library.

Paperback ISBN: 9781036701437

Printed and bound in Great Britain by Clays Ltd, Elcograf S.p.A.

By Jacqueline Beard

The Lawrence Harpham Murder Mysteries

The Fressingfield Witch
The Ripper Deception
The Scole Confession
The Felsham Affair
The Moving Stone
The Maleficent Maid
The Disappearing Doctor
The Camden Killer
Shadow Over Malvern

The Denman & Tallis Cotswold Crime Thrillers

The Girl in Flat Three
You'll Never Escape Me

The Constance Maxwell Dreamwalker Mysteries

The Cornish Widow
The Croydon Enigma
The Poisoned Partridge
The Cheltenham Torso

Prologue

She tilted her head, exposing a smooth, pale neck. Excitement flared inside me, and I knew I would hold my resolve. Her gloved hand carelessly stroked a sinew, her life force throbbing beneath. It would soon be mine. She stood casually against the bar, glass in hand, elbow on the sticky counter, conversing in Yiddish with her moon-faced friend. I did not understand what passed between them, but the woman reached into her pocket and produced a handful of gold and silver coins. She was not penniless as she'd led me to believe, and for a moment, I wondered whether to abort my task. Why would she take a stranger home if not for the money?

I sipped from the foul-tasting liquor I'd selected on a whim from the barman and weighed the risk against the potential reward until an unwanted presence interrupted my musings.

"Care for some company?" asked a whiskered man, not waiting for my response. He slumped on the stool beside me and I cast an irritated glance his way. He returned it benignly, huffing a sigh laced with the smell of rotting teeth and alcohol.

"She's a bit of raspberry," he said.

"Who?"

The man nodded, snorting a dewdrop from his nose. It splashed onto the grimy wooden table, and he rubbed it away with a patched sleeve. My stomach churned.

"Dora. A sight more attractive than the plain Jane she's speaking to."

He nodded to the dumpy woman by her side, smirking as he eyed her broad figure, legs like tree trunks beneath an ill-fitting dress.

"If you say so."

"Both dolly mops," he continued. "But Dora is worth twice as much as the other."

"They are young ladies, not commodities."

The man drew himself up, hands on his hips. "I beg to differ."

"I'm not interested."

"Oh, but you are. You've been watching Dora since you arrived."

"Go away," I said, recoiling from the stench of his body odour as the man slid his hand inside his coat and scratched his armpit.

"You're not very friendly," he replied, sneering beneath hooded eyelids.

I reached into my pocket and felt for my lowest denomination coin. "Take this. Buy yourself a drink and leave me alone."

His bloodshot eyes glinted as he held out a scrawny hand. I dropped the coin in his palm. He raised one eyebrow then the other as if to encourage a further donation. I ignored him.

"Whatever you say, gov. Thanks a bunch."

The man shambled off, propping himself against the bar, temporarily blocking my view of the women. I shuffled left and took another stool, staring through the smoky tavern and contemplating my next move. I would do it soon. Time was of the essence.

The man wobbled to the far end of the room, another drink now in hand. I drained my glass, gagging at the taste, and occupied the space he'd left. The woman stopped talking and stared at me, the larger one smiling as she played with her high-necked lace collar. She was flirting but I didn't want her. Too large, too pasty, and now I was closer, too much facial hair.

"Can I buy you ladies a drink?"

They exchanged glances, immediately recognising me as a good prospect. The barman poured our drinks, and I sipped mine slowly as they clinked glasses and noisily resumed their discussion in a language I did not understand. I knew Dora spoke English, but her friend did not. I realised I must separate them or I'd lose my opportunity, but how? Then nature intervened, and the larger woman pointed towards a gaudy, red-painted door. Dora nodded. I took immediate advantage of her friend's visit to the privy.

"Rotten weather," I said.

"Better than June." Her heavily accented voice was deeper than I'd expected. Polish, perhaps, undoubtedly Jewish.

"Ah, well. Anything is in an improvement on that."

She referred to storm Ulysses and a brutal battering from the worst winds in living memory. I sympathised. I'd bunkered down during the storm and barely left my lodgings. Not so easy when your job is on the streets. She would have been out in it, however uncomfortable.

"I haven't seen you here before."

"It's not my usual drinking abode."

"What brings you to these parts?"

"Well, a man has certain needs."

"I can help you with those."

She stared straight at me with sympathetic, velvety brown eyes and for a moment, I was almost sorry that the light would soon leave them.

"Where?"

"Up to you?"

"Not outside."

"My place then. I must tell Milka."

"I'll wait." We finished our drinks silently, Dora flashing the occasional smile while the room buzzed with chatter. A man stood, drunkenly lurched forward, and fell onto a chair which crumpled beneath his weight. Silence briefly descended, and then the drinking resumed. Nobody assisted him. Nobody cared. Milka strode towards us, barely acknowledging the unconscious man.

Dora jabbered a few words in Yiddish. Milka scowled and uttered more sharp-edged consonants, a nod, then a brief shoulder touch before wandering off without looking at me.

"Ready?"

We walked out together, proceeding down the Tottenham Court Road. I raised my collar. The wind was still high, and a scattering of swirling snowflakes settled on our shoulders. We did not converse. There was nothing to say. We eventually arrived outside a red brick townhouse on Whitfield Street with a short flight of steps leading to the raised ground floor.

Dora fumbled for her key. It slipped and I heard a tinkling sound against the pathway as it fell. She scrabbled in the darkness without success. I lit a match, and she thanked me as her hand closed over the cold metal. The door opened and we entered. All was quiet, the other tenants safely in their rooms. Dora led and I trailed behind her.

"Shall I light the fire?"

"Yes."

I examined the room, noting with satisfaction the gas lamps on the wall. Good lighting was important for setting the mood.

Dora made the fire, prodding at the kindling with a rusty poker. It spluttered to life, and only then did she remove her shawl, exposing, once again, her soft, swan-like neck. I felt a stirring and reminded myself of my purpose. I must not get distracted with earthly desires.

Dora kicked off her shoes, revealing dirty stockings with holes. That wouldn't do, or would it? The contrast of her perfectly white skin against the reality of her condition created an appealing vision. But no. I preferred the idea of Dora in all her naked glory.

"Scuse the draught," she said, gesturing to a pile of glass shards beneath a hastily patched window. What had she used to fix it? The tatty rags looked like underwear.

"No matter."

"Come on then. Don't be shy."

Dora patted her blanketed bed and smiled coquettishly. I glanced at the pile of coins on her bedside table. Why was she doing this if money was no object?

My hands reached for my pocketknife but I thought the better of it. I'd already seen something I could safely leave behind. I accepted Dora's invitation and settled beside her. She placed an icy hand on my trousers and squeezed my manhood. No finesse.

"Take your clothes off."

Dora obliged, stripping off her dress and stays until only clad in a shift. I watched her well-honed performance as the fire spat and crackled.

"How much?"

Dora named her price. Not unreasonable.

"For services rendered."

"Then get on with it."

Her momentary irritation gave me the impetus I needed.

"Lie down," I commanded before reaching for my pocket-handkerchief.

She lay there, voluptuously running her hands through her dark brown hair. Instinctively, I placed mine around her neck and pressed hard. Much too hard. She screamed, eyes bulging, and I knew I must commit to my plan. I grabbed a large glass shard with my handkerchief and set about my task.

Dora did not die easily. She screamed once, thrashed about the bed as blood welled from the wound in her neck, then fell to the floor with a bump, gasping long, drawn breaths.

I watched, intrigued. It was everything I had hoped for and more. Crimson blood pumping from her artery, spewing over a pristine white petticoat. She gurgled. I watched. She clutched her throat, those brown eyes anguished, pleading with me to help her. But I used my time to note every detail of her demise, the way her eyes fluttered, her shuddering frame, rasping breaths, bubbles of sputum glistening in the jagged wound. Her hands were around her throat now, bitten fingernails streaked with blood, trembling hands trying to staunch the flow, a futile effort to prolong her life for a few more minutes.

Dora Kiernicke expired on the cold floorboards of her ground-floor bedroom. But that wasn't the plan. I'd steered clear of her thrashing body and my clothes were still pristine, which is how they would remain. I stripped and dropped my garments by the door, away from the blood. Then I jammed my hands into the tightly fitting gloves she'd obligingly removed and left hanging on the bedstead. Thus protected, I heaved her still-warm body onto the bed, removed her shift and took in every aspect of her now naked body. Her tongue lolled uselessly from her mouth, spoiling the magnificent sight. I tossed the glass shard to one side and fixed my handkerchief over her face, securing it with a knot. Still not right. Work to do.

I placed her hands on her breast. Save for the handkerchief and the gash in her throat, Dora looked angelic. I pushed her hands together in a semblance of prayer. They flopped back again. Not good enough. I tried once more. Still no success, so I gazed around the shabby room with its paucity of furniture, looking for inspiration. There was nothing in the wardrobe, and the drawers were almost empty. But frayed cords swayed beside the curtains. Dora must have used them as tiebacks during the day. They would do. I took one, wound it around her wrists, and set her hands together. It worked like a dream. Dora was now in prayer. Then I tidied the room, hung up her clothes, placed her boots by the bedside, dressed myself and removed the gloves. A tidy job, well done.

Dora lay there in perfect repose while I examined her body from every aspect, prowling the room like a hungry tiger seeking the right vantage point. I knew I must remember the scene and store it in my mind's eye forever. I inhaled the aroma of burning wood, the dry metallic smell of blood against Dora's pungent perfume. Flicking my tongue out, I tasted the air and gently ran a hand over the rough blanket, recoiling at the discomforting cheap, spiky fibres that made my fingers tingle. But details mattered. Then, in one last gesture of respect, I drew the blanket over her naked body and pulled it to her chin. Dora was dead, but I would never forget her. I unlatched the door and slunk into the night.

Chapter One

AN UNWELCOME VISITOR

Thursday, November 18, 1909, Bath Street, Cheltenham

"Well, Lawrence. What do you think?"

Lawrence Harpham stood with his head at an awkward angle, wearing a pained expression as he surveyed the easel before him.

"What is it?"

Violet scowled. "I think it's fairly obvious."

"Not to me."

"Oh, come now, Lawrence. Don't be difficult."

Lawrence sighed, stepped a few paces back, and looked again.

"Pittville Park?" he asked hopefully. Violet beamed.

"Exactly," she said. "Now, that wasn't so hard, was it?"

"No, Violet."

"And you'll take it to the framer on Friday?"

"If I must. Why can't you do it?"

"I'm seeing Miss Faithful at the girl's school."

"Good point. So you are."

"Unless you'd like to come?"

"No. I'm sure you'll create a better impression than me."

"I'll need to if Daisy is to visit the Ashmolean next week with the other girls. Her form teacher doesn't want to take her."

"I don't blame her. Our daughter is a little monster."

"That's a fine thing to say about your child."

"Then she shouldn't have sewn matron's sleeves up. Honestly, Violet, Daisy should be past all this now. She's thirteen, for goodness' sake."

"Daisy has an unusual sense of humour."

"You mean she's immature and lacking good manners."

"Lawrence."

"Don't sound so shocked. Look at this." Lawrence flung a desk drawer open and pointed to the skeleton of a long-dead pigeon.

"Lawrence, it's revolting. Why have you put it there?"

"I haven't. I found it in my desk this morning."

"What makes you think Daisy did it?"

"She's studying science, isn't she? And who else could it be? The housemaid? No. It's our dear girl up to her tricks again, and it really must stop."

"What's wrong, Lawrence?" asked Violet.

"Nothing."

"You're tetchy. I know Daisy tries your patience but there's no need for this outburst. What's upsetting you?"

"I don't know. Boredom, I suppose. Being a wealthy man of leisure is not in my nature. I should be out there pounding the pavements and contributing something useful to society."

"You decided to retire. You could have kept our business going in Cheltenham."

"I couldn't face it."

"Then that's your choice. You must make the best of things as I have."

"But you're busy with your hobbies," said Lawrence, gesturing towards the easel.

"Find some of your own."

"Like what?"

"Well, you always enjoyed carpentry."

Lawrence grimaced and raised his scarred left hand.

"Fine. Then draw, play golf or take up crown green bowling. They have a lovely pitch in the Winter Gardens."

"I might if I were in my eighties."

Violet sighed. "What do you suggest?"

"I wish we were still in Bury. I miss our house and the poky little office in The Butter Market."

"So do I. But we must live with the consequences of our decision."

"If only we'd never met Crossley, we'd still be in Bury now."

"We did what was best for Daisy. We were jolly lucky to get to her before he did. I dread to think what harm she'd have come to if Crossley had reached her first."

"Still, it was a lot to give up."

"I know, Lawrence. But would you rather live in fear like Michael or anonymously as we do?"

"Don't fool yourself, Violet. Crossley could find us at the drop of a hat if he chose to. We might be out of the way, but we are far from safe."

"But Daisy could hardly be in a better place. The teaching staff already care for royalty and heiresses. They'll keep Daisy well protected at The Girls' College."

"I know. But it won't be long before she rails against it. Daisy is wilful and keen for her independence. She keeps asking to go out alone at the weekend, and it's all I can do to stop her."

"We'll make it work, Lawrence. What's the alternative, after all?"

"To live like Michael with a retinue of burly groundsmen ready to swoop on any unsuspecting visitor."

"Very amusing."

"And I have local news."

"I know what you're going to say."

"No, you don't."

"You ran into Loveday Melcham again."

"No. That's not it."

"What then?"

"I saw Tom Melcham at the club. Loveday has pushed him too far this time and he's filing for a divorce."

"How surprising. I thought he'd try to avoid a scandal at all costs."

"Not now, she's openly seeing other men."

Violet raised an eyebrow. "Only a rumour, I thought."

"So did Tom until he ran into a half-dressed chap in his orangery. He chased him off with a twelve-bore, and that's not the worst of it."

"I won't ask what Tom was doing with a shotgun in a townhouse."

"Protecting his assets, presumably. Anyway, Loveday tried to deny it, made out it was all a mistake, but Tom won't be a cuckold in his own home. He's changed half the locks in the house, and they're currently living on separate floors."

"That will cost him a pretty penny."

"He's past caring and happy to live in a flat for the rest of his life if that's what it takes to get rid of her."

"How sad," said Violet, resting her head on Lawrence's

shoulder. He placed a hand beneath her chin and gently tipped her face, brushing his lips against hers.

"Don't worry. I'm not planning anything similar."

"I should think not," laughed Violet. "But you said that's not the worst of it. What did you mean?"

"Only that Loveday has a habit of attaching herself to me if there are no better prospects."

"What about this chap of hers?"

"He won't come near her now. Tom Melcham put the fear of God into the poor fellow."

"Hmm. Well, Loveday has not been too much of a nuisance these last four years. Just don't wear your special cologne."

"I can't. I've run out."

"I'm sure your finances will run to another bottle or two."

"It's not so easy. I bought the cologne in Bond Street. I must write to the shop keeper and ask him to put a bottle in the post."

"Bond Street? Oh, excellent. That could tie in rather nicely."

"With what?"

Violet took Lawrence's hands and gazed up at him. "I'd like to go to London."

"God no, Awful place. Out of the question. And why would you?"

"There's a rather interesting art exhibition in Camden next week. I'd love to attend."

Lawrence pulled away and walked to the window, gazing towards Cambray Baptist Church. "But what about Crossley?"

"He's halfway to Algiers."

"Are you sure?"

"Quite sure. I telephoned Frank yesterday."

"You've been planning this for a while then?"

"Only a few days. I knew we couldn't risk it if Crossley were in London. And I haven't spoken with Frank since he moved to Broughton. I thought it worth a phone call for old times' sake as much as anything."

"At some risk to your reputation."

"Stop it, Lawrence. Frank Podmore is my friend. Who he falls in love with is his business, regardless of gender."

"I think you'll find his interests lie in baser things than love."

"You shouldn't listen to rumours. I'm happily ignorant of the situation and wouldn't dream of asking Frank about his personal life."

"Well, I have it on good authority that his wife left him because…"

"Enough."

"Fine. Have it your way. But you're certain that Crossley is out of the way?"

"Completely. I wouldn't leave Daisy under any other circumstance."

"Leave Daisy? No. She must come too. Either that, or you go alone, and I'll stay here."

"That's another reason for speaking to Miss Faithful. Daisy can board for a while."

"I'm not keen, Violet. Why don't you go alone?"

"Because I'd like you to come with me. I thought we could take a short break, see the sights, relax a little. We've only ever visited London while working. There's a lot to do, and money is no object. Let's enjoy ourselves for once."

"But London," Lawrence grumbled. "Wouldn't you rather visit the countryside?"

"No. I'd like to see the exhibition and spend some leisure

time with my husband before we get too old and jaded to bother."

"On one condition."

"Name it."

"We take Daisy."

"No. Daisy must sit an important test next week, which could determine her future schooling. I completely trust Miss Faithful. And we can't live this strange half-life forever."

"We won't. It's only risky while Daisy is a child."

"Then the older she gets, the safer she is."

"Oh, Violet. You're the intelligent one. I've never said this, but surely you know. The older Daisy gets, the less time Crossley has."

Violet's face paled. "I don't understand why he wants her."

"He doesn't specifically. But when we cost him William and Millicent, he vowed we would pay for it with our children."

"Luna too?"

"Possibly more so. I don't know how Michael sleeps at night."

"The metal gates and guard dogs probably help. But this shouldn't stop us travelling when Crossley is abroad."

"I can't help being cautious."

"Even though Daisy tries your patience daily?"

Lawrence smiled. "My daughter is a minx, but I still love her. And I will protect her until the day I die."

"Don't say that, Lawrence. You must live forever. I insist on it."

Lawrence paced the floor for a moment, then clicked his fingers. "There may be an answer, you know?"

"Go on?"

"What if I ask Cora and Vera to mind Daisy while we are away?"

"That's an excellent idea. Do you think they would?"

"If time allows. I'll pay them, of course."

"Then we can go?"

"Let me make a few phone calls, and I'll let you know."

Lawrence strode towards the stairs, taking them two at a time until he reached the bright drawing room on the first floor. He settled on the leather couch, crossed his legs, and unhooked the earpiece.

"Operator?" he said.

"How can I help you?"

Lawrence opened his mouth to speak as the front doorbell chimed below.

"Just a moment," said Lawrence. He peered over the wrought-iron balcony, his vision obscured by the portico at the front of the building.

"It can wait," he muttered, assuming the housemaid would answer the door and find out who had called. But the operator took it as an instruction and pulled the plug on the call.

"Operator, operator?" Lawrence tapped an irritated finger over the handset just as Violet arrived. "She's rung off."

"Call tomorrow."

"I'd rather get it settled now."

"As you wish."

Violet sat beside him, picked up a book, and read while Lawrence summoned another operator. He was in full flow when their housemaid, Sarah Curtis, entered the room and bobbed a curtsy.

"No need for that," said Violet, looking up from her book. Sarah had come to them keen but inexperienced, showing her gratitude in excessive displays of manners. Fawning obsequiousness, Lawrence called it, finding it almost as galling as if she showed no respect at all.

"Visitor for you, sir and ma'am," she said.

"Really? We're not expecting anyone."

"Here's his card." Sarah passed it over, gave a little shrug, and nodded her head.

Violet's face paled as she took the card. Her mouth dropped open as she made to speak, but the words did not materialise.

"What is it?" asked Lawrence, but Violet remained frozen.

"I'll call back," he said, slamming the handset down.

Lawrence reached over and took the card. His complexion changed from white to florid red. "Where is this man now?" he growled through clenched teeth.

"Downstairs, in the hallway, sir."

"I'll kill him." Lawrence darted through the door, Violet in close pursuit. She dropped the card, which landed face up on the coffee table in the centre of the room. Sarah stared at it, wondering how a simple visitor's card could cause such an extreme reaction. Who was Francis Farrow and what had he ever done to deserve this angry reception?

Chapter Two

PAST REGRETS

Lawrence took the stairs two at a time as Violet struggled to keep up.

"Get out of the way," he yelled as Thomas Greening, the local postman and occupier of the upper part of the building, stepped on the bottom stair tread.

"Oi, watch where you're going," he snapped.

Lawrence ignored him, his temper aflame, and charged forward, pulling up short at the empty hallway.

"Where is he?"

Violet arrived breathlessly behind him.

"Hopefully, long gone."

"I'll kill him," snarled Lawrence.

Francis Farrow stepped from the downstairs reception room and walked towards Lawrence with his hands raised over his head in supplication. "You won't have to, dear boy. Fate has taken care of that."

Lawrence faltered and stood in the hallway. Silence fell, save for his shallow panting breath. Then he lunged forward and pinned Farrow to the front door, his arm squeezing tightly against the older man's throat.

"What the blazes are you doing here? How dare you walk into my home after what you did? Get out now."

Lawrence spun Farrow around and forced his right arm up his back as he wrestled with the door lock.

Farrow moaned, and Lawrence pushed the arm higher.

"Stop. You'll break it."

"Correct. And then I'll break the other one."

"Leave him alone." Violet pushed Lawrence's chest, forcing him away from Farrow. Lawrence lurched backwards as Francis gulped a lungful of air and massaged his damaged limb.

"Leave us," Lawrence commanded.

Violet crossed her arms and stood between the two men.

Lawrence stared angrily.

"How will violence help?" she asked calmly.

"It will rid the world of his foul presence," Lawrence hissed, all self-composure gone.

"I dare say. And you'll be in prison, and Daisy will grow up without a father."

"At least she'll get to grow up. Not like Lily, who burned to death in the fire he set."

Lawrence pointed at Farrow with a trembling finger.

"That was never my intention. It was an accident." Francis Farrow looked up through dim, bloodshot eyes, staring earnestly at Lawrence. He looked thin and insubstantial.

"You killed my wife and my daughter and I don't give a damn about your intentions. Don't come here expecting sympathy from me. By rights, I ought to kill you. I will kill you." Lawrence thrust his hand around Farrow's throat again.

"No," screamed Violet.

"Right. That's enough." Thomas Greening had returned downstairs at the sound of raised voices and stood over Lawrence, brandishing a cricket bat.

"One more move from you, Harpham, and you'll feel the weight of this on the back of your head."

"He's the bloody intruder."

Greening ignored the flecks of spittle and spoke directly to Farrow. "You'd better leave if you know what's good for you."

"Sadly, I cannot. I must speak to Mr Harpham whether or not he wishes to hear me."

"Sarah, fetch the police." Greening gestured towards the door as he instructed the housekeeper.

"Right, you are, sir."

"Stay," said Violet.

"Sorry, ma'am?"

"Don't leave. We'll sort this out like adults." Violet's voice was shaky, betraying her inner fear. Francis Farrow had anonymously terrorised her for months before kidnapping her while alone and vulnerable. She had no reason to side with him. But he'd done worse to Lawrence, depriving him of a wife and daughter. Violet knew Lawrence could easily harm Farrow and the last thing she needed was a policeman on the premises while her husband was volatile and angry.

Sarah looked questioningly, torn between Greening's instructions and Violet's. "Do as your mistress instructs," Greening conceded.

"Good. Now follow me upstairs, Mr Farrow, and we'll speak in the drawing room."

Lawrence darted to the staircase, his arm stretched over the newel post. "Over my dead body," he growled.

Violet raised an eyebrow. "The sooner we hear Francis out, the sooner he will leave."

"I don't want him in my house."

"And I don't want our private business discussed on the doorstep."

Lawrence shot a look of anger towards his wife but conceded, dropped his arm, and climbed the stairs, his face a mask of unrestrained rage.

"This way." Violet stared coldly at Francis Farrow as she gestured upwards.

"Thank you for your assistance, Thomas," she continued, forcing a smile at Greening. "If you would kindly listen for further disturbances, I would greatly appreciate your help if things get heated again."

"And you will have it," Greening said.

Violet entered the drawing room to find Lawrence glowering through the window, chewing his nails, an old habit she hadn't witnessed in years. Francis Farrow had not waited for an invitation to sit and had slumped awkwardly on the settee.

"Any chance of a drink?" he asked.

"None whatsoever." Violet's tone was curt and unfriendly, her usual good manners absent.

"Very well."

"What do you want, Farrow?" Lawrence bristled, hissing the words with venom.

"To make amends?"

"Amends? For taking two lives? And how do you intend to do that? Raise them from the dead?"

"I don't know. I wish I did. But I must beg your forgiveness before I meet my maker."

"Really? I didn't know Lucifer went in for reconciliations?"

"Try not to be facetious, Lawrence. My intentions are sincere."

"You don't know the meaning of the word." Lawrence slammed his palm against the window shutters, making Violet jump.

She shot him another glare.

"Why would you want forgiveness after all this time?" she asked.

Farrow sighed and stroked a day's worth of stubble with yellowing fingernails, his faded eyes sunken into a jaundiced face. Farrow's right eyelid involuntarily twitched as he considered his words.

"I'm dying," he said.

"Good." Lawrence glared narrow-eyed.

"Are you really?" Violet's arched eyebrow suggested unspoken doubt.

"I'm afraid I am."

"Of what?"

"Must I go into the gory details? Do you doubt me after all these years?"

"I might remind you that during our last meal, you shackled me to a table leg before shooting at and nearly killing my husband. So, yes, I have some issues of trust regarding your veracity."

"Cold words, Violet. Have you no compassion for a dying man?"

"She wants details, Farrow. Give them or leave." Lawrence, who had positioned himself opposite his former friend, leaned menacingly towards him.

"Very well. I have tumours in my stomach and all manner of gastric ailments. It's abdominal cancer, according to my doctor, who has given me no more than six months to make my peace with the world."

"That changes nothing," said Lawrence. "It's six more months than you ever gave my daughter. Or rather your daughter, as it transpired." Tears pricked at Lawrence's eyes, and he fought to hold them back.

"I never knew her father's identity," said Farrow. "Neither did Catherine. There's as much chance Lily was yours as she was mine."

"Except that she's nobody's child now. Just a pile of rotting bones."

"If I could turn back time, I would," said Farrow. "I never intended to kill Catherine."

"No, only me, your friend of several decades." Lawrence spat his bitterness, still as raw as if the intervening years had never happened.

"I was mad with jealousy. Had I realised the consequences and understood the terrible effects of my actions, I would not have set the fire."

"Or tormented me with messages, kidnapped Violet or endangered your brother. It's all talk, Farrow. God forgive my ignorance, for I should have realised sooner, but it always was."

Francis Farrow licked his lips, his once plump frame reduced to skin and bone. "I kept bad company and allowed evil men to influence my life. Rather than confront my guilt and make amends, I glorified it and made excuses, courted sin, and welcomed ungodly men into my life. And it worked. Membership of the order left me free to satisfy my desires at any cost. Social norms, the law of the land, none of it applied. Crossley believed in following his urges and encouraged us to do the same. He liberated me from the weight of my guilt when it threatened to overwhelm me."

"Oh, hark at you, feeling sorry for yourself. What about me? I lost my family because of your desires. First, you took my wife's virtue, then her life. And if that wasn't enough, you stole my child."

"I know what I have done. And as I approach my darkest hour, I beg for your forgiveness."

"Have you fallen out with Crossley?" Lawrence cocked his head, eyes glinting with suspicion as he sought the real reason for Farrow's unwelcome arrival.

"Not exactly. I am tired of Crossley and his relentless pursuit of self-gratification. It's all too much in the end."

"You mean there was trouble at the temple? Crossley left Mexico, didn't he? He hasn't been back for some time, I hear. Has his influence waned? No, don't answer that. I know exactly where your master is. Do you?"

Farrow flushed.

"You don't then? He's dropped you, and that's what this is all about. There's nothing left for you in Mexico, and nobody wants you here. You have no home, no family, and zero chance of reconciling with anyone who ever knew you."

"You're wrong," said Farrow, shaking his head. "I would have left Mexico a long time ago and returned to England but for my illness. I seek forgiveness and reconciliation. Nothing more and nothing less. Just a kind word from you and my brother and sister, those I have wronged and who lived to regret my folly."

"You've left Violet out."

"Intentionally. Violet, I believe you already have forgiven me. It's not in your nature to hold a grudge."

Violet shifted uncomfortably in her seat. "Don't take my good nature for granted," she said.

"But you don't deny it. I can hope?"

"Never," said Lawrence. "Violet despises you. Why Farrow? Why? Why when you had so much to give, did you ruin so many lives? You say you want to put things right, but how do you think it feels when you arrive uninvited and dredge up all the hurt and upset again? Your behaviour is utterly self-indulgent and typical of the selfish man you became. I've heard enough. Get out of my house or I'll throw you out."

"I'm sorry I caused you pain," said Farrow, his hands clasped nervously around a battered felt hat. "I've said my piece, and I'll leave you alone now. But if you can find it in your heart to forgive me..."

"Get out." Lawrence stood and approached the broken man before him, but Farrow backed away.

"I'm leaving," he said, squeezing his hat on his head, as he turned slowly away and left the room. Lawrence and Violet silently sat as they listened to the soft footfall on the stairs. The front door opened and closed.

Lawrence wrenched the handset from the telephone. "Operator," he barked. "Cheltenham 253 Frederick G Adams, estate agents."

"What are you doing?" whispered Violet.

"Calling the rental agent. We're relinquishing our let. That man will never darken my door again."

Violet waited until he turned his back before deftly removing Farrow's card from the table and putting it in her purse.

Chapter Three

TRIP TO THE CAPITAL

Saturday, November 20, 1909 - Cheltenham Spa

Lawrence inspected his watch for the sixth time as he paced the platform. "She's cutting it fine," he muttered.

"It doesn't matter," said Violet. "Cora knows what to do if we miss her."

"I'd rather have time to talk things through. It's only fair."

"Coralie Cream is a competent young woman," said Violet. "She's one half of a successful detective agency and will manage perfectly well, with or without our help."

"Even so…" Lawrence stalked up the platform and exaggeratedly stared beyond. Moments later, he returned.

"Sit down," said Violet. "You're like a cat on a hot tin roof. I don't know what's got into you lately. I hope this trip of ours will sort you out."

"I don't need sorting out."

"Whatever you say."

The loud rumble of an approaching train drowned out

their bickering. The burly stationmaster blew his whistle and beckoned his assistant.

"About time," said Lawrence. "Stay here with the bags."

"Happily. Now off you pop."

Lawrence stalked towards the now stationary train and wrenched open a door. Two elderly men slowly filed out and, mistaking Lawrence for an attendant, proffered their bags. Violet watched his face redden as he visibly bit his lip and turned away. A steady stream of passengers emerged while Lawrence waited. He looked up and down the station but saw no sign of Coralie Cream.

"I don't believe it," he said, thundering back to Violet. "That bloody woman has missed the train."

"What bloody woman?" asked Coralie, following a few paces behind him.

Lawrence blushed beetroot red. "Ah. I thought I'd missed you."

"No such luck. Sorry, I didn't mean to hold you up. I was assisting a young mother with her perambulator in the luggage compartment."

"Excuse my husband," said Violet, pecking Cora on the cheek. "He's increasingly losing patience as he descends into old age."

"I quite understand." Coralie returned the kiss and patted Violet's arm. "How are you both?"

"Very well," said Lawrence. "And I am sorry. Truly, I am. It's just the thought of leaving Daisy. You know how it is."

"I do," said Coralie. "Why don't we discuss it over a hot drink? There's a sweet little tearoom over there."

"Good idea," said Violet.

The ladies meandered to the station cafe while Lawrence paid a porter to mind their bags until the London train arrived. By the time he joined them, Violet had already ordered tea, and a piece of lemon drizzle cake was waiting for him. He disposed of it in a few bites, feeling better for the welcome snack.

"So," said Coralie, leaning forward. "How are you both?"

Lawrence and Violet exchanged glances. "Tolerable, until recently," said Lawrence.

"What changed?" Coralie cocked her head, quizzical blue eyes revealing a perceptiveness that acknowledged all was not well.

Lawrence hesitated, momentarily stilled by the scent of her perfume. He remembered it from their last meeting and focussed his attention elsewhere before he became tongue-tied or worse.

"An unwelcome visitor," he said.

"Who?"

"Francis Farrow."

"The old devil." Coralie shook her head and reached high for the cup of tea the waitress was about to deliver on a tray. She plucked a sugar cube from a silver dish and plopped it into her drink. "Did you shut the door on him?"

"I tried to," said Lawrence, ignoring Violet's gaze.

"And I stopped him," she retorted. "We only air our business privately."

"What did he want?" Cora quickly interjected to head off any escalation of the apparent tension between husband and wife.

"Forgiveness," Violet responded first.

"That's a lot to ask."

"Isn't it?"

"But why, after all this time?"

"Farrow says he's dying," Lawrence explained. "Not sure

I believe him. If he said it was raining, I'd go outside and check."

"Understandably."

"But I will never reconcile with the man. I wish him nothing but suffering."

Violet detected the tremor in her husband's voice that Coralie missed. Farrow's visit had brought a host of painful memories, but although Lawrence hadn't acknowledged it, she recognised an emotion that Lawrence would never admit. He missed Farrow's friendship despite all the dreadful things he had done. Lawrence would never forgive his old friend, but he still grieved their lost closeness.

"Do you expect him to turn up again?" Coralie took a cake fork and set to work on her slice of lemon drizzle.

"No," said Lawrence. "I've asked the agent for another let, but it was an overreaction on my part. Farrow's illness has rendered him physically harmless, and Crossley could locate us whenever he wanted. I wouldn't have left Daisy if Farrow was a threat, and I don't believe his visit makes things worse. If you pushed him, he'd fall over."

"He sounds very frail," said Coralie.

Violet gazed earnestly in her direction. "He is. Lawrence thinks he was lying about his illness, but it's obvious to me he's suffering."

"Well, Violet, your daughter has my full protection, I promise. Miss Faithful is an old acquaintance of mine. I telephoned her yesterday, and she asked me to tea, so I'll join her and collect Daisy afterwards. Now, I know you were expecting me to lodge at your property, and that's fine if you prefer it. But Miss Faithful has offered me a room at the school. Daisy and I could stay there together if it suits the situation."

"That's a splendid idea." Lawrence smiled for the first time that day.

"I thought you didn't want Daisy boarding?" asked Violet.

"Not alone. But it's ideal with Miss Cream there to guard her. Under those circumstances, it's safer than home."

"Very well," said Violet. "I hope you have an interesting time."

"I'm sure we will." Coralie finished her tea, wiped her lips with a paper napkin and got to her feet. "I'd better press on," she said.

Lawrence hailed a porter who took Coralie's bag. They waved as she crossed the bridge.

"You seem happier," said Violet.

"It's another worry out of the way. Ah. That sounds like our train."

Five minutes later, they were sitting in a first-class carriage on the way to London. Lawrence stretched his legs in front, briefly closing his eyes before Violet spoke.

"Do you think we should tell Michael?"

Lawrence's eyes snapped open.

"About Francis?"

"Yes."

"I suppose so."

"The sooner the better, Lawrence. I wouldn't want him finding out from someone else. Aurora will be terrified."

"We'll telephone tomorrow. Talk it through with Michael. He'll worry less when he hears how frail his brother has become. God knows where Francis has gone, but that's not Michael's problem."

"Are you sure? If Francis wants forgiveness, he's bound to contact Michael."

"Yes. And he'll get short shrift when he does. Michael will protect Aurora at all costs."

"I'm sure you're right, dear."

"What's that?" Lawrence gestured towards the white card Violet had idly pulled out and replaced in her bag.

"Francis left his card," she replied.

"Why have you kept it? Hand it over, please."

"What will you do with it?"

"Tear it into tiny pieces naturally."

"Then no. It won't do any harm to have a point of contact."

"Why would either of us want to call him?"

"No reason. But what purpose is there in destroying it?"

"Oh, keep it if you must. Where is Francis staying?"

"In London, and you'll recognise the address on the card. You've been there before. Francis is lodging at the Crescent Moon headquarters."

Lawrence frowned. "I suppose staying in London was inevitable. Where else could he go? Still, as long as he doesn't bother us, I don't care. Blythe Road is a good few miles away from our hotel."

"You haven't told me where we're staying."

"With good reason. I am treating you to a suite at The Grafton Hotel."

"In Fitzrovia?"

"That's right."

"How lovely, Lawrence. But a little self-indulgent compared to our usual accommodation, don't you think?"

"Not at all. We rarely treat ourselves. You're keen on this London trip, and if we're going to do it, we'll do it in style."

Violet beamed. "Thank you."

"Not at all. You're worth every penny, my dear."

The Grafton Hotel did not disappoint. From the moment they left their cab, with their bags miraculously reaching the room before they did to the enormous vase of flowers on the occasional table, the experience was truly magnificent. Lawrence despised excessive shows of wealth and preferred to stay in the familiar hotels he frequented before receiving his inheritance. He lived well within his means, was never ostentatious, and Lawrence was the benefactor of several local Cheltenham charities. The only thing he valued enough to deviate from his modest way of life was Daisy's school fees. But a private education had served Lawrence well, and he wanted his only living child to have the same excellent start. And Violet, never having much money of her own, was happy to continue in the same vein. She would have preferred to work, but when Lawrence retired, he wanted her to make the most of her free time while they were both in good health. So, frugality became second nature. Yesterday, in the aftermath of Farrow's visit, Lawrence decided to upgrade from their usual hotel in Battersea to something grander. Life was too short, and Violet deserved a treat. So, after a quick apology, he wired a generous and unnecessary compensatory sum to the obliging manager of the original hotel and booked a junior suite at The Grafton.

Violet approached the vase of roses, closed her eyes, and inhaled the floral scent. Then Lawrence opened the door to the knock of a smartly dressed porter pushing a trolley laden with champagne and a box of chocolates. They clinked their glasses and toasted London, Violet's eyes sparkling with pleasure. Lawrence smiled indulgently. He'd recognised Violet's frustration at his behaviour in the station and during Farrow's visit and was glad to make amends. His tolerance for London was low, but Violet wanted to be here, and Cora had mitigated his worries about Daisy. It was time to relax.

"Well, this is lovely, Lawrence. What a fabulous start to our break."

"Isn't it? We'll dine here tonight if that suits you. The menu is excellent."

"Good. I shall enjoy that."

"And I thought we might take a stroll down The Embankment tomorrow. For old time's sake."

Violet's face fell. "Oh. But there's an exhibition of fine art at the Sackville Gallery. I'd love to see it."

"Can't you go the following day?"

"No. That's the first day of the Camden exhibition."

"First day? How long is it running?"

"Most of the week. But I dare say I'll skip the last few showings."

"Oh. Right. I'm not sure I'll manage that much art."

"You don't need to. I can cope alone."

"Then I'll come along tomorrow and we'll play the rest of the week by ear."

Violet licked her lips, prepared to speak, and thought the better of it.

"What's wrong?"

"Nothing, Lawrence. Oh, just a thought though. Hadn't we better contact Ann while we're in town?"

"Gosh, yes. I'd like to see the Brocklehursts. Let's arrange something straight away. I'll call now."

"Must we leave so soon? I'd like to freshen up before we find a telephone."

Lawrence smiled and gestured to the polished black

apparatus on the sideboard. "No need to set foot outside. We have our very own handset."

"Goodness. What will they think of next? The world is modernising at an alarming rate."

"Will you do the honours, or shall I?"

"I'd love to talk to Ann and tell her about our lovely room."

"Get her to visit. We can ask the receptionist if they will serve afternoon tea here. I'm sure they will oblige."

"Wonderful. I'll ask Ann."

Violet sat by the handset and called the operator, who quickly passed her through to the Brocklehurst household.

"Yes, I'll wait, thank you," said Violet. Covering the mouthpiece, she whispered, "That was the housekeeper. She's fetching Ann now."

Lawrence nodded, removed his shoes, and reclined on the bed, staring at the ceiling rose and the elaborate golden light fixture. His eyes grew heavy as he contemplated the craftmanship.

"Ann. How lovely to hear your voice. Guess where we are?" Violet paused for a moment. "That's right. How do you know? You've had what? Ann, no. Oh, my goodness. We should have called sooner and warned you. I'm so sorry."

Violet's hand flew to her mouth as her eyes widened.

Lawrence looked towards her and mouthed, "What's wrong?"

"It's Francis," she whispered. "No, not here, Ann. I was telling Lawrence. He's with me. When did you see him?"

Violet grimaced as she spoke, beckoning Lawrence to join her. He padded over, pulled out a second chair, and sat beside her.

"He turned up last night. To the house? At a quarter to midnight? What was he thinking?"

Lawrence shook his head and growled, "Mark should have called the police."

Violet ignored him. "Did you see him? Oh, I see. Mark dealt with it. How? He did what?"

"I can't hear," hissed Lawrence.

"Mark chased him from the premises with his horsewhip."

"Good man." Lawrence smiled wryly.

"Did he say what he wanted? I see. That's more or less what he asked of us. Lawrence gave him short shrift. Mark felt the same. No, I was a little more circumspect. You feel the same way too?"

"No room for that," said Lawrence. "Give the man an inch. He's completely untrustworthy."

Violet clapped her hand over the mouthpiece. "Can you fetch me a handkerchief, please?" she asked.

"Now?"

"Yes, please."

Sighing, Lawrence entered the bathroom.

"Yes, I know where he's staying," she whispered. "He left a card. The Order of the Crescent Moon in Blythe Road. Number thirty-one, if memory serves. I wouldn't, Ann, at least not alone. What good could it possibly do? You want to hear him apologise directly? But what then? Ah, thank you, Lawrence."

Lawrence handed her a polished silver box, and Violet removed one of several laundered handkerchiefs. She rubbed it daintily under her nose.

"Perhaps we can discuss it over tea?" asked Violet, nodding her head. "I'll let you know when. Sometime this week, I hope. Just be careful, Ann." She replaced the handset.

"Be careful of what?" Lawrence eyed her suspiciously.

"Of everything. Francis might return."

"Not if he knows what's good for him. Mark Brocklehurst is a crack shot."

"Ann didn't see or speak to him. Mark should have told her before turning him out."

"Why? He was only protecting his wife."

"Because Francis is her brother, and she still bears a heavy burden from his actions. Ann would like to know why he betrayed them."

"What difference would it make?"

"That's not the point. It's easier to understand someone's behaviour in context."

"Then Ann will be sorely disappointed. There are no excuses for his loathsome actions."

Lawrence clenched his fist as if to bang it on the table and tightly closed his eyes before visibly relaxing. "He's not worth it," he said. "Come on, wife. Let's freshen up and have a snifter at the bar before dinner."

Chapter Four

EXHIBITION

Monday, November 22, 1909

Lawrence paused outside the four-storey townhouse and shrugged. "Are you sure this is a gallery? It looks more like a residence to me."

Violet reached into her purse and retrieved a dog-eared leaflet. "Number twenty-eight Sackville Street," she read. "Ah, look." Violet pointed towards a polished gold plate engraved with the words Sackville Gallery. "However did we miss that?" she asked.

"I can't imagine. Let's get it over with."

Violet glared. "Don't be like that. If you don't want to come inside, then find something else to do. I thought you liked the old masters?"

"I'm sorry. I was unnecessarily short. And you're right. I draw the line at those awful modern compositions, but I'm happy to pass the morning inspecting real works of art. Ladies first." Lawrence cast his arm towards the door before walking ahead and pulling it open.

"Thank you."

The door opened into a black and white tiled hallway where a large blackboard stood on an easel announcing *Rothschild Fine Art* in stylish calligraphy. A sharply dressed man appeared to the rear and introduced himself as Harper Rolman. "And who do I have the pleasure of addressing?" he asked.

"Mr and Mrs Harpham," Lawrence replied, sizing up the man before him. With greased-back hair, a heavily starched collar, and a suit that surely came from Savile Row, Mr Rolman appeared more monied than the average art dealer. And when he flashed a Breitling watch beneath diamond-studded cuffs, Lawrence felt suddenly out of his depth. But Violet remained serene.

"Is sir an art dealer or a critic, perhaps?"

"Just a private citizen."

"And how did you hear about us? The Burlington Club, I fancy?"

"No," said Violet, proffering her leaflet.

"Oh. I wasn't aware we advertised that way," he said, handing the paper back to her between index finger and thumb. "We are a modern gallery for connoisseurs, you understand?"

"Better than you realise," said Lawrence, ignoring Violet's glare.

"Where are the paintings?"

"On the next three floors. Take the stairs. You might want to start with the gallery on the left. The other is likely to be full."

Lawrence nodded curtly, took Violet's hand, and led her upstairs.

"Pompous idiot," he mouthed.

"Shhh. He'll hear you."

"Wouldn't you be better off at The Royal Academy?"

"No. I'd like to see these paintings today. Tomorrow's exhibition is a little more contemporary. I'm aiming for a juxtaposition between the two."

Lawrence paused. "You're taking this hobby very seriously, Violet. There are limits, you know."

"To my ability? My understanding? I'm not stupid, Lawrence. I paint for pleasure, and I won't set the world on fire with my art. But I want to do the best I can. Besides, I don't work for a living, and there's little else for me to do."

"This way," said Lawrence as they reached the top of the stairs. He gestured towards the empty gallery to the left. Violet turned sharply right.

"Hello," she said, heading towards a group of men clustered around a gloomy Renaissance portrait of a man in a wide-brimmed hat.

They turned away briefly, and the older man nodded. "Good morning," he replied, before resuming his discussion.

"It's the sensitivity in the face," he said, before turning to his colleague. "Look. What do you see?"

"The concentration of light, obviously," said the second man. And the bright accents across his cheeks. Here, in this reddish spot."

"Good, good," the older man said, resting his hands on his hips as he regarded the work.

"If the concentration of light matters, then why the dark tones?" asked Violet. "They dominate the picture. What did the artist intend?"

The man raised an eyebrow, regarding Violet through quizzical eyes. He was handsome with lightly greased hair, even features, and piercing blue eyes.

"That's an excellent question, madam," he said. "It represents a show of strength. See the powerful curve from the subject's hand resting over the shoulder and touching his collar. You will note one of the few bright accents in the pleats, but the collar darkens as it extends beyond his neck. Almost threateningly, don't you think?"

"I do. But I also see nobility," said Violet.

"Indeed. This man was undoubtedly a member of the aristocracy. You read a painting very well, Miss, er?"

"Violet Harpham," said Violet, offering her hand.

"Mrs Violet Harpham," echoed Lawrence as he approached.

"Walter Sickert," replied the man, lightly kissing Violet's hand and taking Lawrence's with a firm shake. "And these are my fellow artists Freddy Gore and Leonard Covington."

"Pleased to meet you." Freddy smiled, his blond hair flopping slightly over his ears, seemingly in need of a good haircut. He smelled faintly of turpentine. Leonard Covington lingered in the background, evidently shyer than his more flamboyant friends.

"Are you a fellow artist?" asked Sickert, turning back to Violet.

"Only a rank amateur. But I love it."

"Oh, come now. Show some confidence. Do you have a preferred style?"

"To paint or admire?"

"Either," said Sickert.

"Naturally, I adore the great masters, and I have tried my hand at landscapes. But I'm leaning towards a more contemporary style. Something freer and less restrictive. I'm hoping to find inspiration in Camden tomorrow."

"I say. Are you attending the exhibition?" Freddy stepped towards her with the eagerness of a working spaniel.

"Yes, I am. Will you be there?"

"There and exhibiting," said Sickert.

"How wonderful."

"Do look us out," he continued.

Leonard glanced at his watch. "We must push on," he said. "I must be in Hackney by three o'clock."

Sickert touched his forelock. "Excuse us," he said. "We must give the remaining floors our best attention. Young Leonard is writing an article for The Burlington Magazine."

"Of course."

Would you like to join us? You are very welcome, although you may find it rather technical."

"That would be perfect," said Violet. "As long as we won't be in your way."

"I can't," said Lawrence, removing his notebook from his pocket and glancing at an empty page as if remembering a long-standing appointment.

"I understand. Another time then."

"My husband might be otherwise indisposed, but I am free," said Violet. "And I'd love to take you up on your kind offer."

Lawrence frowned. "How long will you be?"

"A couple of hours," said Sickert, glancing at his watch. "I'll return for you at midday."

"No need, Lawrence. I'll see you back at the hotel."

"But Violet…"

"Don't worry. I'll take a cab."

"Very well." Lawrence hesitated, then left the room, plodding downstairs, reluctant to leave Violet. But she was flushed with pleasure at her luck in unexpectedly falling in with a group of artists. They could teach her more during a two-hour conversation than she would ever learn alone. And this trip was for her benefit, after all. Lawrence continued onwards, knowing he should trust her judgement and find another way to occupy his time.

"Has sir seen enough?" The languid voice of Harper Rolman interrupted his introspections.

"For now," Lawrence replied.

"And you won't be purchasing anything today?"

"Not on this occasion."

Rolman cast a disdainful eye to Lawrence's jacket, and Lawrence wilted as he looked down at his frayed cuffs. Dapper and precise while working, Lawrence had largely ignored his appearance since moving to Cheltenham. Now retired, moneyed and with no need to work, he'd taken his eye off the ball, neglecting to replace his suits, his shoes showing visible signs of wear. And Rolman was judging him for it.

"Tell you what. Why don't you send me a catalogue?" Lawrence tossed the hotel card onto a small table. "Suite three," he continued as he strode towards the front door.

"Of course, sir. Do visit again soon," said Rolman, but Lawrence was already several yards up the street.

Chapter Five

SPARKING INTEREST

The clouds had opened while they were in the gallery, leaving deep puddles along the pavement. Lawrence pulled up his collar and stepped briskly onwards, trying to decide what to do with two unexpectedly free hours. He headed towards the hotel but thought the better of it. There was no point in being holed up indoors with nothing to do. He removed his glove and placed his palm to the side, testing the strength of the rainfall. They'd been indoors and oblivious for most of the shower, but thankfully, it was diminishing. Cheered, Lawrence powered onwards, striding vaguely north with no other plan than to walk and enjoy the sights. He soon found himself heading towards Russell Square, favouring a stroll down Montague Street rather than the notorious Southampton Row. Keeping to the pathway, Lawrence soon passed a newly painted cabman's shelter and spent a few moments stroking the muzzle of a piebald pony. But before long, the cabman returned, removed the nosebag, and prepared the horse for another journey across the city. Lawrence considered paying a fare for a ride through the finer parts of London. He had hours to kill and no real purpose. But trotting aimlessly through the high streets of the metropolis would not hold his interest for two hours. So, Lawrence had a long, hard think about what he wanted to do and concluded that as he was alone, he'd enjoy a pint. Ten minutes later, he found himself on the Euston Road, passing one dingy public house after another, each less salubrious than the last. But the pitter-patter of another rain shower soon changed his mind about the need for ambience. Any establishment with an intact roof would do the trick. Twenty yards later, he found himself outside the red-stoned pillars of The Rising Sun and went inside.

Lawrence was not the only customer dodging the rain. The small lounge bar buzzed with chatter. A listing coat stand was close to toppling under the weight of damp overcoats, umbrellas peppered the floor, and one man had discarded his goloshes, which lay abandoned by the door nearest the convenience. Lawrence sighed, knowing he would not cope with the disorderly room for long. Whether raining or not, he must leave before he publicly manifested his compulsion to tidy. Lawrence turned towards the door, which suddenly shot open as a young man entered and breathlessly signalled outside.

"What is it, Sam?" asked the barmaid as she polished a glass with a dirty-looking towel.

The man gulped like a fish and pointed again.

"Well?"

"The Mutton Shunter's got Jimmy."

"Got him? Why?"

"I dunno. They took 'im by the arms and tried to cart 'im away."

"For what reason?"

"Mafficking in the streets, Bet."

Lawrence stepped aside as the man continued excitedly. Silence had descended, and the pub clientele were waiting for more news. Now would be the time to slip out, but Lawrence found himself eager for information.

The barmaid deposited the glass on the counter and put her hands on her hips.

"They can't arrest him for that."

"Well, they bloody well did. 'Spect the gun didn't help."

"What in the world was he doing with a gun?"

"Shooting pigeons, probably. I don't know. But he's diggin' 'is heels in, and two dirty great cops can't move the bugger."

"Ha. Got to see this," said a balding man, grabbing his jacket and heading to the door.

"Me too."

Lawrence retreated towards a nearby table as, one after another, the men rushed out for a look at their beleaguered friend. Within seconds, he was the only male remaining, apart from another barman who appeared from the rear.

"Blimey. Where did everyone go?"

Bet explained while Lawrence wandered towards the bar, taking advantage of the lull to order a pint. He tossed a few coins in payment, perched on the barstool, and took a long gulp, smiling as the amber liquid hit the spot.

"Looks like you needed that, mister," said the barman.

Lawrence wiped his lips. "You pull a good pint."

"There's plenty more where that came from. It's a new keg, hauled up by my own fair hands this morning."

Lawrence glanced at his watch. "I expect I'll manage another. Must take it easy though."

"Trouble and strife not keen on your whetting your whistle?"

"I doubt she'll mind."

"Have a mint, in case," chuckled the barman, handing over a humbug.

Lawrence smiled. He shouldn't need to disguise his breath. Violet didn't mind him drinking at the club. But then again, it had been a long time since he had graced the doors of a public house. Perhaps she would be unhappy on this occasion? Especially if he overdid it and returned to The Grafton, slurring his words. He decided he ought to stick to one pint and opened his mouth to inform the barman.

"Don't think too hard about it," he said, as if reading Lawrence's mind. "Go with the flow. Looks like you need a few good drinks."

Lawrence grimaced. "Does it?" he asked.

"Excuse me for saying so, sir. But you have the air of a man fed up with life."

"Do I?"

"I'm afraid so. Dull eyes, you see. I can always tell."

Lawrence withdrew his calling card holder and peered into the polished silver. His eyes looked perfectly normal, considering the slightly bevelled metal. "I don't know what you mean," he said, making no attempt to disguise his irritation.

The barman held his hands up in mock horror. "Don't shoot the messenger."

Lawrence drained his glass and prepared to leave.

"Have another," said the barman.

"I'd rather not."

"Go on. It'll do you good."

Lawrence shook his head. "I came in for some peace and quiet, not for a discussion about the lack of sparkle in my eyes."

"So you admit it then?"

"What?"

"That you're glum."

"I'm perfectly happy."

The barman leaned forward, put his elbow on the counter and cradled his chin in his palm. "If you say so, gov."

"I do."

"Oi, Sid. Stop bothering the punters." Bet sidled behind the barman and placed a veiny hand on his shoulder.

"Give over. I'm only offering an opinion."

"Well, keep it to yourself, you old fool."

Lawrence slid off the barstool and removed his gloves.

"See what you've done, Sidney?"

"Don't be like that, sir. Have another pint. I'll shut my big mouth. If you leave now, she'll give me grief for the rest of the day."

"I was going anyway. It's time to return to my hotel."

"Where? To your lonely room?"

"Don't start that again."

Lawrence prepared to leave, but the words had hit their mark. He was reluctant to return to his room before Violet, fearing too much waiting might make him irritable. The barman was an inconvenience he could do without, but the beer was a different matter. He reached into his pocket and slammed two coins on the counter. "Another ale without the running commentary, please."

"As you wish." Sid poured another pint and passed it over, then retreated to a respectful distance while Lawrence took another large draught.

Ten minutes later, Lawrence was nursing the final dregs, feeling warm and mellow. The pub was filling up again, and Sidney had stayed out of sight, but when he saw an almost empty glass, he drifted over.

"That's better," he said. "Now. Are you amenable to telling me all about it?"

Lawrence sighed. "I'm bored," he confessed.

"That'll be the size of it."

"How did you know?"

"It's my job. Part purveyor of fine ale, part judge of character. It all comes down to keeping the customer happy."

"But what to do about my tedious existence? That is the question?" Lawrence's usual reticence had disappeared halfway through the second pint, and he mused aloud as he considered his life.

"What are you missing?" asked the barman percipiently.

Lawrence puffed his cheeks, blowing out air as he considered the matter. "The thrill of the chase, I suppose."

"You're a sportsman then?"

"Me? Good lord, no. But I was a private detective."

"Well, I never."

"What?" asked Bet as she poured a large measure of gin into an already-used glass.

"You'll never guess the occupation of this fine gentleman," said Sid.

"Gentlemen don't have occupations."

"Well, this one does."

"Go on then. What do you do for a living, love?"

Lawrence squirmed at the familiarity despite the mellowing effects of the beer. He wished he hadn't mentioned his former job. Sidney seemed unusually impressed, making Lawrence self-conscious and uncomfortable.

"Nothing. I'm retired."

"Oh. Good for you."

"Yes, but he was one of those. The kind who took Jimmy," whispered Sid, pointing outside.

Bet narrowed her eyes. "Then you're not welcome here," she said.

"I don't mean a rozzer. A private detective."

"Oh. Was he really?"

Their wide-eyed exchange of glances did not escape Lawrence's notice. "Yes, until three years ago. Then I gave it up."

Sid pulled a pint and slid it silently towards Lawrence.

"I didn't order that."

"It's on the house."

"Thank you, but I've had enough."

"Drink it down now. I want to tell you a story."

Lawrence checked his watch. He'd successfully killed one hour and fifteen minutes. Another pint wouldn't hurt. "Go on," he said.

"If you'd have come here a little over two years ago, you might have met a girl called Emily. Emily Dimmock. Now, she liked a drink, didn't she, Bet?"

"Oh yes. Always a large gin. Never short of cash, that one. The gin flowed all night long when she was in the mood for a good time. A nice girl. I miss her."

"Me too, Bet."

The two bar staff chattered for a moment, reminiscing over old times. Lawrence sipped his beer, now feeling slightly woozy, and wondered whether he should find a coffee shop on the way back to sharpen his senses. "Your friend sounds jolly nice," he said. "But why are you telling me about her?"

"It's like this," said Sid, pulling up a stool on the other side of the bar. He leaned forward conspiratorially. "Emily died."

"How sad. I'm sorry to hear it."

"Aren't you curious about how she died?"

Suddenly, despite the beer fog, Lawrence's senses were on high alert. His pulse quickened and his heart skipped a beat. A frisson of excitement snaked through his body. And he knew what Sid was going to tell him.

"Someone killed her," he said before Sid could open his mouth.

"There. That got your attention," said Sid. "Now, you don't look so tired of life."

"But when, how? Is he rotting in Pentonville?"

"Ain't that the question? No, he ruddy well ain't because they never caught him. He cut Emily up like the Ripper himself and went off into the night."

"They must have had suspects?"

"Plenty. And a particular one who went to trial. But he got off. Now, some say it was a travesty, and others like me think he shouldn't have been there in the first place. Robert Wood's trial was all over the papers. I'm surprised you never came to hear of it."

"I rarely read them," said Lawrence.

"Why's that then?"

"Too many memories," replied Lawrence candidly.

"You need to get back out there." Sid pulled a pipe from his jacket pocket, filled it with tobacco and packed it down with a grubby thumb.

"Care for a pinch of snuff while I'm about it?" he asked.

"No, thank you." Lawrence recoiled as Sid lit the pipe, and a plume of smoke left his mouth.

"So, do you want to know more?"

"Well, yes."

Sid's eyes narrowed at Lawrence's hesitation.

"Not exciting enough for you?"

"I'm only in London for a week or so."

"Time enough to give it a go, though? You couldn't do worse than that lumbering oaf from the yard."

"Hmmm. I'll need to know a little more before deciding."

"Then I'll tell you. But first, here's another little offering to whet your appetite."

"Go on."

"It ain't the first."

"What ain't? I mean, isn't?"

"Young Esther Prager died in Bloomsbury last year. The same mode of dispatch." Sid grimaced as he ran his hand along his neck in a throat-cutting gesture.

"Really?" Lawrence reached into his pocket and removed the notebook he could never bring himself to abandon. He opened it and licked the tip of the pencil.

"That's got your interest, Mr Private Detective."

"Isn't that what you wanted? Now, tell me more."

"I will. But first, I'll let you into a little secret about Emily."

Chapter Six

EMILY DIMMOCK

"Go on?" Lawrence held his pencil ready, his hand shaking in anticipation.

"Emily wasn't her only name."

"She had another?"

"Yes. A professional moniker, if you take my drift."

"Ah. Emily was an unfortunate?"

"Get away with your fancy words. The girl led a charmed life and wanted for nothing."

"Sorry. I misunderstood. You mean Emily had an occupation?"

Sid crooked his finger at Bet, snorting with laughter. Eyes heavenward, she moved across the room.

"What's tickled you?"

"Our investigator friend, whatever your name is."

"Lawrence Harpham."

"Yes, Mr Lawrence Harpham thinks Emily Dimmock had a calling."

"She did," said Bet, pursing her lips. "Not one I'd choose, but it takes all sorts."

Lawrence flipped his notebook closed. "You've pulled my leg, Sidney, and I fell for it. Time to go."

The barman placed a weather-beaten hand on Lawrence's sleeve. "No. Please don't. I've told you the truth – every word. Emily Dimmock was a dolly mop, make no mistake. She called herself Phillis and met her acquaintances in the local public houses. But it wasn't for money. She didn't need it. Her husband worked on the railway. Not the tracks. Not hard labour. Bert was a dining car attendant and earned a pretty penny for it. No. Emily did it because she enjoyed it. And that's likely what killed her."

"I see." Lawrence opened his notebook again and scribbled a few silent lines.

"Well?" asked Sid, after a while.

"Bert's surname, please?"

"Shaw."

"Age?"

"Nineteen or twenty. Younger than Emily."

"And you say they were married?"

"Not actually married. Living in sin, more like. Bert just told people that. She only cared about appearances because Bert said he wouldn't marry her if she didn't give up her ways. So, he put it about that they'd wed. And Emily, well, she just put it about."

"So, Bert knew about her proclivities?"

"He thought Emily was safely at home keeping the house tidy. He trusted her and didn't know what she was up to. How could he? The poor chap was on the train to Sheffield six days a week. He barely had time to sleep, much less check what his old lady was doing."

"I presume he had an alibi?"

Sidney nodded. "As solid as a rock. He was on the train serving food to the passengers while Emily was dying. He couldn't have killed her. Besides, the poor sap adored the woman."

"How do you know?"

"Papers, gossip, policemen ferreting for information. It's all anyone discussed for weeks around here."

"What else do you know?"

"Well," said Sid as he stood and drew half a glass of ale. "Emily's death gave Bert's mother the shock of her life."

"Why? Was she around?"

Sid downed the liquid in one gulp, wiped his mouth, and belched. "'Scuse my manners, gov."

"I was asking about Mrs Shaw." Lawrence, never tolerant of vulgarity, was rapidly losing patience.

"Yes. Hold your horses. I'm recollecting hard. Now, Bert's mother travelled to Camden to give Emily the once-over. Not sure what she'd heard, but Bert wasn't much of a man and seemed to think he needed his mother's consent before putting a ring on Emily's finger."

"You don't seem to like him much."

"I barely knew the man. We spoke, but he was too much of a namby-pamby mother's boy for me. Don't know what a good-looking girl like Phillis saw in him, but there's no accounting for taste."

"Moving on."

"Alright. I'm getting to it. Mrs S arrives, knocks on the door, looking for Emily, and nobody answers. So, she waits and waits some more. Eventually, the landlady brought her a chair to sit on. More waiting and all the time she's seething, fair mad with the girl, or so I'm told. Finally, Bert arrives just after eleven o'clock."

"Morning or evening?"

"Morning. He started late afternoon and finished about eleven. So, he comes home, sees his mother, and tries the door, but it won't open. Locked, you see. His mother asks him to open the ruddy door, but he can't. Because his wife always lets him in, and she keeps the key. There's a bit of to-ing and fro-ing before the landlady produces her spare; Bert goes inside and finds Emily with her throat cut from ear to ear. Proper deep it was too."

"What time did Emily die?"

Sidney shrugged. "I don't know. Others might."

"Hmmm." Lawrence nodded uncommittedly, internally debating whether to use his contact at Scotland Yard or a friendly reporter for more detailed information.

"You mentioned a man called Robert Wood."

"I did. And if you had paid a bit more attention to the press, you'd know that he entered the courtroom as a suspect and left as a ruddy hero. A lucky escape. They could have hung him by the neck if he hadn't found a decent barrister. Now, who do you think he used?"

"No idea."

"Go on. Guess."

"I'd rather not."

"You're no fun. Only Mr Edward Marshall Hall."

Lawrence raised an eyebrow. He had heard of the celebrated lawyer, well respected in his field and a formidable opponent.

"Mr Wood must have had a bob or two to afford him."

"Not really. But Wood had the benefit of a well-off father."

"So, Hall got him off?"

"Yes. Without a blemish on his character. Even though Wood gave a false alibi and wrote the bloody postcard."

"Postcard?"

"Yes. The stupid fool wrote a card, addressed it to Phillis, and sent it to her home, asking her to meet him here on the night of the murder. He might as well have advertised it in the newspapers."

"Did she meet him?"

"Apparently. I didn't actually see them. And if that wasn't bad enough, he got Ruby Young to lie for him."

Lawrence sighed. He'd met people like Sidney before. Men who assumed everyone around was as well acquainted with the locals as them. It made following the story exhausting, not to mention deeply frustrating.

"Who is Ruby?" he asked through gritted teeth.

Sidney slowly answered as if Lawrence were half-witted. "The girl Wood was betrothed to before he took up with Emily, of course. Wood promised he'd marry Ruby if she gave him an alibi."

"How on earth did a man with so much reason to be in court get off scot-free?"

"His father, for starters. Said Wood was at home all night."

"And no doubt covering for his offspring."

"He was a proper gent and very well respected."

"Even so."

"And there was a lot of circum... circular..."

"Circumstantial?"

"That's the one. Circumstantial evidence. Marshall Hall sliced through the prosecution like a scythe through the corn. I wouldn't mind him on my side if the chips were down."

"And Wood walked free?"

"As a bird. Far too much doubt in the jury's minds to risk a conviction."

"And you agree with the verdict?"

Sidney nodded. "Wood was a fool. He lied to protect his

reputation. But I don't think he had a good punch in him, let alone the ability to carve up a girl he barely knew."

"Were you acquainted with Robert Wood?"

"I poured him a pint or two. We chatted a bit in passing. Can't say I remember much about him."

"Well, I think that's all. Thank you for your time."

"Are you going to look into it?"

"Probably. What can you tell me about the other girl?"

"Esther Prager? Nothing. I never met her."

"No matter. I have other sources."

"Promise you'll do what you can?"

"Why? Were you fond of Emily?"

"She was a nice enough girl."

Lawrence raised an eyebrow and waited.

"I have a daughter," said Sidney. "She's a headstrong girl. Don't always know where she is or what she does. But I'd like to think she's safe."

"I have a daughter too. And rest assured, I'll do what I can in the time available."

Sidney forced a smile as his happy-go-lucky facade crumbled. His lip trembled, and for an uncomfortable moment, Lawrence thought he might cry. "Bless you, Mr Harpham. I won't forget this."

Chapter Seven

SETTLING IN AT THE GRAFTON

Lawrence had been back at The Grafton Hotel for one hour and twenty-five minutes by the time Violet flew through the door, carrying a large sketchbook.

"There you are," she said as if Lawrence had unexpectedly been somewhere he shouldn't.

"Where else would I be?"

"Don't be grumpy. I've had the most marvellous day. You'll never guess what I've got here."

"An African mountain gorilla? Or could it be a Faberge egg? No. Sorry, you'll have to tell me."

"Oh really, Lawrence. Look."

Violet opened the front cover and thrust a set of bound drawings in front of him. "Well?"

"Very nice, dear."

"Oh, for goodness' sake. Walter Sickert gave me his sketchpad to learn from. I mean, he's a well-respected artist and out of nowhere, he took this from his bag and said I should borrow it and use it for further study. How unbelievably generous. I'm overwhelmed."

"Well, I'm pleased for you," said Lawrence, rising above his instinctive lack of regard for artists in general and ugly drawings in particular. Lawrence liked carvings, sculptures, and things you made with your hands. Not peculiar sketches of jowly faces. He quickly turned the page only to encounter the naked rear of a large woman in her later years.

"Good God!" he exclaimed.

"It's only art."

"Even so. He must have copied it from somewhere or, God forbid, drew a living person."

"The latter. Walter and the boys often use live models."

Of course, they do, thought Lawrence, wisely keeping his opinion to himself.

"How about a spot of dinner now you're back?"

"That would be lovely." Violet returned the drawings to their waterproof bag, reverently tying a cord around them and straightening the ends until they looked just so.

"Capital. We'll freshen up and have a drink first."

"Oh, but I must call Michael."

"I suppose you ought. You do that, and I'll start planning the rest of our week after seeing the exhibition tomorrow afternoon."

"About that."

"Yes?"

"Change of plan. I'm not going."

"Marvellous. We'll have the day to ourselves."

"Not exactly." Violet approached her husband and took his hands. "I'll go on day three. I know you won't mind, but Walter has invited me to one of his get-togethers at his home in Mornington Crescent."

"God. How awful. But fine if it means that much to you. Can I assume we will attend fully clothed?"

"Oh. I didn't think you'd want to come."

"I'll take any man's hospitality. We don't need to stay for long."

"It's not a social event. At least not in that way. And I would like to stay for as long as possible."

"Not a social event? You're not modelling for them, are you?"

"Lawerence! That's low."

"No insult intended. But I'm rather confused about what you mean by a get-together. I'm not fond of the term, but I understood it implied a social element."

"You are formal sometimes, my dear. Mr Sickert and his artist friends see each other weekly to display their paintings, talk about art and exchange information on the latest techniques. They usually meet on a Saturday but were busy and postponed until tomorrow. It's an excellent opportunity for me to learn. They'll all be there. Freddie, Leo, and Walter, of course. He's passionate about the work of another young artist and wants me to meet him."

"Any women artists?"

"Yes, as it happens. Are you jealous?"

"Not a bit of it. I'm only protecting your honour."

"I can do that perfectly well alone. This is the 1900s, Lawrence. Women can look after themselves."

"The least I can do is escort you there."

"And I would welcome it." Violet leaned into her husband and pecked his cheek. "I will introduce you, of course. Perhaps you can catch up with Ann or go to one of your clubs after. Have some fun while I work."

Lawrence returned the kiss, stood, and offered Violet the telephone handset. "Call Michael then. I'm gasping for a drink, and I've barely eaten since breakfast."

"You and your stomach," said Violet, patting Lawrence's ever so slightly rounded abdomen.

"Get away with you."

Still laughing, Violet summoned the operator, but her jocular mood did not last. A few moments later, she sat ashen faced, listening as if she could not believe her ears.

Chapter Eight

BOMBSHELL

Lawrence's first instinct on seeing Violet's shocked face was to ask what was wrong. But he decided against it, adopting the second instead by taking her hand and leading her straight to the bar, where he ordered two gin slings. He gave her a moment to take a few sips before reaching out and stroking the back of her hand.

"What is it, old girl?"

Violet lowered her eyes, took another mouthful, and whispered. "He's already there?"

"Who?"

"Francis."

"Damn his eyes. The nerve of the man."

The bartender stared in their direction, disturbed by Lawrence's raised voice.

Violet put her finger to her lips. "Be careful," she said.

"Of what?"

"Drawing attention to ourselves. Things are bad enough as it is."

"How is Michael?"

"Confused, upset, worried. He wasn't making much sense. We should have warned him sooner."

"I know. But I didn't expect Francis to go high-tailing it to Suffolk when he's allegedly on his last legs."

"You say that as if you don't believe him."

"I remain unconvinced, Violet."

"Don't start that again. I've cared for enough elderly patients to know the signs. Francis is skin and bone. He's not a well man."

"Then why are you so worried?"

"Michael is living at Netherwood, which belongs to Francis. Aurora is terrified of the Order that Francis still belongs to. I know she's come out of herself since they married. And she's a wonderful mother to little Luna. But this could prove a dreadful setback, and I fear it's a recipe for disaster."

Lawrence stirred his cocktail for the fourth time, wiped the silver spoon on his napkin and, lining it up with the edge of a black bar tile, placed it down again.

"Please stop," said Violet.

Lawrence steepled his hands.

"Better."

"The question is, my dear Violet, will Francis want his home back?"

"I don't see how he can. It's morally awful. Michael has spent a fortune in the ten years since Francis left. He's invested everything he owns in Netherwood. It's a happy home. Well, now that he's nailed the door shut on that dreadful room."

"Francis is utterly amoral. He won't care."

"He must do. Why come to us asking for forgiveness?"

"Who knows? I don't trust him."

"Neither does Aurora."

"Did you speak to her too?"

"No. Only Michael. But he said she was there when Francis arrived."

"Did they speak?"

"Apparently so. He knocked on the front door and Aurora admitted him. She'd never met him before and did not know anything was wrong."

"Should be impossible for him to get inside," said Lawrence. "With guard dogs and two ex-soldiers in Michael's employ, Netherwood ought to be as safe as Barings Bank."

"Unfortunate timing," said Violet. "Francis arrived late last night while the dogs were being fed. Michael's taken to having family only Sundays and stands his staff down so they can do the same."

"He's taken his eye off the ball."

"Perhaps he knows Crossley's in Africa."

"Maybe. How awful for Aurora."

"Yes. Michael said he feels terribly guilty."

"No harm done now he's turned Francis out."

"Except that he didn't," said Violet, draining her glass. Lawrence nodded to the barman, and moments later, another two cocktails appeared together with a small salver of hors d'oeuvres.

"Please tell me they didn't sit down to a family dinner, and all is now forgiven?"

"Of course not. But they talked in a civilised manner in the drawing room."

"Good God. Has Michael forgotten what happened in Swaffham?"

"No. But he's a man of God, and I know him so well.

Michael teaches forgiveness. He'll be wrestling with his conscience."

"What did Francis want?"

"The same thing he asked from us. To make amends and let bygones be bygones."

Lawrence snorted. "Not much to ask from a brother who has spent the last decade mopping up his mess. Francis could walk into the Freemason's hall, and they'd greet him with open arms. Between Michael and I, we've suppressed every criminal act he committed. I wish we hadn't, Violet, and I hope we won't live to regret it."

"Hopefully not. Francis said he would only spend a few days in Bury before returning to London to die."

Lawrence winced, then put his head in his hands. "I dread to think of the effect that well-crafted statement will have on Michael."

"I thought so too."

"How long did Francis stay?"

"About half an hour," I believe.

"But did he leave the premises?

Violet nodded.

"With no plans to return."

"None."

"Where is he staying?"

"At an inn. Michael didn't say which one."

"Shouldn't be difficult to find out."

"To what purpose, Lawrence?"

"Not me. I've no intention of contacting him ever again. But if I can find out where he's staying, so could Michael."

"He has Aurora to consider. Michael will want to protect his family."

Lawrence reached for a fork and stabbed it into a

devilled kidney, raised it to his mouth, and then reconsidered.

"Not hungry."

"Not anymore."

"Don't worry. Michael will do the decent thing."

"Pray God you are right."

Chapter Nine

MORNINGTON CRESCENT

Tuesday, November 23, 1909

Lawrence was still mulling over the Farrow situation when he rose the following morning. He hailed a cab for Mornington Crescent, staring bleary-eyed as one driver after another trotted past, oblivious to his presence. Then he snapped out of his reverie, waved his hand, and summoned a driver.

"Come on," he said, casting an irritated glance at Violet, who was sheltering from the early morning rain shower in the hotel foyer.

She nodded to the hotel doorkeeper before darting towards the cab door where Lawrence stood, holding it open.

After giving directions to the driver, he joined her inside, immediately alert to a tension in the air.

"You've upset the porter," Violet whispered.

"Me? How?"

"They don't expect you to find transport yourself."

"I don't mind," said Lawrence, who had never taken well to being waited on.

"But the hotel staff do. It affects their income."

"Oh. By way of tips?"

"Exactly."

"Fine. I'll remember next time."

Lawrence stifled a yawn and leaned back in the cab, his eyes half closed.

"You should have stayed in bed."

"No point. I haven't slept all night."

"It isn't easy, Lawrence. I had a disturbed night too. But we must go on as best we can."

"I'm torn between dashing home to Daisy and heading for Netherwood."

"Please don't. We must live our lives. Francis is a fool but a frail one. He won't hurt anybody, and Crossley is far away. I overreacted yesterday. Michael is a sensible man."

"I know," said Lawrence. "I wish I had your optimistic nature. Your moments of fearing the worst are transitory. Mine last until I'm proved right."

"Have faith," said Violet. "Let's enjoy the day."

They pulled up outside a small crescent of handsome townhouses, uniformly red-bricked with railings and balconies. Lawrence leaned forward, glancing towards them with evident approval.

He paid the driver, and they approached the black door of number six.

"Ready?" asked Violet, watching Lawrence's smile slip away as he faced the prospect of greeting people he didn't much care for.

"As I'll ever be."

Violet rapped the door knocker, which opened almost immediately.

"Mr Covington," she said delightedly. "Lawrence. This is Leonard Covington. Leonard, you met my husband yesterday."

"Good to see you again," said the young artist, extending his hand.

Lawrence grasped it and encouraged by the firm grip, smiled.

"Do come through," Leonard continued. "Freddie and Walter are upstairs with the paintings. I thought you might like to meet our honorary artist, Ethel Sands. We don't admit women to our membership," he continued ruefully. "Not as progressive as perhaps we should be. But Miss Sands is a regular visitor, and we greatly appreciate her work. Ethel, this is Violet Harpham."

"Pleased to meet you," said Violet, taken aback when Ethel answered in an American drawl.

"Charmed, I'm sure. Have you brought something along to delight us with?"

"Goodness me no. I'm a novice, quite inexperienced. Mr Sickert has been extraordinarily generous in allowing me access to this group. I can't quite believe I am here."

"You're very welcome. And who is this?" She stared pointedly at Lawrence as if he were an unnecessary accessory.

"My husband, Lawrence."

"Does he paint?"

"No, I don't," snapped Lawrence.

"Then what are you doing here?" Ethel's question was curt, but though irritated, Lawrence recognised a straight-talker and tried to exercise patience.

"Dropping off my wife," he explained. "I thought it only polite to call in."

"Good for you." Ethel's face softened. "I'll see you later, Mrs Harpham."

Violet stood still, momentarily registering the back of Ethel Sands' head as she moved on to more pressing matters.

"Come along," said Leonard. "And don't mind, Ethel. She's very driven."

They followed him upstairs into a light, bright drawing room with two sash windows perfectly situated to make the most of the weak November sun. Walter Sickert stood, brush in hand, behind one of several easels, a red scarf fastened around his neck. His paint-spattered overalls reeked of turpentine.

"Ah, Mrs Harpham. Excuse my appearance. I've just returned from Fitzrovia with my latest work. Unfinished, I might add."

"It's marvellous," breathed Violet.

"And will be even more so when it's complete. But of course, I couldn't just bring it untouched. I spotted an imperfection and became hopelessly distracted trying to fix it. What a palaver it was lugging a wet painting halfway across London in a cab."

"You do exaggerate," laughed Freddy. "Fitzroy Street is a bare twenty minutes from here."

"Yes, but facts make a dull story," said Walter. "I do so love a drama. Now, let's get started. Freddie, why don't you pop downstairs and give them all a ten-minute warning while I introduce Violet to the others."

"Right you are." Freddie winked and went on his way.

"Good," said Walter, approaching a man crouched in the corner. "Come this way. On your feet, Len."

The young man moved away from a heavily pregnant Dalmatian.

"She's gorgeous," he said, reaching down for another ear tickle.

Walter frowned. "Yes. But quite why Ethel felt the need to bring her, I don't know. God knows what will happen if she whelps here."

"You'll manage perfectly ably, as in any situation."

"Or toss her out on the street if the mood takes me."

"Don't listen," said Leonard, covering his hands over the dog's ears. She nuzzled into him as if sensing a friend. "Uncle Len will look after you," he whispered.

"Enough now." Sickert scowled, his impatience on full display. "Tell Mrs Harpham of your tremendous success. We are all very jealous of young Covington."

"Do rein it in, Walter. You know I hate bragging."

"But you must. You owe it to all of us. Blow your own trumpet loudly and often. No point in having a bloody trumpet if you don't."

"Whatever you say."

"Leonard is too modest to recount his wildly lucrative career. The rest of us starve in our garrets while he cavorts around London in a Bentley. And he's now removed to a very nice place in Holborn and no longer needs to slum it in Camden with the rest of us."

"Oh really, Walter. Mornington Crescent is hardly a slum."

"It's a charming house, Mr Sickert," said Violet, instinctively working to keep the peace.

"Indeed, it is. I'm only teasing. Well, let me tell you about Leonard's work because he hasn't painted much this year and has nothing to display for your pleasure."

"I have, and I do," said Leonard. "It's back at the workshop, and unlike Walter, I was unprepared to risk transporting it here only to take it back again."

"And what is the name of this mysterious work?"

"To be advised," said Leonard firmly.

"Very well. Now, Violet. Leonard's most notable painting was a masterpiece, a gloriously blended work called Sunset over Primrose Hill, which he sold to a gallery for a sizeable sum. The rest of us have spent six years trying to emulate his success, to no avail. Although filthy lucre aside, Freddie excelled himself last year, and young Mr Lightfoot has recently produced the most remarkable drawings."

"And there he is," said Leonard, pointing to a much younger man who had just entered the room.

Lawrence watched disinterestedly. If he cared more, he might wonder why no one had the manners to address him directly. But he was only here for Violet, with no interest in scraping further acquaintance with the bohemian art-loving crowd. And if young Lightfoot was anything to go by, they were a motley crew. Tall, thin and with a neck so slender it looked like it might snap in a gust of wind, the young man wore an expression of abject misery.

"Over here, boy," blasted Walter Sickert, crooking his finger.

Lightfoot raised a hand in acknowledgement and made his slow-paced way across the room.

"Violet Harpham, meet Maxwell Lightfoot." Sickert rushed the introduction, placed his arm around the young man's shoulders, and guided him away. "Come, Mrs Harpham. You must see this."

Violet eagerly followed while Lawrence mustered sufficient enthusiasm to catch up with them after re-tying his shoelace. They stood, clustered around three drawings pinned to an empty frame while Violet cooed over the picture.

"Aren't they marvellous, Lawrence?" she said. "Just look at the expression, the shadowing. It's exquisite."

"They're preliminary drawings," said Lightfoot.

"To what end? How will you develop them?" Lawrence felt the first stirrings of irritation at Violet's rapt features as she probed the young artist.

"How kind of you to ask. Well, a larger version of this using graphite with watercolours, I fancy."

"That would be wonderful. It's such an emotive piece."

Lawrence felt his lip curl and adjusted his face to something more benign. The angst-ridden drawing of a girl holding her face in utter despair did nothing for him but lower his already unsettled mood.

"You don't approve," said Walter Sickert.

"Me? What do I know?" Though tempted to give his opinion, Lawrence had no wish to upset Violet.

"It needs a great deal of improvement," said Lightfoot eagerly, almost relieved at the implied criticism.

"I beg to differ. It's a marvellous work. You're heading in the right direction, and I'm sure you'll end up nipping at Covington's heels." Sickert gazed paternalistically at his younger colleague.

"Oh, I could never."

"Of course you could," said Leonard, beaming. "Stick with me, and I'll do my best to guide you."

Lightfoot's face fell again. "You've already done so much for me, and I don't deserve it."

"You both deserve the benefit of my experience," said Sickert, winking at Covington and patting Lightfoot on the shoulder. "Come on. Rally yourselves, and let's get on with it."

"My cue to leave," said Lawrence. "Will you make your own way back, my dear?" he asked.

But he didn't hear Violet's reply. Sickert had walked over to the larger easel and snatched away a black covering to reveal a young lady surrounded by rumpled sheets, fast asleep on her bed.

"Don't say a word," hissed Violet as Lawrence stood, mouth agape at the sight of an anatomically detailed nude.

Sickert coughed, then introduced the painting to the occupants of the now crowded room. "Ladies and gentlemen. This young lady has accompanied me to Paris, where I'm delighted to say she was very well received. I will not be exhibiting her here for a while. The general public is not quite ready. So, I offer you a unique insight into one of my many current works."

Sickert launched into a detailed description of the techniques used on the muted tones, but Lawrence had seen enough. He didn't care for dingy settings in seedy rooms and found the picture depressing and voyeuristic.

"Are you sure you want to stay?" he whispered. Violet shot him a glare, and with that, he exited stage right and went to find something more appealing to do.

Chapter Ten

AN INNOCENT MAN?

Lonni Carpenter was sitting behind a desk jabbing tobacco-stained fingers onto the keys of a solid-looking Royal typewriter when Lawrence approached. Lonni did not look up from his desk.

Lawrence coughed, then coughed again while listening to the industrious sounds. Three more keystrokes, a bell ringing at the end of the line and a flourish as Lonni removed the page. Then the reporter looked up, his face faltering in vague recognition before the penny dropped.

"Lawrence Harpham. Well, I'm blessed. What are you doing here?"

"Looking for you, Lonni."

"Ah. Marvellous, I mean, it would be if I wasn't on a tight deadline." He glanced at his pocket watch. "My editor needs this now."

"Will you break for lunch?"

"Yes, and for a little mid-morning snack, I daresay. I was in the office before six today. I could eat a horse."

"Then let me treat you, but you'll have to guide me. I'm unfamiliar with the area."

"There's a cafe on the corner. See it?" Lonni pointed outside.

"I do."

"Meet me there in half an hour, but don't worry if I'm a few minutes over. The new editor is a stickler. I haven't trained him yet."

Lawrence was halfway through his second coffee when Lonni finally arrived, slumping inelegantly into the opposite seat while loosening his collar.

"How are you?" asked Lawrence.

"Carrying too many pounds. I married last year, and my wife is an excellent cook. I've gone up three neck sizes and must exercise some restraint."

"A pity," said Lawrence. "Those pies smell delicious."

"They are not to be missed. Restraint can wait until tomorrow."

Lonni placed orders at the counter for himself and Lawrence and returned with a large mug of tea.

"Hearty food, but good," said Lonni. "You will enjoy it. Now, I'm delighted to see you, Lawrence, but I'm guessing there's a reason. It's been several years since you sent me that excellent letter confirming the fate of the psychopath Connolly."

Lawrence grimaced. Like Lonni, he was relieved that Dickie could do no more harm, but he had never come to terms with delivering the blow that left Dickie a paraplegic.

"There is a reason for my visit," he confessed, pushing the vision of the rusty pitchfork from his mind.

"Go on?"

"Are you familiar with the Camden murder?"

"Of course. Isn't everyone?"

"Apparently so. But I've only recently come to hear of it."

"Have you been abroad?"

"No. But I stopped reading newspapers."

Lonni waited patiently through the growing silence until Lawrence spoke again. "I retired. Too early, perhaps. It was easier to ignore the news."

"I see. So why take an interest now?"

"It's a long story. I met a man in a pub, and he told me all about Emily Dimmock and the many clues that remain unsolved. It disturbed me in ways I can't explain."

"I can. Rotten detective work," said Lonni. "Which your instinct will despise."

"What happened?"

"Have you ever worked a case with only one obvious suspect?"

"Not that I remember."

"Me neither. Not that I investigate for a living, but I've reported on many crimes. Yet never have I seen so much effort into going after one man at the expense of any other. They marked Robert Wood's card from the start."

"Yet it seemed justified. He lied and obfuscated at every turn."

"Circumstantial though, wasn't it? What would you do if you'd been a damned fool, and somebody died? Any of us might underplay the facts."

"So, you don't think he's guilty either?"

"It doesn't matter what I believe. They cleared the man in court."

"It matters to me. I value your opinion."

"Why, thank you. Alright. I don't think Wood is the guilty party, though he didn't help himself. There's much more to this murder than meets the eye.

"Meaning?" But Lawrence was interrupted by the delivery of a steaming hot pork and apple pie. He salivated as the waitress placed it on the table.

"In what way?"

"Emily Dimmock had a shady past. I presume you know how she made a living?"

"I do. And I've heard it was unnecessary."

"Correct. But it didn't stop her. She'd been seeing men for so long it became second nature."

"Tell me more."

"Miss Dimmock came to London from the country. I can't remember where, but she arrived in the capital and lodged at the house of a small-time crook."

"Address?"

"I can't remember that either, but his name was Crabtree. John Crabtree."

"A criminal, you say."

"Yes. Thieving, horse stealing. That kind of thing. And they charged him with keeping a disorderly house on several occasions."

"I see."

"Yes. Crabtree was undoubtedly running a brothel."

"Did they interview him for the murder?"

"No. He had a cast iron alibi."

"They all seem to have one of those."

"Not like this. He was serving time when Emily died. Anyway, she'd long moved on from him, and they only saw each other occasionally."

"Then why mention him at all?"

"To give you an insight into the kind of girl she was. Very pleasant from all accounts, but hardly innocent."

"Do you think her profession had something to do with the murder?"

"Probably. But not necessarily. The killer might not have been a client. Emily knew many people, some of whom were violent and some of whom were wrong 'uns. Yet, her partnership with Bert brought respectability. Emily rubbed shoulders with all kinds of people."

Lawrence, who had demolished his pie in no time, straightened his cutlery and pushed the plate away.

"I heard something about a postcard. Can you tell me more?"

"Certainly. I wrote a piece on it last year. So, Emily Dimmock enjoyed collecting postcards almost as much as suitors. She plied her wares, as it were, in the local pubs. And she was at The Rising Sun this particular evening with Robert Wood when a postcard seller arrived. Now, Wood was a glassware designer for a manufacturing company and fancied himself a bit of an artist. And when Emily wanted to purchase a postcard from the vendor, he poo-pooed the idea, saying he'd draw one himself. Then he whipped out a card he'd brought back from a recent holiday, wrote a quick message, and drew a picture of a Rising Sun. To represent the pub, you see. A decent cartoon it was too."

"Interesting."

Lonni slurped his tea and gestured to the waitress for another. Then, stifling a belch, he reclined before continuing.

"Now, Robert Wood didn't give the card to Emily. He posted it to her house. Which would likely rouse Bert's suspicions if he used his own name, so he signed it Alice."

"Any reason why he chose that particular name?"

"I don't know. Not sure it matters. The point is someone posted the card in the early hours of Sunday morning or possibly even Monday. Regardless, it arrived several days after he wrote it."

"What did the police make of it when they investigated the murder?"

"Nothing. Because they didn't find it. Someone had ransacked Emily's rooms and her postcard album lay on the floor with the cards scattered around the room as if someone had torn them from the album."

"Yet another reason to suspect Robert Wood," said Lawrence. "I have every sympathy with the police for arresting him and cannot understand why Wood got off scot-free. Nor why everyone thinks him innocent."

Lonni shrugged. "It helped to follow the story and sense the public mood at the time."

"Miss Dimmock only died a few years ago."

"The sentiment hasn't changed. Few believe Wood killed her."

"Still," said Lawrence, about to launch into the many reasons why he couldn't write Wood off. But Lonni stopped him.

"You haven't asked how anyone knew about the postcard," said Lonni.

"Go on."

"Emily had other men on the go, not just Robert Wood. But conveniently, a chap called Robert Roberts was a regular companion that week. Having spent three consecutive nights with Emily, he was keen for more. He turned up at The Rising Sun the night before the murder, expecting to meet up with her again. Only she wasn't there."

"Is he a suspect?"

"He was. But it never came to anything. He had an alibi too. Anyway, Roberts got speaking to a friend of his."

"Name?"

"Frank Clarke. A regular at The Rising Sun. It might be worthwhile having a chat if you can find him. And that shouldn't be hard. He was more or less a fixture there. Can't see that changing."

"Good point. I'll visit the pub and track him down."

"Do that. So, Emily showed the postcard to Roberts. He saw it and confirmed its arrival at her house."

"Yet the police didn't find it?"

"No. Because she hid it. Bert Shaw found the card beneath a drawer several days after her death and turned it over to the police. Very hard on him, that was. He didn't know she was still meeting other men. The postcard must have been a bitter blow."

"You said Wood signed it from Alice."

"I did. But by the time Shaw found it, they'd already told him about Robert Wood. And Robert Roberts, for that matter. Poor chap."

"Well, Lonni. I couldn't have asked for a better account, short of being at the trial. Thank you very much."

"My pleasure," said Lonni, accepting a second cup of tea from the busy waitress. "Now, here's another tip. If you don't mind a trip to one of the shadier parts of the town, you might get a chance to speak to Ruby Young."

"I know that name."

"You should. She was Robert Wood's intended. She gave him the alibi, but they're not together now. He emerged the hero and she lost her reputation completely, not that it was much to start with. So poor Ruby still solicits on Southampton Row. I saw her there recently."

Lawrence raised an eyebrow.

"In the line of work. I'm a married man now, don't forget."

"I know." Lawrence smiled. "Well, there's no time like the present. I'll see if I can find Ruby now."

"You do that. And call me if you need me."

"I will do. There are other cases, I hear."

Lonni stroked his chin. "One that I know of."

"Really?"

"Yes. Tell you what. Come by again later this week. I'll need to do some digging, but there's something in the back of my mind that happened a few years ago. We might be talking more than two killings, you know."

"Right you are," said Lawrence calmly, remembering Sid's allusion to another crime. His heart raced as he left the cafe, his senses alert and fired. Lawrence knew with certainty that he was onto something. And he had never felt more alive.

Chapter Eleven

SOUTHAMPTON ROW

Southampton Row did not scream ignominy, thought Lawrence as he headed past the tram subway. Quite the opposite. It was a lively shopping district dominated by substantial, well-built townhouses and various motorised and horse-driven vehicles. And it was brimming with people. Unfamiliar with the area, Lawrence had assumed the streetwalkers would be obvious, clustered perhaps by some well-known vantage point. But if that were the case, he couldn't see it. Nor could he differentiate a lady of ill repute from any other woman going about her lawful business. A fine detective he was.

Lawrence paused momentarily, found a public bench, and contemplated his next move. Ten minutes later, he was still ruminating and would have continued to do so had a uniformed man not sat beside him, engaging him in unwanted conversation.

"Nice day for it."

"Indeed," Lawrence replied as the cold November air began to bite earnestly.

"Yes. A bloody fine day indeed."

"Quite."

"Shall I tell you why?"

Lawrence edged two inches away from the man. "By all means," he said coldly.

"I've just become a father."

"Good for you." Lawrence smiled, feeling more well-disposed towards the man. He was always happy to acknowledge a new life.

"Yes. A little boy. Well, not so little. The nurse thinks he's over six pounds. Plump and healthy as babies should be."

"Congratulations to you and your lady wife."

"Why, thank you." The man beamed. "I couldn't be happier. Really, I couldn't. When Ivy left me, I thought that was the end of it. Then I met Carrie, and bless her heart, she's a good 'un. This is just the icing on the cake."

"What will you call him?"

"Carrie likes Vincent, but I'd rather name him after my old man, God bless his soul."

"What's he called?"

"Maxwell."

"That was my uncle's name."

"Then it's a sign. I'll tell Carrie. Vincent Maxwell Dobbs or Maxwell Vincent Dobbs. Either is fine by me."

"I say. Do you know this area well?"

"Yes, I ruddy well do. See that shop over there?" The man pointed towards a greengrocer.

"I do, and I should have realised. Your uniform bears the signage."

"It does. I cart the veg to and from the marketplace. Have done for last six years."

"Good, good," said Lawrence, trying to work out how

best to phrase his question. "Then perhaps you can help me."

"Happy to, gov."

"I need to find someone."

"What's his name?"

"Hers, but she may not use it."

The man's brow furrowed. "Oh, I see."

"I'm a private detective."

"Fair enough."

"I need to find a young lady named Ruby Young. She's one of the unfortunate kind."

"I've never heard of her."

"Unsurprisingly. But if I wanted to find another woman like her, where might I go?"

Lawrence ran a finger around his collar as he spoke, hoping to distract himself from blushing. Asking where prostitutes congregated was not a good look, even in the line of duty.

"Try Cosmo Place," said the man. "It's a little alleyway up there and quite active at night if you take my drift."

"Very helpful," said Lawrence. "I hope your young boy thrives."

Lawrence stood, tipped his hat, and strode up the road, still feeling self-conscious. He wasn't sure if the man believed him, which shouldn't matter, but it did. And Lawrence gritted his teeth as he tried to ignore the intrusion of awkward thoughts that echoed through his mind.

But one foot onto the junction with Cosmo Place, and he knew the man had been right. Several single women loitered in the narrow alley, using it as shelter from the cold, each one eyeing him with interest as he gazed in their direction. One woman winked from afar, and another called out.

But the third, more resourceful, approached him directly and asked if he wanted a good time.

"No," spluttered Lawrence.

"Are you sure, dear? You seem to be looking for something. I know a molly house not far from here. I'll tell you where it is for a penny."

"Certainly not. Good grief, woman."

"Get off your high horse, Mr la-di-dah. You've got that look in your eye. What do you want?"

Lawrence sighed and reached into his pocket for the inevitable bribe. "Do you know a girl called Ruby Young?"

A sly smile slid across the woman's face. "Happen, I do, but it'll cost you."

"I never doubted it," said Lawrence, dropping a coin into her extended hand.

She stared belligerently back.

"Here's another."

"You're heading in the right direction," she said.

Sighing, he dropped a third coin. "That's your lot. Where will I find her."

The woman pocketed the coins, placed her thumb and middle finger in her mouth and emitted a piercing whistle. A girl looked up further down the alley.

The woman gestured for her to join them, and moments later, she arrived slightly out of breath.

Chapter Twelve

RUBY'S DOWNFALL

"Ruby. This gentleman wants a word."

Lawrence examined the young woman's face as she cocked her head and smiled, her plain, almost manly visage marked with an outbreak of sores. She squinted at him through dark brown eyes, one slightly off-kilter.

"Show us your coin," she said.

"I only want to talk."

"Time is money."

"Very well." Lawrence held a penny aloft. "You shall have this if you answer truthfully."

"What are you? The ruddy police?"

"No."

"Then what?"

"An interested bystander."

"Give over," said Ruby. "But the answer seemed to satisfy her. What do you want then?"

"Tell me about Robert Wood."

Ruby's eyes fluttered as a look of pain crossed her face. "I've forgotten all about him," she muttered.

"But you'll remember for this penny."

"I thought he loved me. But Robert left me high and dry after the trial. Some gentleman he turned out to be."

"Why don't you start at the beginning?"

"I would if I weren't so damned cold."

"Come with me." Lawrence returned to Southampton Row, turned left, and walked for a few yards until he reached the spot where he'd earlier passed a street vendor.

"Would you like a coffee?" he asked.

Ruby's eyes grew round. "Rather," she said.

"Take a seat." Ruby settled on a rickety stool near a trestle table. The stall holder raised an eyebrow, but Lawrence shot him down with a stare.

"Two coffees and a round of bread and butter," he said.

"Right you are, sir."

The vendor poured a tarry substance into a pair of sturdy mugs, and Lawrence topped them up from a jug of milk.

"Don't loiter too long," the vendor whispered as Lawrence turned away. "I've got my reputation to consider."

"We'll be quick. And if we are a second over ten minutes, I'll purchase more coffee and some of that fine-looking fruit cake."

Lawrence did not stop to register the vendor's reaction but joined Ruby, sitting opposite her.

"Dig in," said Lawrence, placing the bread and butter in the centre of the table. Ruby took a slice and crammed it into her mouth as if she hadn't eaten all day. She swallowed one piece, then another, glancing nervously up as if Lawrence might suddenly spirit it away.

"Robert Wood," said Lawrence as Ruby wiped her hands on a fraying jacket. She followed his gaze to the patch on her elbow, now peeling away where the stitches had failed.

"I got the worst of it," she said bitterly.

"Of what?"

"The trial. Bob got off scot-free, and I left the Old Bailey in disguise."

"Why?"

"They blamed me for his arrest. The crowd turned hostile, and the prosecutor had no use for me after he lost his case. He tossed me a tatty old charwoman's frock and got his boy to show me to the rear exit. I could hear the jeers from the crowd as I ran for my life through the streets."

"That sounds a little extreme?"

"You weren't there," said Ruby, slapping the table in frustration. Both coffees wobbled and dribbled their contents down the sides.

"Steady on. You'll waste it."

Ruby snatched her drink and ran her tongue along the side of the mug before blowing the steaming hot liquid and taking a tentative sip. Her eyes closed in momentary pleasure.

"Start from the beginning," said Lawrence. "What was Robert Wood to you?"

Ruby's eyes misted over. "He was my sweetheart for a while," she said. "We walked out together back in the days where I sat for paintings more often than walking the streets."

"You were an artist's model?"

"Yes, for a while. And it was a sight better than going out in all weather, even if it paid poorly."

"Did Robert know?"

"Of course. That's how I met him. I sat for him once or

twice and then gave him a bit of the other for free. We saw quite a lot of each other, but he didn't like me out on the streets even though he saw other girls. We argued and didn't meet for a while."

"What changed?"

"Robert came to see me in my flat in Earl's Court to tell me he was in a spot of bother. I didn't ask him why because I already knew. I'd seen a copy of his postcard in the *News of the World*, and I recognised his style. It's quite distinctive, you know."

"The rising sun postcard?" asked Lawrence.

"Exactly. So, I asked him what's what, and he admitted he'd written that one but not the others found burned in Phillis Dimmock's grate. I asked him what he would do about it, and he said that he'd been alone on the night of the murder and had no alibi."

"Did he ask you to provide one, or did you offer?"

"He asked and was quite pushy about it. Ruby, he said, will you be true to me? And I asked him what he meant. He asked me to say I was with him on that Wednesday night. And I said I couldn't do it because he wasn't. Robert pleaded with me to trust him. If I were true, my word would stand against the world, he said. Now, Mr, whatever your name is."

"Harpham," said Lawrence.

"Now, Mr Harpham. I wasn't happy about lying. I didn't want my name in the papers for my mother to see. She didn't know what I was doing for a living, and I didn't want her to find out by seeing it splashed across the front page. I told Robert as much, and he said if they besmirched my name in any way, he would make an honest woman of me."

"So, you agreed?"

"Eventually. But I didn't like it."

"What happened next?"

"Robert told his family that he had known Emily Dimmock, but not to worry because he wasn't with her on the night she died. His brother said he must tell the police, but Robert would not. The following day, we met again in the Gray's Inn Road and Robert treated me to lunch in the Express Dairy. Proper nice it was too. But he kept on about the alibi, bothering me about being true to him and not changing my mind. I got fed up in the end and left him. He was getting on my nerves. Then I ran into a friend."

"Who?"

"Never you mind."

"A client?" Lawrence persevered as he scribbled the information in his journal.

"You might say that. But I hadn't seen this chap for a while. His name was McEwan Brown, if you must know," said Ruby, eyeing the notebook suspiciously. She reached for another slice of bread and took a bite.

"I was fretting by then," Ruby continued. "It didn't seem right to lie in court. So, I asked my friend what I should do about telling a lie under oath. I didn't mention Robert, of course. But I asked Mr Brown's advice on what might happen to me if I gave a false alibi. And he said I must not. I should go directly to the police and report it."

"Did you?"

"Not exactly. Robert visited me at home again on Thursday evening, and I asked him to release me from my promise."

"Of the alibi?"

Ruby nodded and licked her lips. "He asked if I had spoken to anyone else about it. I did not answer and Robert began to worry. He said if I had allowed someone to influence me against him, I could not love him. And I replied that it was true. I did not love him anymore because he should not ask such a thing of a woman he cared for. Robert left the house and that was that. But Mr Brown, unbeknown to me, had recounted my conversation to a friend at *The Weekly Dispatch*. He guessed my alibi was for Emily Dimmock's murder even though I did not tell him and asked Mr Brown to arrange a meeting in Regent Street. I didn't know what else to do, so I did as he asked. McEwan Brown escorted me, and I met Mr Dilnot, his journalist friend. I showed him other postcards Robert had sent me and agreed to help the police with their investigation. I met Robert after work, and two police inspectors followed me. They arrested him on sight."

"You did the right thing, Miss Young," said Lawrence, patting her hand.

"Then why am I reduced to walking the streets now? My name is mud, my reputation ruined, while Robert left the court a hero." Ruby sighed, and a tear trickled down her face.

"How was it for you in court"?

"Unpleasant. They frightened me, firing question after question, all the time trying to trip me up."

"What did you tell them?"

"The same as I just told you. Then Mr Newton showed me some fragments of a letter found in Miss Dimmock's fireplace and asked if I recognised the writing. I said I did, and that it was Mr Woods'. He continued questioning me and wanted to know where I was that night and if I could have seen the defendant. I said no. I could not, and that was that. He left me sobbing on the witness stand until they came to take me away. I have regretted my day in court ever since. I wish it had never happened."

"I am sorry for you, Miss Young. Truly. One should never suffer for telling the truth."

"Perhaps not. But my life is harder than ever. Still, thank you for the bread. I will take your penny now and go. I have a living to earn."

Lawrence withdrew his wallet and handed a crisp five-pound note to Ruby. She stared, eyes wide. "I can't take that."

"Yes, you can," he said, closing her hand over the money.

Ruby's eyes filled with tears. "God bless you, sir."

Lawrence stood and prepared to leave, but Ruby stopped and turned around.

"You never asked me if I think he did it," she said.

"I thought that was self-evident."

"You're wrong. Robert Wood asked me for an alibi because he didn't have one. Not because he killed Miss Dimmock. I never thought he did. But I was brought up to tell the truth. Robert was foolish, but there are darker forces at work. Whoever killed Emily Dimmock probably killed Esther Prager the following year. You need to find the connection between them."

Chapter Thirteen

A MINOR SQUABBLE

"Are you squiffy?" Lawrence shot up from his seat at the dressing table as Violet opened the hotel room door and stumbled into the room. She righted herself and glared at him.

"No. My foot buckled for a moment."

"So, you haven't had a drink?"

"A small sherry, but that's the extent of it."

"Good. That's alright then."

Violet drew herself to her full height. "I don't need your permission. If I want a few social drinks, I shall have them. You'd do it."

"You're right. I'd indulge, and I know you wouldn't fuss. Come here."

Lawrence embraced Violet and kissed her cheek. "I missed you, that's all. It's been a long but interesting day."

"Mine too. I've learned so much from The Camden Town Group."

"That's an official-sounding name. I thought it was an informal gathering?"

"It was. But Walter is an integral part of this organisation. We ought to do something similar in Cheltenham."

"If you wish. It should certainly keep you busy."

"Not me, dear. I'm still learning how to paint. Perhaps an art group already exists. I must find out. Anyway, I shall be going to Fitzrovia next. Walter and Freddie Gore have invited me to their studios."

"What am I supposed to do while you're gadding about London?"

"Come with me if you like."

"I don't."

"Then go and visit Ann."

"Yes. I might."

"What's that?" Violet pointed to an envelope by the telephone table.

"I don't know. I must have missed it when I returned."

"I can't see how. It's very obvious. Have you only just arrived?"

"I've been here for half an hour but working hard since I set foot through the door."

"Doing what?"

Lawrence hesitated for a moment, not sure how Violet would react. "I visited Lonni Carpenter earlier."

"Who?"

"The reporter who helped me track down Dickie Connolly."

Violet blanched at the memory. "Did you. How is he?"

"Very well. Lonni married not long ago."

"Good for him. I didn't know you had kept in touch."

"I hadn't. But I thought I would look him up, anyway."

Violet raised an eyebrow. "That's not like you, Lawrence. Are you harbouring an ulterior motive?"

"Well, now you come to mention it."

"What then?"

"You know I stopped in for a drink the other day."

Violet nodded.

"I got chatting to the barman."

"What about?"

"A murder."

"Lawrence?"

"It was an interesting case."

"In what way?"

"It remains unsolved."

Violet sighed, took her husband's hands, and led him to the edge of the bed, where they sat together.

"Are you sure you're ready for this? You haven't so much as opened a newspaper since we moved to Cheltenham."

"I'm bored. There's nothing better to do, and you are busy with this blasted artist colony."

"Yes. But we're only in London for a short time. And who would you help by prying into a dormant case?"

"Me, Violet. I'd be doing it for me. My life is currently meaningless."

"Don't say that. You deserve your retirement. Having no occupation does not make you less important."

"In your eyes, perhaps."

"What is so fascinating about this particular murder?"

Lawrence cupped Violet's face, holding his hand there momentarily, before kissing her forehead. "They found a young woman locked in her room with her throat cut from ear to ear. The man she lived with had an impeccable alibi, but the police arrested another man she had been seeing and took the case to court."

"And the second man got off?"

"Without a stain on his character. Robert Wood attained hero status."

"Robert Wood? I know the case. I read about it in the newspaper."

"Really?"

"It was front-page news. But not the sort of crime that would normally appeal to you."

"I agree. Yet they freed Wood, and nobody thinks he did it even though all the evidence pointed against him. I met his former lady friend earlier today. He pressurised her into giving a false alibi, and she still thinks him innocent of the crime."

"I do too," said Violet.

"Why?"

"The evidence was circumstantial."

"Granted. But they found a postcard he'd written in the victim's lodgings."

"From my understanding, Mr Wood didn't deny it."

"That doesn't make him innocent."

"No. But did they find anything in the victim's rooms that proved Mr Wood had ever been there?"

"Not that I know of. But your average murderer is a bit more careful than to leave evidence lying around. I'll tell you something you probably didn't know."

"What?"

"Emily Dimmock's postcard album was lying on the floor when they found her with several of the cards ripped out."

"Ripped out? Are they sure? Could the album not have fallen during the struggle, and the cards spilt when it hit the floor?"

"Possibly. It's one of the many things I need to discover."

"You sound committed to solving this, Lawrence."

"I am if such a thing is possible in a short space of time. But looking into it can't do any harm."

"And it will give you something to do while I paint." Violet smiled and examined the envelope she had collected from the telephone table, staring quizzically for a moment.

"What is it?" asked Lawrence.

"A letter bearing a Bury St Edmunds postmark, but I don't recognise the writing. It isn't Michael's."

Lawrence peered over her shoulder. "Definitely not," he agreed.

Violet peeled open the envelope and began to read. Then she clutched the letter to her breast. "Oh, Lawrence. Terrible news. Michael has succumbed, as we feared. We must do something, and soon."

Chapter Fourteen

LIVING IN FEAR

"What does he say?" demanded Lawrence.

"Michael didn't write this. It's from Aurora. I'll read it to you."

"Do so. At once."

Dear Violet

Forgive me for corresponding while you are away from home; I am in a terrible quandary, and I don't know where else to turn. Thank God you gave Michael the name of your hotel, or I would not know how to reach you.
Michael's brother visited Netherwood a few nights ago. But as we were unacquainted, I harboured no suspicions when I answered the door and admitted the frail-looking man. I welcomed him inside and Michael took him to the drawing room, where they spoke alone for a while. It wasn't until after he had left that Michael finally told me the truth. And the thought of him being so close after the horrors of that night at Akenham terrified me. I confronted Michael, asking him why he had spent so much time with a man who almost killed his closest compan-

ions, abandoned his family, and built the terrible room upstairs. But Michael couldn't explain himself. I made him promise to keep away from his brother, but he slept fitfully that night, worried about familial obligations.

Francis Farrows' visit happened on a Sunday evening when the groundsmen were away, and we were alone and vulnerable. I could hardly wait for them to turn up the following day so Michael could brief them to stop his brother from entering our home again. They arrived as usual, and Michael greeted them. Naturally, I assumed he had instructed them to keep Netherwood safe from Francis, but he had not. Later, when delivering hot drinks, I discovered they knew nothing about the plan. Michael hadn't said a word. My husband was out, and when he returned, I confronted him with my discovery.

Michael admitted to visiting local hotels, searching for where his brother was staying. He told me they talked again, and when he came to leave, Michael could not bring himself to walk away. He said he could not bear to leave Francis alone in his hour of need. Michael begged me to allow Francis into Netherwood and I refused. Not because of my fear, though he truly terrifies me. But because of little Luna. She is small and innocent and deserves our protection. Deep in his heart, Michael knows this but thinks that if he is nearby, Luna cannot come to harm. I disagreed, reminding him about his brother's close association with Felix Crossley. But Francis has convinced Michael that their acquaintance is over, and he is no longer under Crossley's influence. Don't judge me too harshly, but I told Michael that if he did not give up his brother, I would take Luna far away from Netherwood and never return. Michael understood my concerns but asked me to trust him. Any reconciliation with Francis would inevitably be short-lived as he has little time left on this earth.

In the end, humanity got the better of me and I agreed. But only because Michael left me feeling guilty and with little choice. I love my husband too much to leave him, and my idle threat to take Luna away did not work. Michael knows me too well. He is a good man and loyal to his Christian faith. Michael wants to make this situation work for everyone. But I fear it cannot. I do not trust Francis Farrow, and I never will.

Michael brought his brother home last night and settled him in the guest bedroom farthest away from our room. I removed Luna from the nursery, and she will sleep with us while this unwelcome house guest resides in my home. Meanwhile, I am sick with worry and did not sleep a wink last night. I know you will understand, dear Violet, and perhaps you and Lawrence can help me protect my darling girl from harm. I would not ask you if I did not think it was a serious risk. Michael is doing what he thinks is best. He treats Francis like a prodigal son, welcoming him back into the fold as if he had squandered a few pounds or broken a young lady's heart. He seems to have forgotten about the loathsome company Francis keeps and his past violence towards you both. I have not. I cannot forgive, and I will not forget. Please help me, dear Violet. I shall not sleep safely while this man invades my sanctuary.

Your loving sister-in-law

Aurora

"The bloody fool," said Lawrence, snatching the letter from Violet and dashing it to the floor. "What the hell does he think he's playing at?"

"Being a good Christian, as we feared."

"Michael's loyalty is better placed protecting his family. I would sell my soul to the devil if it meant being there to save Lily from his foul clutches."

Violet wrapped her arms around Lawrence, pulling him close. "Don't say that," she whispered. "You're too good a man to turn to the dark side. I understand Michael. I love and respect him, but he's tied to Francis by brotherly bonds.

He can see past the evil, though Michael should remember he does not own forgiveness. But it's different for you, Lawrence. How could you ever rise above the harm he did to your family? I cannot find it in me to pardon a man who has caused my beloved husband such grief."

Lawrence held her tightly, unable to speak for a moment. "I love you," he whispered before releasing her. Lawrence strode towards the window and looked out over London town.

"But what can we do about it?" mused Violet.

"I know." Lawrence spun around and faced his wife. "Can you spare a few hours tomorrow?"

"Of course. Anything."

"Good. I know just the person to call on."

Chapter Fifteen

VERA TO THE RESCUE

Wednesday, November 24, 1909

"Wait one. I'll be with you in a jiffy." Vera Ponsonby gestured at the door without properly looking. Lawrence and Violet loitered uncomfortably by the expansive front window.

"She hasn't recognised us," whispered Lawrence, listening to Vera's heated conversation.

"A bay mare? Bay, you say. Of course it matters. There's no point searching for the wrong-coloured horse. What will he say if we bring him back a piebald? Honestly. Details count." Vera sighed as Violet coughed and caught her eye.

Vera's head snapped up. "Lawrence, Violet," she boomed. Then, staring at the receiver, she raised her eyes heavenward. "No, I did not say a violet pony. When did you ever see a purple horse outside of the circus? Just listen. Actually, don't. I'll call you later. Something's cropped up."

Vera slammed the handset onto the cradle. "How are

you both?" she said. "And what are you doing here? Cora didn't mention you were visiting."

Violet embraced her while Lawrence offered his hand. "We didn't plan it," said Violet. "Have you got a few minutes?"

Vera glanced at the wall clock. "Of course. I have an appointment in half an hour, but I don't much care for it. I'm sure they will wait if I overrun."

"We won't keep you." Lawrence stowed an umbrella under the chair and took a seat.

"Have you heard from Cora?" asked Vera.

"Yesterday," said Violet. "She said all was well."

"Excellent. And what brings you here?"

Violet smiled to herself. Cora could talk all day long, but Vera Ponsonby was a different animal: efficient, frank and to the point. Small talk was not her forte.

"Some advice, please," said Lawrence, marshalling his thoughts.

"Go on."

"Francis Farrow has returned."

Vera whistled and crossed one trousered leg over the other. "Cora said Farrow was back, but it's hard to fathom even now."

"Yes, I shall never understand how he has the brass neck to cross my threshold. I should have shot him with a twelve-bore."

"You don't have one," said Violet.

"My bad planning and soon remedied."

"No, you don't."

"Be that as it may," said Vera, trying to lighten the tension. "Francis has returned, but Daisy is safe. Cora will see to that."

"We know. It's an enormous relief to have her. Not that

Farrow presents much of a physical threat. He is all skin and bone. It's more about the company he keeps."

"Crossley?"

"Yes. Though I am reliably assured he has decamped to Africa."

"Then why are you so worried?"

"Because of Aurora," said Violet.

Vera tilted her head. "Remind me?"

"Michael's wife."

"Of course. What about her?"

"Michael has allowed Francis in, against all reason."

"You mean he is living in Netherwood?"

"I do." Lawrence grimaced, his jaw set tensely.

"Good God. What was he thinking?"

"Religious nonsense," said Lawrence. "Forgiveness and all that. Michael feels torn between his family and his profession. As a priest, he must forgive; as a husband, he must protect; and as a friend, he must be loyal. He is trying to be all things to all people and offending everyone."

"Except Francis."

"Indeed. As my dear wife says, we all suffer apart from Farrow."

"I hear he is dying," said Vera.

"So he says."

"Don't you believe him?"

"My heart does not, but my eyes say otherwise. Francis is frail and unwell. He must be telling the truth."

"Then why worry?"

"Aurora is beside herself," said Violet. "After Crossley imprisoned her, she found sanctuary at Netherwood. At least until she discovered the unholy room Francis built for the order. Then she ran away to escape him again."

"It was the devil of a job to retrieve her," continued

Lawrence. "I wouldn't want to go through that again. And then, there's the matter of the child."

"Ah, young Luna," said Vera. "How old is she now?"

"Almost four years old," said Lawrence. "And a dear little thing. You'd never think…" His voice trailed away.

Vera Ponsonby cleared her throat. "I've never asked, but the time feels right somehow."

"She's Crossley's child," said Lawrence. "Though Michael is the only father she has ever known."

"Is Crossley aware?"

"We think not, though danger exists either way. Crossley has never forgiven us for losing William and Millicent. They were the orphaned children of a holy man, and Crossley intended to use them in one of his awful rituals. Crossley thinks Luna belongs to Michael and is the child of a clergyman, which brings its own risks. But she'd be in even more danger if Crossley knew she was his. He'd come after her in a heartbeat."

"A terrible situation. Michael's actions seem even more foolhardy." Vera's eyes glinted with unconcealed disgust.

"He thinks he's doing the right thing," said Violet. "Michael is torn between family and duty."

"I could cheerfully kill him," said Lawrence, shaking his head.

"But what can I do about it?" asked Vera. "I presume that's why you are here."

Lawrence and Violet exchanged silent glances.

"Oh, I see. You want me to go to Netherwood?"

"Could you?"

Vera opened an ink-splotched, tan-covered journal, licked her fingers, and flicked through the pages. "Hmmm," she said. "I could cancel that appointment and move this one into December. Oh dear. This one's unavoidable. Ah, I know. Cedric can deal with it."

"Who is Cedric?" asked Lawrence.

"Our new trainee and completely bloody useless. He's the fool who couldn't tell a brown horse from a piebald. Still, we'll whip him into shape soon enough. This will be good on-the-job training. So, yes. I can go to Netherwood, but will Michael have me?"

"That's the sticking point," said Lawrence. "On balance, we think it's better to present him with a *fait accompli*."

"Oh, you do, do you?"

"He can't refuse if we don't give him the chance."

"But he can turn me off the premises."

"He wouldn't. Michael isn't made that way."

"So, what do you propose?"

"That you catch a train to Bury as soon as possible. We will pay a handsome fee."

"Very well."

"Violet will write to Aurora and tell her you are on your way. Aurora will settle you into the other guest room before telling Michael. It will be too late for him to object, and he will have no choice but to go along with it, leaving Aurora with an ally in Netherwood."

"You've thought of everything," said Vera. "It's a good plan and the best course of action. But what about Francis? Will he know why I'm at Netherwood?"

"No," said Violet firmly. "It's best if you masquerade as Aurora's friend. Use your real name by all means. Francis won't know who you are. But he mustn't learn your true occupation in case he has malign intentions."

"Right," said Vera, steepling her hands. "Well, that's altered the course of my week, but I'd like to take on this assignment. It feels like the right thing to do."

"You look a little shell-shocked, Vera dear," said Violet. "Shall I make you a hot drink?"

"No, I'm fine. Truly. But a cup of tea is a jolly good idea. Stay here, and I'll do the honours."

Lawrence waited until Vera had left the room. "That went well," he said.

"Vera's a good sort, Lawrence. We didn't leave her much room for refusal."

"She wouldn't have said no."

"But have we put her in danger?"

"I doubt it. This assignment is purely precautionary. And it will boost Aurora when she badly needs it."

"Here you go," said Vera, bustling through the door with a tray of mugs. "Now, is tomorrow too soon?"

"It's perfect. We'll telegram Aurora today and return to the hotel when we finish our drinks."

"Not me," said Lawrence, but I'll find you a cab."

"Sorry?"

"I'll hail you a hansom back to The Grafton and join you later. I have a few things to do in town."

"I can make my own transport arrangements without your help, Lawrence. What things?" Violet's voice sounded slightly shriller than usual.

"The investigation."

"Oh, that."

"What investigation?" asked Vera.

Lawrence sighed and lowered his head as if slightly embarrassed. "What do you know about Emily Dimmock?"

"As much as anyone who reads the newspapers."

"And Robert Wood? Guilty or innocent?"

"Innocent in the eyes of the law."

"But in yours?"

Vera chewed her lip. "Innocent, I would say. After all, he didn't kill the other girls."

"Interesting. You're the third person to mention a second victim."

"Esther Prager, I should think."

"That's right."

"If you want my advice, you'll look at Dora Kiernicki too."

"Who is she?"

"Another young lady, murdered in similar circumstances. Now, I can tell you all about Esther. It only happened last year. But Dora is a different matter. She died in 1903 while we were setting up this place, and the details rather passed me by. But I know a man who knows a little more. He took a keen interest in the case."

"Really?"

"Yes. Though whether you will want to re-acquaint yourself with him is quite another matter."

"Go on?" Lawrence waited, intrigued at Vera's tone.

"Roslyn D'Onston."

"Good God. I assumed he was dead."

"Not yet. Though he is ailing and poor."

"That's a big fall from grace since his investment in the cosmetics business."

"Not helped by his addiction to alcohol."

"Then why should I seek his opinion on the Prager murder if he is in dire straits and too ill to help?"

"Not that murder. The earlier one. D'Onston had many connections with the press from his days as a reporter. And he collects murders, as you know. I ran into him a few years ago with a reporter friend, and it came up then. We were both impressed at his recall of local murders, particularly

Dora Kiernicki. D'Onston was adamant her killer would strike again. You should talk to him."

"Where does he live these days?"

Vera scribbled an address on a card and passed it to Lawrence. He raised an eyebrow. "How are the mighty fallen?" he said.

"Do you want to hear more about the Prager girl?"

"Very much so."

"Count me out," said Violet. "I must write a letter."

"Are you sure you don't mind?" Lawrence smiled ruefully.

"Not at all. I may go to the exhibition or risk an early visit to Fitzrovia. We'll see what the day brings. Goodbye, Vera, and good luck in Bury. I will keep in touch."

Lawrence jumped up and opened the door, pecking Violet's cheek as she sailed past.

"Now to business," he said, turning back to Vera. "Tell me everything you know about Esther Prager."

Chapter Sixteen

ESTHER PRAGER

"Let me refresh my memory." Vera strode to the rear and pulled open a filing cabinet. Rifling inside, she retrieved a brown paper package and dropped it on her desk. "My archiving system," she explained, slitting the fold with scissors. Lawrence watched as she shuffled through layers of newspaper. "Ah, here it is." Vera withdrew a notebook and turned over the hardcover.

"Why were you taking notes?" asked Lawrence.

"We were setting up the company. Business was slow."

"I see."

"So, we kept ourselves entertained with significant local news stories. We jotted them down and worked out how they might have come about. The unsolved ones, that is."

"Could be useful."

"Let's hope so. Ah, yes. Now, this is sad. The poor young girl was only seventeen."

Lawrence whistled. "That's unusually young to be alone in London."

"Not as much as you would think. The boarding houses are full of such girls."

"Do you know Esther's background?"

Vera turned the page. "Yes. She was a Jewish girl from Warsaw and had only lived in England for a few years. Esther lived on Bernard Street. That's near Russell Square if you know the area."

"I do. And it's rather pleasant. Did she have resources?"

"Doubtful. Esther lived in the back bedroom of a lodging house. She probably couldn't swing a cat in there."

"Which floor?"

Vera glanced at her notes. "The second. Hmmm. That implies she must have let him in."

"Her murderer?"

"Yes."

"What happened to Esther?"

"Oh, that's odd," said Vera distractedly.

"What?"

"The landlady's son found her, according to my notes. I wish I'd recorded the newspaper they came from."

"What was he doing there?"

"My point, precisely. It doesn't say. Only that he went into her still dark room and found her dead under a pile of clothes."

"Perhaps somebody sent him to check on her?"

"Possibly. Anyway, do you want to hear the gory details or not?"

"I can't assess the murder without, though I'd prefer not to hear too much blood and guts. Is it explicit?"

"I'm afraid so. Someone had tied a towel around her neck and strangled her."

"Anything else?"

Vera paused and ran a finger across the page. "Yes.

Over a dozen abrasions to her neck and throat and a wound on her right breast. She died from asphyxia."

"Nasty way to go."

"Agreed. The poor girl must have been terrified. One of the other lodgers heard her screaming."

"When?"

"About two o'clock in the morning. He thought she yelled *Ga Volt*, a cry for help in her language."

"Then why didn't he?"

"Help her? He wasn't sure whether the noise came from inside or outside the building."

"And they never apprehended the killer?"

Vera shook her head. "Sadly not. But they discovered where she'd been the previous night."

"Where?"

"Down Southampton Row with a young man. Pale-faced with dark eyes and what the reporter fancifully calls a staring expression. Someone else thought they saw the same man standing outside her window in Bernard Street on the night of the murder."

"I was in Southampton Row yesterday," said Lawrence. "Looking for Ruby Young, who you might remember was Robert Wood's lady friend."

"And is she that kind of girl?"

Lawrence nodded. "Yes. A lady of the night. Presumably, Esther was too?"

"I believe so. The papers said she was from the unfortunate class."

"So, the killer might be a client."

"I expect so."

"Could Esther have known Emily Dimmock?"

"Perhaps. But I don't know for a fact."

"Then we'll assume not. Anything else in your notes?

Vera scanned the journal. "A couple of interesting points. Esther also went by another name and called herself Mrs Marks."

"Was she married?"

"It's unlikely."

"Then why the false name?"

"To account for men in her room, perhaps? Here. Take this. It's only a brief clipping, but it describes the suspect."

Lawrence folded the paper and placed it underneath the page he was writing on. "And the other oddity?"

"Not relative to this crime at all, but fascinating, nonetheless. Did you know that more than a hundred murders committed in Great Britain in the last thirty years went unpunished?"

"No, and it seems rather a high number."

"Because it is. The Penny Illustrated Paper claims that 495 out of 500 French murderers stood trial."

"Are you sure?"

"I've no reason to doubt their statistics."

"That is truly troubling. What are the police doing all day?"

"Not solving murders."

"Then I will do everything in my power to ensure these girls don't end up as another unsolved statistic."

Chapter Seventeen

PAST ACQUAINTANCES

Lawrence approached the east gates of High Hill infirmary, shuddering as he raised his collar against the biting wind. A cluster of people milled around the entrance beside a horse-drawn carriage, which looked suspiciously like a hearse. Coughing, he gestured for the crowd to part, pushed his way through, and stood outside the gates, wondering which part of the impossibly large structure to head for.

Lawrence entered the complex through stone pillars, passing several ancillary buildings along the way. One door stood wedged open, giving a clear view of two stacks of coffins. Lawrence pressed on, past a stretchered man carried by two elderly bearers who looked too slight to manage the weight. He finally arrived at a portico annexe, pushed open the door and headed inside. Lawrence knocked on a sliding window and bent down to remove a leaf from his shoe. When he stood up, an auburn-haired nurse greeted him with a cheery hello.

"I'm looking for Mr Roslyn D'Onston."

The nurse frowned and glanced down a list of names. "He's not here."

"Are you sure?"

"Positive. Are you looking in the right building?"

"I don't know. How can I tell?"

"Does your relative have smallpox?"

"He's not my relative, and no."

The nurse sighed. "What is the nature of his complaint?"

Too nosy by half, thought Lawrence but wisely kept his counsel. "I don't know."

"Then how do you expect me to help you?" A frown had replaced the nurse's earlier smile, and she impatiently tapped a pencil on the counter.

"He likes a tipple," said Lawrence, as Vera's earlier reference to D'Onston's drinking came to mind.

"In that case, try that building over there." The nurse jabbed her pencil in the air, and Lawrence noted the trajectory.

"Thank you," he said, doffing his hat before walking across the courtyard towards a pair of dark double doors in the distance. Once inside, it took Lawrence a matter of moments to get directions to D'Onston's room. He approached it and sighed as he spotted the long, thin dormitory containing at least twenty beds without the slightest nod to privacy. He entered the room to the glare of a white-robed matron.

"Name?" she thundered.

"Lawrence Harpham."

"Then you're in the wrong ward. There is no one of that name here."

"My name is Lawrence Harpham."

"I'm sure it is. But why should I care? Who are you

looking for?"

A grey-haired man sitting in a bed a short way up the room raised his hands. "I rather think that would be me."

Roslyn D'Onston had not fared well in the eighteen years since Lawrence had last seen him. His moustache, once thick and well-groomed, hung limply from his upper lip and sagged against sallow skin. Black bags hung beneath fading eyes like smudges of charcoal.

Lawrence held out his hand and D'Onston shook it suspiciously, recoiling from the sensation of his touch. "I recognise you, but why are you here?" he growled, a flash of interest momentarily lighting his eyes.

"For information."

"Who sent you?"

"Vera Ponsonby."

"Vera," said D'Onston, rolling the name around his mouth. "Vera, oh yes. I know the woman you mean. Tall, wears slacks, and has a manly walk. Why would she think I want to talk to you?"

"Because you collect murders."

D'Onston flashed a smile. "Collect is too strong a word for it. But I am interested, as you know."

"Though your theories leave something to be desired."

"Nobody could have predicted the Ripper was the doorman at the SPR."

He doesn't know, thought Lawrence. Shall I tell him or let dead doctors lie? Opting for the latter, he swiftly changed the conversation. "Regardless, I would value your opinion on another matter."

D'Onston placed a hand behind his back and shuffled into a more comfortable position, then reached for a glass with a shaking hand. Lawrence's gaze lingered too long.

"Paralysis agitans," said D'Onston.

"I'm sorry to hear that." Lawrence felt a genuine surge of sympathy for the man he'd assumed to be nothing more than a drunkard. A progressive brain disorder was a tricky illness to bear.

"Not your problem, though, is it?" said D'Onston. "And anyway, my disease is in the very early stages. I drink to forget."

Lawrence decided against probing further and got to the point. "What do you know about Dora Kiernicki?"

D'Onstan's eyes briefly widened before he turned away, vainly attempting to conceal his interest. "A little," he muttered. "Why?"

"Vera said you could help me."

"With what?"

"Something that looks like a pattern."

"Of murders?"

"Exactly."

D'Onston slugged a gulp of water and eagerly leaned forward. "Let me guess: Kiernicki, Dimmock and Prager."

"How did you know?"

"Sit down," said D'Onston, gesturing to the end of his bed. "And whisper. Just look around you, and you'll understand the need for discretion."

Lawrence glanced behind to a sea of eyes. Sick men bored with institutional life hung on his every word.

"Noted," he said. "Go on."

"I agree the crimes were similar. The same man could easily have committed all three. There were quite a few years between Dora and the other girls, but not so much to spoil the theory.

"So I'm learning," said Lawrence. "It's unfamiliar territory."

"Don't you read the papers?"

"Actually, no."

"An odd point of view for a detective."

"Former detective."

"I see." Lawrence resented the satisfied expression on D'Onston's face as he comprehended Lawrence's situation.

"You're missing your old life?"

"Not really. I'm a man of leisure."

"Then why are you poking your nose into matters that don't concern you? I'll tell you why. Old habits die hard. I still write even though my handwriting is illegible," said D'Onston, holding a shaking hand. "Once an author, always an author. And once a nosy detective. Well, you get the gist."

Lawrence removed his notebook from his pocket. "Are you going to help or not?"

"Of course. I'm terminally bored in this prison. God knows when they'll let me out. What do you want from me?"

"Everything you've ever heard about Dora Kernicki."

Chapter Eighteen

DORA KIERNICKI

"Dora was the first," said D'Onston, teasing the end of his moustache as he gazed vacantly across the ward. "No previous killings fit the pattern and only two after Dora. There are similarities, and you'll understand more when you hear the details."

Lawrence waited as D'Onston paused for breath, eager to move things along but reluctant to prompt him.

"The killer used an identical modus operandi to that of Emily Dimmock."

"He cut her throat?"

"Yes – a terrible gash across her neck; blood everywhere. A gruesome sight."

"Was she at home?"

D'Onston nodded. "As I said, virtually the same sequence of events. Dora was twenty-nine years old, to Emily's twenty-two years and Esther's nineteen. But the women were all unfortunates, leading lives of vice and depravity."

D'Onston trembled as he spoke, a tic by the side of his nose giving the impression of unbridled disgust.

"What nationality?" asked Lawrence, scribbling in his notebook.

"A Polish Jewess."

"The same as Esther Prager?"

"Indeed."

"Did they know one another?"

D'Onston shrugged. "Perhaps. Who knows? Anyway, they found Dora bound and blindfolded in her room, having suffered a left-to-right knife wound. She was naked and partly covered by a blanket, with a handkerchief tied tightly around her mouth. Her arms, bound with cord, rested on her breast in an attitude of prayer. There were no signs of a struggle in the room. Now, guess what the Home Office expert suggested?"

Lawrence paused. "Not murder, I suppose, if you are asking me to speculate. That's too obvious."

"Correct."

"Manslaughter then."

"Try again."

Lawrence frowned. "Surely not an accidental death?"

D'Onston leaned forward. "Suicide," he said, crossing his arms and fixing Lawrence with a bemused stare.

"Preposterous."

"I couldn't agree more."

"Why would an expert arrive at that conclusion?"

"I cannot imagine. Certain points taken on their own merit might support such a verdict, but not in conjunction with each other. And importantly, they never found Dora's missing rings."

"That's certainly suspicious."

"Agreed. But the doctor fixated on the direction of the

wound. A left-to-right cut could be self-inflicted. He saw no blood stains or finger marks to indicate foul play, and the police saw no disruption to the furniture, which might have suggested a struggle. In the doctor's opinion, Dora probably killed herself, but owing to several bruises on her body, he could not rule out murder."

Lawrence shook his head. "I should think not, but I will try to keep an open mind. What else can you tell me?"

"Plenty," said D'Onston. I say, reach into that wardrobe and pass me my writing case."

Lawrence did as asked, opening the door to find a substantial leather briefcase box occupying the bottom of the wardrobe. He hefted it up and placed it on the bed.

"Kindly open the clasps. It's not locked."

Once unfastened, Lawrence saw three voluminous drawers.

"In there," said D'Onston, pointing a shaking finger.

Lawrence pulled open the bottom drawer.

"Not there. Close it at once." D'Onstan's face flushed florid, his eyes starting, fingers trembling in time with the tic on his face.

"Sorry. No harm done." Lawrence wondered what he might have seen had he opened the drawer another inch, but the contents had remained out of sight.

"The second drawer," said D'Onston, avoiding any further misunderstandings.

"Very well. Is this what you are looking for?"

"Give it to me," said D'Onston, raising his hand towards the black-bound jotter.

Lawrence thrust it towards him, and D'Onston took it almost tenderly, his fingers unusually firm as he grasped the back cover and turned it over to reveal a pile of newspaper cuttings.

"Well, well," said Lawrence, impressed.

"As Miss Ponsonby says, I collect murders. Now, let's give you a little more background."

D'Onston straightened the papers, ignored the first, and unfolded the second with a satisfied sigh. "So, Dora Kiernicke came home with a young man on the night of her murder."

"This is starting to sound familiar."

"As well it might, hence my theory that these crimes are connected. Now, Dora lived in Whitfield Street."

"I don't know it."

"Off the Tottenham Court Road."

"Why, that's no more than fifteen minutes from Bernard Street, where Esther Prager died."

"Quite right. And a bare thirty minutes from Emily Dimmock's home."

"Are the police investigating these crimes as if a single person committed them?"

"They are barely investigating them at all. The force is a complete waste of money."

"You mean the Metropolitan Constabulary?"

"Yes," spat D'Onstan. "They are incompetent buffoons. I have taken the time to write and offer my opinion as I did during the dreadful days of the Ripper. But having heard nothing, I can only assume they are uninterested."

"Shocking," said Lawrence.

"Isn't it? But I refuse to waste my words on that shower. A French fellow living in the Whitfield House basement said he heard Dora come home in the early hours. Later, around daybreak, a woman cried out as if in pain. He was so concerned that he roused another lodger who went to check on her, waiting and listening at her door. He heard three long drawn breaths, then nothing further, and returned to bed. They found Dora at six o'clock that evening when a friend visited the flat and raised the alarm.

"Anything else?" asked Lawrence.

D'Onston's eyes darted across the page. "Yes. Not from the Frenchman though. Dora went out the night before she died in the company of a young Polish Jewess."

"Name?"

"It doesn't say."

"No matter."

"The young woman met Dora on Tottenham Court Road, and they started chatting outside a public house. Miss Kiernicki showed the girl a handful of coins, amounting to about eight pounds."

Lawrence whistled. "Not short of funds then."

"Not at all. And she was wearing a clutch of rings, ripe for pawning if she needed money."

"But you said the rings were missing?"

D'Onston nodded. "That's right. They thought someone had taken the money at first, but it turned up in her room after all."

"Was the other girl a close friend?"

"More than that. The young woman was her sister-in-law."

"Dora Kiernicki was married?" Lawrence stopped scribbling and scratched his temple with the end of the pencil.

"Yes, but her husband was in prison, which is why she lodged alone."

"Dear, oh dear." Lawrence mused for a moment, contemplating the selfishness of a man whose behaviour was so bad he languished in gaol while his wife faced a murderous attack. Visions of Daisy and Cora Cream clouded his mind, filling him with an unjustified anxiety about their safety. He felt a terrible pull towards home and a burning need to gather his child into his arms and protect her with his life.

"Are you well, Mr Harpham?"

D'Onston's eyes creased with concern.

"I'm fine," said Lawrence. "Really. Do go on."

"Where were we?"

Lawrence glanced at his notes. "Actually, I'm missing a vital piece of information."

"Yes?"

"The man who accompanied Dora home. Did anyone give a description?"

"They did. He was a clean-shaven man with a thin face, medium height and wearing a light grey suit with a cap. An Englishman, according to the press report."

Lawrence stopped writing and looked up, startled. "Show me," he said.

D'Onston passed over the paper. Lawrence took it, eyed the page, and passed it back again before licking his finger and flicking through his notebook. "Here," he said, unfolding Vera's clipping.

"Suspect location, Southampton Row, male, four foot nine, pale face, dark hair and eyes, clean shaven, slim build, broad shoulders. Goodness me, a grey striped suit and matching cloth cap. They might be describing the same man."

"I agree."

"Look, keep me informed, will you? I can do nothing from here."

"I will if you do something for me."

D'Onston eyed Lawrence suspiciously. "It depends on what it is. But, Mr Harpham. Don't play games. This killer won't stop. You can be sure he will murder again and soon."

"He might," said Lawrence.

"He will. I know it. Don't toy with me, Mr Harpham. Keep me involved. I can help."

"A reporter friend is assisting me."

"Who?"

"I'd rather not say."

"I worked with all of them at one time or another. Tell me."

"Lonni Carpenter. Do you know him?"

"A little. He's a good man. You can trust him. Now, will you keep me informed?"

"Yes, but tell me something. I remember hearing that you ran a business with Vittoria Cremers."

"I did, for my sins, and I have no desire to dwell on it."

"Did you cross paths with Felix Crossley?"

"D'Onston gasped and reached for a glass of water with shaking hands. It wobbled precariously. Lawrence grabbed the glass as water sloshed onto the bedclothes.

"Your reaction suggests you did."

"That monster nearly ruined me," said D'Onston, his eyes darkening with ill-concealed rage.

"How?"

"He was in cahoots with Cremer. They said I was Jack the Ripper and told the police, who hauled me in for questioning. It left a terrible stain on my character. But you know this. So why bring it up now?"

Lawrence ignored the question. "Have you had any more dealings with Crossley since?"

"Never. The man is not to be trusted."

"I know. Our paths have crossed."

D'Onston nodded. "Then you'll know what I mean."

"I do. But I remembered your connection with Crossley. If I'm to trust you, I must know you are not a part of his organisation."

"Do I look like I could conduct a black magic ritual?" hissed D'Onston.

"I am sorry you are unwell."

"My brain still functions adequately. My reason is intact."

"And I will use it. I will visit again, I promise."

"With news of your investigation?"

"Absolutely."

"What steps will you take now?"

"I thought I might take a trip to The Eagle and speak to the bar staff. I'd like to know more about Emily Dimmock's last night and the people she encountered in the public house. That is, if my dear wife doesn't mind."

"Best not tell her," said D'Onston.

"It was my little joke. Violet is too busy with the Camden artists to give me a second thought these days."

D'Onston frowned. "Which one?"

"All of them."

"Not Walter Sickert, I hope?"

"Yes, as it happens."

"Then, Mr Harpham, I would be vigilant. Don't let your lady wife out of your sight."

Chapter Nineteen

FIRST SUSPICIONS

"I'm glad you enjoyed your visit," said Lawrence, lounging on the bed with his shoes off and his cravat undone.

"So you keep saying." Violet lowered her book for the fourth time in as many minutes.

"I mean, it's nice to have friends who can show you a thing or two about your hobby only I can't help wondering…"

"Wondering what?"

"What do you really know about them?"

"What do I need to know? I'm not interviewing them for employment."

"No, but even so."

"I don't know what is bothering you, Lawrence, but I wish you would stop beating around the bush."

"It's nothing. I worry you don't know them very well."

"Nor will I if I don't make an effort. I like people, even if you don't."

"Come now, Violet. That's hardly fair."

"You could have joined me earlier if you were interested."

"I was busy."

Violet raised an eyebrow. "I daresay. And I'm glad you've found something to occupy yourself, but you could have joined us."

"I met an old acquaintance."

"Who?"

Lawrence was about to answer but decided against it. Violet might not appreciate his encounter with Roslyn D'Onston. "Did you learn anything new today?"

"I did, actually," said Violet, her eyes sparkling. "Freddie showed me some of his new paintings, and then we went next door to see a room full of other works. Afterwards, Walter asked if I would like to see his sketches."

"I bet he did."

"I just said so, didn't I?"

"Carry on."

"Walter took me into his unit and taught me a quick charcoal drawing technique. Then he critiqued my attempt."

"Alone?"

"Yes. He has a huge workshop. Quite the largest I have seen. But he locks his most valuable works away."

"Somewhere else?"

"No. In his workshop, but out of sight."

"Why?"

"I don't know. In case someone steals them, I suppose."

"I'm surprised you didn't ask to see them anyway."

"I did, but Walter said no. He's just returned from France and had exhibited them there. Walter thinks the works are too controversial for English eyes."

"Did he say why?"

"No. And I respect his privacy, so I dropped the subject. There must be quite a few locked away behind an opaque window. I saw a shadow floor-to-ceiling high with an odd little tailor dummy silhouetted inside. It was really quite bizarre."

"Remind me where you went again?"

"Fitzroy Street. Are you losing your memory?"

"No. Only I got confused when you said you'd been to number three."

"I said no such thing."

"Are you sure?"

Violet turned her book over and splayed it over the bed cover before locking eyes with her husband. "Of course, I'm sure," she said. "Walter's friends have many units in Fitzrovia, but none numbered three."

"I was sure you said three."

"Walter has number eight Fitzroy Street," said Violet. "Freddie rents number twenty-one, and they share number nineteen. A few other artists also use workshops there, but I don't know which units, and I didn't refer to number three." Violet's voice rose as she tried to keep her temper.

"Right you are," said Lawrence.

"Where are you going now?"

"To brush my teeth."

"Good. It's about time you settled down for the night."

Lawrence entered the bathroom while Violet resumed reading, surreptitiously reaching into his jacket pocket for his notebook. He sat fully clothed on the toilet while scribbling a list of addresses in the journal before shoving it back in his trousers. Then he flushed the lavatory and washed his hands.

"There you are. It's getting late."

Lawrence proceeded to the window and leaned on the ledge as Violet spoke.

"Lovely evening, isn't it?" he said.

Violet checked her wristwatch. "It's three-quarters to midnight."

"Yes, but it looks mild out there. Just right for a late-night walk."

"Lawrence, are you feeling well?" Violet's eyes creased with concern.

"I'm fine. Don't worry, dear. It's just a little headache. A short stroll might set me right.

"Do you mind if I don't join you?"

"I wouldn't dream of asking. You enjoy your book. Don't wait up." And with that, Lawrence laced his shoes, grabbed a coat and set out into the night.

Chapter Twenty

ILLEGAL ENTRY

Lawrence descended the hotel stairs, cast a cheery nod to the reception clerk, and strode into the night. A short walk later, he turned onto Fitzroy Street, finding number eight near the top of the road. The elegant townhouse bore no resemblance to the cavernous studio Violet had described earlier. Lawrence struck a match before checking and rechecking his notebook. But unless he had misheard her, this was the property that Violet had been inside earlier that day. Lawrence ascended the steps towards a wide, black front door, admiring the fanlight just visible from the gentle glow of a nearby gas lamp. The house stood still and quiet as Lawerence slowly turned the doorknob, but he found it firmly locked. Lawrence pushed the nearby window, pausing as a young couple walked arm in arm towards him, excitedly chatting. They abruptly stopped while contemplating what he was doing.

"Lost my key," said Lawrence, ruefully.

"Oh dear. I wish I could help." The young man was polite but indifferent. He shrugged and placed a protective arm around his lady, guiding her away. Silence fell over Fitzroy Street again.

Walter Sickert had secured the building against intruders, forcing Lawrence to reconsider his options. He could try the back door if he could find a rear passage, assuming it was easy to get to. But roaming around without attracting attention at a quarter to midnight was not a sensible plan. He could try putting a stone in his handkerchief and breaking the lower window. But that was far too risky and Violet, who knew his tactics only too well, was bound to find out if she came to hear about any damage. He glanced at the stairs and noticed another set running towards a basement entrance. It looked promising. Moments later, he stood outside an almost identical door, squinting in the moonlight. The door was closed, but to his amazement, a thick iron key stood solidly in the lock. Hardly able to believe his luck, Lawrence turned it and let himself in before almost tripping over a dining table in the middle of the entrance hall. Lawrence found a candle in a small kitchenette, lit it and examined the rest of the lower ground floor. Nothing leapt out at him, but he was beyond caring. Lawrence felt active and alive. His heart quickened at the prospect of being caught in the act and taking a risk for once instead of mouldering away in a Cheltenham townhouse waiting to grow old. Things would be different when he returned.

Downstairs was a disappointment, and none of the pokey rooms were big enough to accommodate the myriad paintings Violet had seen. Lawrence crept upstairs, treads squeaking as he cautiously ascended to the first floor. Lawrence opened the nearest door and went inside. This was what he'd been looking for: a room occupying the whole frontage with a range of sash windows like those in

Mornington Place. Sickert, a creature of habit, clearly enjoyed painting in familiar conditions.

At some point in its history, the first floor of 8 Fitzroy Street had been partitioned into several rooms. But not now. Instead, an expansive area tapered towards the rear of the building, bridged halfway by a range of frosted glass doors, precisely as Violet had described. Lawrence approached them and stood, nose to the glass, trying to peer into the gloom. But without the benefit of daylight, he could see nothing. Pushing the door handle repeatedly, he futilely continued before kicking the bottom in temper and retracing his steps. Sickert might have the key back home in Mornington Place, though this was uncertain. If something had sufficiently distracted him enough to leave an outside key in the lock, the inner key could be anywhere. But there was another floor to explore, and it was worth checking.

Sighing, Lawrence made his way upwards to a dusty, seldom used level with several doors tightly locked and one room that looked promising. Inside was an unmade bed, covers rumpled and needing a good wash. Perhaps Walter Sickert slept here occasionally to be closer to the city's heart. But an easel dominated the area to the right of the window, and Lawrence wondered if the bed was a painting prop and somewhere to bring his models. Lawrence shuddered, remembering Sickert's enthusiasm for nudes while hosting in Mornington Crescent. He still found the concept distasteful and consigned it to the outer reaches of his memory. Then he opened the bedside cabinet, discovering a bunch of keys on top of a book with minimal effort. Lawrence grinned – this was more like it. He descended the stairs triumphantly, striding towards the glass doors and turning the key with a click.

The door opened, and Lawrence stared at a large heap

of junk. The shadow he'd thought was a tailor's dummy turned out to be a life-sized sculpture of an old man leaning heavily on a stick. He gazed admiringly. The statue showcased technical brilliance that Lawrence hadn't expected from Walter Sickert. Yet someone had carelessly draped a tattered jacket and red neck scarf over the carving. Lawrence reached a cautious hand into the jacket pocket, finding only a used handkerchief, which he quickly replaced.

The candle wick spluttered as Lawrence pressed on, skirting a dusty, unloved desk through a narrow walkway and into a larger room at the rear. Raising the light, he cast his eyes upon a row of easels standing side by side at the back of the room. He set down the candle, lit a gas mantle on the wall, and examined the room. Large cream dust sheets covered six easels, the other two standing empty. Lawrence reached for the nearest covering and lifted it, stepping back in puzzlement. Then, grasping the cloth with both hands, he threw it from the painting. Underneath was the unedifying sight of a naked woman, her head flopping to one side, while a man sat, head bowed, at the foot of her bed. Lawrence stared in horror, not at the seedy, unromantic view of the fleshy, unclothed woman. But at the card inserted in the bottom of the frame. Sickert's title, written in italics and painted in 1908, was *What shall we do for the rent?* subtitled *The Camden Town Murder*.

Chapter Twenty-One

STALKING LONDON

I stride through London town, dressed head to toe in black. Not that I need to set foot outside today. Someone else acts for me, actively searching for suitable subjects. But I am restless, my senses alive. I smell the earthy odour of impending rainfall, but it does not deter me. I yearn to feel the elements, savour them, and revel in their discomfort. Only then can I bring them to mind on demand, visualise and feed my soul.

Catlike, I pick through the alleys; the smaller, the better, making the most of the weak moonlight, collecting the atmosphere. I started in Camden but soon walked away. It has lost its allure, too many people. The brash, loud, repellent specimens of humanity spill from public houses, gossiping on pavements. Chitter-chatter echoing in my ears, interrupting my carefully curated memories.

I consider using the newly opened underground station, enjoying the thought of deep descent below the streets of London. Trains snake through tunnels beneath my feet in cold, dark spaces where no human dares to tread. I venture inside and watch from afar. But people flood onto the escalator, top hats and bonnets bobbing beneath my gaze. They surge downwards, men in suits barging past, women clinging to the rail. I can't face their closeness, a claustrophobic nightmare, and quickly turn away.

Hands in pockets, head bowed, I take the Hampstead Road at a pace, homing towards a quieter part of London. But it is too early. The city is alive, writhing and twitching like mating serpents. I stop in Regent's Park, take stock, settle on a bench, and wait. Dusk falls, and the temperature drops. Still, I pause, cemented to the spot. Then, a nearby clock chimes the hour, breaking the spell. I rise, wander the streets, and find myself heading towards Fitzrovia, stealthily prowling through Grafton Mews with a light tread, footsteps inaudible. I know where I am going, though I did not plan it.

I turn onto Fitzroy Street, cautiously stepping across the wide pavements. But they are not free. The chattering voices of a young couple tell me I am not alone. But they are moving forward and will soon pass. Yet they don't. They stop and share a word or two with a tall, dark figure. He seems familiar. But what is he doing here?

I shelter in the lee of a building, watching as the pair depart. The man looks furtively over his shoulder, then disappears from sight. I stir myself and move quickly towards the property, never taking my eyes from the front door. But when I get there, he is gone. A glance at the basement door tells me everything I need to know. I reach for the key, then stop. I should not enter. It is not right. Yet I must know who he is and why he is there under cover of darkness, I find a viewpoint near a gas lamp on the street and begin the long wait.

Time drags, each second a long, drawn-out measure of boredom. I almost give up, but an occasional faint light source flickers from window to window, floor to floor. He is in there, creeping across the floorboards, violating the place like an uninvited wraith in need of exorcism. I can only wait and wonder. And I do.

A sudden movement startles me awake as a moth wing brushes my cheek. I move swiftly away from the gas lamp to linger yet again. After half an hour, my ordeal is over. He crunches up the basement stairs, turning right towards the square. He is almost on top of me before I hear him. I instinctively flatten myself against the wall, holding my breath as he strides past, eyes aflame with a scarf wound tightly around his jaw.

There is something familiar about this man. But whether I know him or not is immaterial. He should not be where I found him. He should not have gone inside. So I follow him for a few yards, and then he turns. And as he extends his walk, making no directional sense, I am seized with fear. Where is he going? Does he know my secret? How could he? But curiosity has bitten deep. Where he leads, I must follow. Yet I resist. I have avoided this street for five long years, and now he inadvertently leads me past the door I first accessed when this all began. My hands search deep in my pocket for the blade I always carry, sheathed safely inside a hidden opening. I stroke the cold metal, feeling a surge of anger. Who does he think he is playing with? And what does he know? I move closer towards him as the pace of my stride matches his. I am moments behind, rage flaring through my body, with my arm raised high and my knife only inches from his back. And then he turns, as if he had always known I was there, places his hand across his face, crying out in terror. My eyes start. Has he recognised me? Of course not, for I turned my collar high and wore a scarf over my face. It is late, and darkness cloaks me. The nearest lamp is yards away. He cannot recognise me. So, I strike, plunging the knife towards him. It hits fabric, slices through, and I rip it upwards. He turns and runs, charging down Whitfield Street like all the devils in hell were on his tail. A sigh hisses from my mouth as my bloodlust remains unsated. And my heart sinks at the purposelessness of my actions; once so pure, so necessary up to now. What have I become if blood spill becomes the point of the act? I am no worse than a street thug. It must never happen again.

Chapter Twenty-Two

UNDER ATTACK

The hotel door clicked open and Lawrence crept inside, his heart pounding, breathing laboured. Tiptoeing across the carpet, he pushed open the bathroom door, locked it and sat on the lavatory, undoing his coat buttons with shaking hands. Once open, Lawrence ran the tap, emptied his toothbrush from the glass, and filled it with water. He slugged one glass back and half-emptied another. Still, his hands shook, and his heart thudded too loudly to contemplate joining Violet in bed. She would feel the tension and know.

Finally, his breathing quietened, and Lawrence peeled off his coat and examined the sleeve. A long, jagged tear snaked up his arm, now damp with blood. Lawrence placed a tentative hand on his arm and held it under the bathroom light. Rusty wet blood streaked his palm, and now unprotected by his coat, pain throbbed down the back of his arm. He probed the wound with his fingers. It was deep and probably needed stitches. Damn it. He'd have to tell Violet. But what would he say? He thought for a moment. Perhaps he didn't need to say very much at all. He could so easily have been a random target, the subject of attempted thievery. Which was probably all it was anyway. Lawrence had been trespassing onto another man's property. But the house was empty. He had got away with breaking in, and nobody knew he was there. He'd simply been unlucky and run into a passing thug who seized the opportunity to rid a wealthy man of his wallet. His story decided, Lawrence opened the bathroom door and switched on the side light.

"Violet," he whispered.

"Shh," she said, still half asleep.

"Wake up, my dear." Lawrence gently pushed Violet's homemade sleep mask away from her eyes.

"What is it?" she asked.

"Can you help me?"

"Oh, Lawrence." Violet sat up, bristling with indignation, before noticing Lawrence's pale face.

"What have you done?" she asked, clapping her hand to her mouth at the sight of her stricken husband.

"Just a little flesh wound," he said.

"Good grief. Stay here." Violet took Lawrence's hand and led him to the chair by the window. "I won't be a second." She darted to the bathroom, where the sound of opening and closing drawers clattered through the night.

"Nothing suitable." She sighed, repeating the same exercise on their chest of drawers and nightstands. "There's only one thing to do," she said before standing and ripping the lower length of her nightdress away. She grabbed her robe and tied it around her middle before pulling the torn nightie into lengths of fabric. Then, removing Lawrence's shirt, she cleaned the wound with a flannel before binding the lengths of the makeshift bandage around his arm.

"Better?" she asked.

Lawrence nodded. "You've ruined your nightdress."

"No matter. I have another. Now, we must get you to hospital."

"Is that necessary?"

"Yes. I've no liniment. Your wound could easily get infected."

"Can't we leave it until morning?"

Violet frowned. "I'd rather not. If we go now, we'll be back in a few hours. We've both got appointments tomorrow, so it makes sense."

"Please, Violet. I'm tired and can't face travelling at this time of night."

"Very well," sighed Violet. "But what on earth happened to you?"

"I don't know. Someone attacked me."

"Did he get your wallet?"

Lawrence pointed to a bulge in his discarded jacket. "Fortunately not."

"But he tried?"

"I'm sure he would have. I caught him unawares?"

"How?"

"He was behind me and did not expect me to turn around."

"Stalking you?"

"So it seems."

Violet crossed her arms. "It sounds so logical, and yet…"

"It was an opportunistic thief, my dear. That's all."

"I'm sure you're right. But it's the hospital and the police station for you tomorrow, Lawrence. No further investigations until you have the all clear."

Chapter Twenty-Three

PATCHING UP LAWRENCE

Thursday, November 25, 1909

Lawrence had slept badly, his dreams punctuated by visions of a raised arm and sharp-edged knife descending in slow motion until the blade punctured his forehead and pierced his brain. He woke with a start somewhere around six o'clock, having barely managed two hours of rest all night. Violet was already in the bathroom, and, taking advantage of a few moments of privacy, Lawrence unwound the bandage and peered at the blood-encrusted mess beneath. He gently stroked the wound, flinching as he touched the angry, swollen skin around the puncture marks.

"That is infected," said Violet sternly as she strode into the room with a towel wrapped around her head.

"I know."

"Then get dressed. We'll head straight to the hospital."

"I'd rather not."

"Naturally. But you must."

"I mean it."

Violet perched beside him on the edge of the bed. "Look at you," she said, cupping his face with her hand. She moved it to his forehead for a moment. "You're overheating. If your temperature goes any higher, you'll get a fever."

"I'll sleep it off."

"Really?"

"Or walk it off."

"Absolutely not."

"I'm not going to the hospital, and that's the end of it."

"Why?"

"I can't."

"Can't and won't are two different things. You must tell me what's bothering you. Think about it while we travel. I know you too well, dear husband. You are keeping things from me."

"Travel where? I'm not going to the hospital."

"And I'm not wasting time arguing with you. We'll take your reluctance for medical aid as read. But this wound needs urgent attention, and you can jolly well get it from Ann Brocklehurst if you refuse to see a doctor."

"Ann might be working."

"Except that she isn't. We swapped appointment schedules a few days ago, and I happen to know she is free all day. Now, get dressed right away, and I'll hail a cab.

Half an hour later, Lawrence and Violet disembarked outside Ann Brocklehurst's ornate front door. Lawrence paid the fare while Violet rang the doorbell. "Take this to your mistress," she said as an unusually scruffy maid stood uncertainly in the hallway.

"She's asleep, miss."

"Then wake her."

The maid waited, her mouth opening, goldfish-like, as

she considered the ramifications of an early morning alarm call. "I don't think I should."

"Then I will." Violet pushed past and strode into the hallway before taking the first few stairs two at a time in an unladylike burst of energy."

"Stop. Please stop. I'll do it," shrieked the maid, pushing past Violet and bolting upstairs.

"I say, Violet. Do steady on. She's trying her best."

"I wouldn't need to bother if you'd agreed to go to hospital."

"I wish I had," grumbled Lawrence.

Violet shook her head, pushed open the drawing room door, and perched anxiously on the daybed. Lawrence joined her, placing a hand on her shoulder.

"I feel ridiculous," he said.

"Let Ann be the judge of that."

"She has far better things to do."

They silently waited until the door opened again and Ann Brocklehurst appeared, followed by her half-dressed husband.

"What is it?" he asked, crossing his arms.

"Lawrence has an injury." Violet gestured towards her husband.

"He looks alright to me." Mark Brocklehurst, seemingly unimpressed, curled his lip derisively.

"Take off your jacket." Ann sprang into action, helping Lawrence disrobe. "And your shirt."

Lawrence glanced around, reluctant to bare his chest for all to see.

"Come on. I've seen it all before."

Lawrence obliged and Ann peeled back the bandages. Her face turned ashen at the sight of his wounds.

Mark Brocklehurst frowned, approached Lawrence, and looked for himself.

"You've got some explaining to do," he said.

"Someone attacked me."

"Obviously. Another few inches and those stab marks could have been fatal. So why are you here and not in the hospital? Have you called the police?"

"Not yet."

"Then you must be on a case," said Mark, his eyes twinkling.

"Well, in a small way. But that has nothing to do with this."

"Then why the reluctance to tell the authorities?" Mark persisted while Ann rang for the maid.

"Put some boiling water in a bowl, dear," she said. "Then bring bandages and liniment from my workroom."

The maid scuttled off, returning a short time later with the requested items.

"Stay still," hissed Ann as Lawrence flinched at the boiling water against his skin. She worked methodically, cleaning the wound, and squeezing the flannel until the water bowl turned pink.

"That's the worst of it," she said, plastering thick, white liniment over the wound before tightly winding bandages across the back of his arm. "Any deeper or nearer your torso, and you'd have been in real trouble," said Ann. "You got off lightly."

"This time," said Violet.

"What happened?" Mark remained dissatisfied with Lawrence's explanation.

"Someone attacked me."

"Where?"

"I don't know. Between Fitzroy Street and our hotel. Just off Grafton Way."

"Must be Whitfield Street," said Mark, exchanging glances with his wife."

"Yes, dear. What were you doing there, Lawrence?"

"Whitfield Street? Is that where I was? I hadn't realised, but the name rings a bell." Lawrence scrabbled for his jacket and extracted his notebook. "Good God. That's where Dora Kiernicki died."

"Who?"

"The first of the stabbings in 1903. D'Onston told me. There, look." Lawrence pointed to an underlined paragraph.

"What a coincidence," said Mark.

"Lawrence doesn't believe in coincidences," said Violet coldly. "And never mind the Whitfield address, Lawrence. Exactly what were you doing in Fitzroy Street?"

Chapter Twenty-Four

AN INFORMATIVE STROLL

Lawrence trudged along Tottenham Court Road feeling thoroughly sorry for himself. Ann and Mark Brocklehurst had offered a hot breakfast, which Violet had accepted, but they had conducted the cab journey back to The Grafton Hotel in frosty silence. Lawrence tried to open a conversation, which Violet quickly closed down with a few choice words, leaving Lawrence in no doubt that she knew about and disapproved of his previous night's work.

"Have a nice day, dear," he had said as she flounced off towards the shops to pick up a bottle of turpentine before joining the Camden artists in yet another workshop. Violet had shot back another withering glance. "How could you," she'd offered as her parting shot.

Lawrence longed to hold her in his arms and tell her about the sickening nudes Sickert had produced. But in the cold light of day, were they so awful? Camden must have been rife with stories about Emily Dimmock after the slaying, and it was only natural that a painter of Sickert's self-importance would insert himself into the news of the day.

He had probably copied his revolting art directly from the penny dreadfuls. Sighing, Lawrence returned to the hotel foyer and ordered a coffee while he contemplated his plans for the day and decided he felt well enough to continue with them.

"I say. Mr Harpham, isn't it?"

Lawrence looked up to see the sandy-haired man he'd met at Mornington Crescent earlier in the week.

The man extended his hand. "It's Freddy. Freddy Gore. You probably don't recognise me. Can't say I blame you when you last saw me dressed in a smock with paint in my hair." Freddy smiled as Lawrence firmly shook his hand.

"Pleased to meet you again," said Lawrence half-heartedly. "What brings you to my hotel?"

"I was hoping to find your lady wife. Walter asked me to collect her. A change of plans, you see. She won't know where to go."

"I'm afraid you've just missed her."

"Damn it. That's Leonard's doing. He insisted on visiting the men's room. Which way did Mrs Harpham go?"

"I've just dropped her off over there," said Lawrence, waving vaguely ahead. "But you're in luck. She's off to the hardware store in Euston Road for some art supplies."

"Capital. I know the one. I'll catch up with her there. Be a good fellow and let Leonard know."

Lawrence opened his mouth to say he doubted he would recognise Leonard if he tap-danced across the lobby on the back of a lemur, but Freddy Gore was gone. Lawrence waited momentarily, half irritable and half nervous, uncomfortable with the direction this London visit was taking. Violet was his wife, and all she wanted to do was hang around with a bunch of self-obsessed artists of doubtful talent and not much in the way of personality. And she'd been snappy over the last few days, unusually intolerant and showing no interest in his investigations. The old Violet would be all over London looking for ways to solve the case. Yet now, she barely gave it a second thought. For a horrible, panicky moment, Lawrence wondered if he was losing her. But then he remembered her concern over his wound, her insistence that he get help, and the moment she practically mowed down the maid to get to Ann for medical aid. No, it wasn't that. Violet loved him as much as she ever did. But she had moved on from a private investigator's life. Perhaps her newfound regard for art was her self-protection in the same way that avoiding newspapers was his. He must talk to Violet soon, especially as he lacked trust in Walter Sickert.

"Don't I know you?"

Lawrence jerked his head at the sound of a refined male voice and found himself face-to-face with Leonard Covington.

"Lawrence Harpham. We met a few days ago in Mornington Crescent."

"Of course we did. And naturally, you'd be staying at the same hotel as Mrs Harpham."

Lawrence didn't deign to reply, but Leonard Covington barely noticed.

"Have I missed her?" he asked.

Lawrence glanced at his watch. "She'll be on the Euston Road by now, with Mr Gore in hot pursuit. He asked me to let you know."

"Good. I won't try to follow them, or we'll all end up in disparate parts of London. He knows the plan."

"The plan?"

"Yes. Walter has organised another of his little gatherings at home."

"Not Fitzroy Street?"

"No. It would have been far more convenient. I'm sure Freddie will arrange a carriage. But it's a nice day out there. I think I'll take a stroll."

"I'm heading that way," said Lawrence, the words out of his mouth before considering the consequences of sharing a journey with a casual acquaintance.

"Jolly good. We can walk together. Where are you going?"

Lawrence consulted his notebook. "The Eagle," he said.

"Which one?"

"Royal College Street."

"That's a fair old trek. The ale must be excellent."

"I'm meeting a friend," said Lawrence, unsure whether it would be the case. He'd escaped from the breakfast room at the Brocklehurst residence long enough to telephone Lonni Carpenter's number, but Lonni was out of the office. A squeaky-voiced youth had answered, reassuring Lawrence that he would pass on the message that Lawrence would be in The Eagle for a few hours later that day. But the boy couldn't get off the telephone quickly enough, and Lawrence was far from convinced he would bother relaying the message.

"Well, it will be nice to have company," said Leonard, affably.

They spent the first ten minutes chatting about the weather and how living in the regency spa town of Cheltenham compared to London, but after a while, the conversation stuttered to a halt. Silence usually suited Lawrence, but he was still uneasy about Walter Sickert and his influence over Violet. He decided to dig deeper and get to know the man through a convenient third party.

"How long have you been an artist?" asked Lawrence as they strolled past the station.

"All my life. Never wanted to be anything else."

"Did that involve studying?"

"Indeed. I won a few prizes at school, and my tutors expected still greater things. But I was among talented peers and far from being the best artist in my year. Father wanted more from me. He had no respect for the creative world, but the headmaster talked him around, and I finally applied to the Slade School of Fine Art, where I met Freddy Gore. Young Lightfoot studied there too, but he was a good few years behind us. Anyway, that's my background. How about you? Not keen on art, I hear?"

Lawrence scowled. He could take or leave art and found the Camden painters largely insufferable. But Violet had no business publicly bandying his opinions around. A man should be able to have private thoughts. "I'm ambivalent," he said eventually. "Carving is more my thing."

"Clay, marble?"

"Wood," said Lawrence. "Not so much now, but I was handy with a knife once upon a time."

Covington nodded without comment, leaving Lawrence relieved he did not need to explain his damaged left hand.

"So, how did you meet Walter Sickert? He looks a little older than the rest of you."

"I'll tell him you said that," laughed Leonard. "But you're right. He has a decade on Freddy and me. We've known each other on and off since the turn of the decade, mainly socially, but occasionally, we met to share ideas. But after my lucky break with *Sunset over Primrose Hill*, Walter asked me to discuss my technique with the other artists."

"I'm sure it was more talent than luck," mumbled Lawrence, feeling obliged to politeness.

"There is no difference between us when it comes to craftsmanship," said Leonard loyally. "I was lucky to fall on my feet and happy to share my experience with other artists. We met more frequently, and Walter created The Fitzroy Group a few years ago. We've been regularly supporting each other ever since."

"Does Mr Sickert lead the group?"

"You could say that. It would be less without him."

"I find his pictures rather dark."

"Then he would appreciate your opinion. He has spent years studying Degas and Pierre Bonnard to achieve the perfect blend of seedy contemporary work. Real life, he calls it."

"That's not quite what I meant. There is something sinister about his work, something secretive and almost otherworldly."

"I don't think so," laughed Leonard. "What you see is what you get. Walter paints his models warts and all."

"Is he a good man?" Lawrence threw caution to the wind, knowing that subtlety was rapidly failing to get results.

"It depends on what you mean. Walter is a talented artist and loyal friend. But he started his career as an actor and is all things to all men. Why do you ask?"

"No reason."

"I know. You've been listening to rumours and wondering why the Whitechapel affair fascinated Walter."

"What rumours?"

"Pure silliness. Walter is curious and loves a mystery. I wouldn't say he was obsessed with the Ripper murders, but he was more interested than most. You must disregard what you hear if it sounds sinister. His interests come from an artistic perspective. It's good that they caught up with that miscreant or poor Walter might have fallen under suspicion."

Chapter Twenty-Five

THE EAGLE

By the time they reached Mornington Crescent, Lawrence had lost all tolerance for conversation. He knew very well that Sickert had played no part in the Ripper killings, but the man's fascination for the crimes horrified Lawrence. What was he doing allowing his wife to spend so much time in the company of a man invested in the darkest depths of human depravity? Lawrence was glad to part ways with Covington and strode through Camden, wondering how he would break the news of Sickert's personality to Violet. He must tell her the truth even if she railed against it. He would ask her to break with the Camden artists and hope she still respected him enough to comply.

Lawrence approached the black-painted wooden front of The Eagle public house, hoping he would not have to sup alone. He wasn't in the mood for casual conversation but had come with a purpose in mind. Crossing his fingers, he hoped the means to that purpose would be around today. He pushed open the door and entered to find a quietened establishment, some hours away from the lunchtime rush.

Two men played cards to his right, barely glancing up as he walked past them. The only other signs of life were a woman sitting alone with half a glass of an evil-looking beverage, a one-eared house cat cleaning its paws by the rear door, and a bored-looking barmaid. He approached the counter and waited. The barmaid looked up, eyeing him with a half-smile. "What do you want?" she demanded, opening her mouth to reveal a hang tooth.

"Half an ale," said Lawrence.

"Come now. That's hardly worth the bother. You look good for the money. Have a pint."

"Very well. A pint then."

"Here you go," she said, passing the beer and holding her hand out for coins.

"Thank you, Miss, er…"

"Lillian," she said.

"Ah. Lillian Raven?"

The barmaid flicked her dark hair over her shoulder and glanced suspiciously at him. "Who's asking?"

"Lawrence Harpham. But that won't mean anything to you. A friend of mine suggested we speak."

"What about?"

"Emily Dimmock."

"Now why would I want to do that?"

"Because you're a decent human being. And you'd like to help."

"Help who? Phyllis is worm food. It's too late for her. Anyway, why do you want to know?"

"Because no one has been held accountable for her death."

"And who are you to put that right?"

"A private investigator who cares that a young woman lies dead in the ground."

"I care too."

"Then help me."

"Very well. What do you want to know?"

"I hear you were serving behind the bar on the night of the murder."

Lillian nodded. "I was. But you must understand. I didn't know Phyllis. I mean, I work here, and she came in occasionally, but our paths didn't cross until that night."

"Did you see anything else?"

"Nothing of note. She came in with one man and was about to leave when another man came in. He approached her and they had a drink together. After Emily died, the police came to see me and took me to Kentish Town Police Station to identify a man. A chap called Lambert. Joseph Lambert. Truth to tell, I could identify him easily enough, but he did nothing other than talk to her. And not for long either. So I said to them as I'll say to you. You'd be better off asking him."

Lillian Raven pointed to one of the pair of men.

"Who?" asked Lawrence.

"Him. Frank Clarke. He comes and goes between public houses, but Miss Dimmock was in The Rising Sun that night too. And so was he. Have a chat with Frank. He'll know far more than me."

Chapter Twenty-Six

QUESTIONING FRANK

Lawrence was on his way to introduce himself to Clarke when the door opened and Lonni Carpenter bowled in with his hair stuck up and covered in a greasy substance.

"Well, hello," said Lawrence, relieved to see him. "Better late than never."

"You're jolly lucky I'm here at all," said Lonni, wiping dark grease stains over his jacket.

"What happened?"

"My bicycle chain fell off."

"Oh dear."

"And that's not the worst of it. The damned totter couldn't keep his mare under control. It bit me on the behind as I was fixing my cycle."

Lonni turned around and lifted his jacket to reveal a large tear in the seat of his trousers. Lawrence stifled a laugh.

"Don't. It would be funny if it happened to anyone else, but I am not in the right frame of mind."

"Have a drink," said Lawrence. "On me. Anything you

like. I'm sure you'll feel much better when you've wet your whistle."

"A pint of ale. That will do."

Lawrence ordered the drink while Lonni stomped to the table nearest the window, lowering himself gently onto the wooden stool.

"Did she bite through to the skin?" Lawrence aimed for a sympathetic tone but realised he'd missed the mark when Lonni shot him a glare.

"Never you mind," he said, reaching for the beer and taking a long gulp. His frown eased as he reclined farther back in the chair. "Now, what was so important to fetch me halfway across London?"

"A slight exaggeration, I think."

"That's what it felt like."

"If you say so. Anyway, you said you would look into this potential second murder."

"I know. I made a start, but time ran away with me. It's been a busy news week."

"Well, I went ahead without you, and I believe that the man who killed Dora Kiernicki and Esther Prager also murdered Emily Dimmock."

"On what basis?"

"The method of murder, the proximity of the locations, and above all, the way the three women made a living."

"I expect you know more than I do. But with my limited knowledge, yes, I agree it's possible, but proving it is another matter altogether."

"I know. I've been speaking to Roslyn D'Onston."

"That's nothing to be proud of."

"You know him?"

"I know the name. It's not a good one."

"He's a knowledgeable man who also sees a pattern."

"What can I do about it?"

"Dig out the old newspaper reports, especially those relating to Dora Kiernicki. I believe she was the first in the series."

"Right. I will. But why here, Lawrence?"

"D'Onston told me to find Lillian Raven, which I have, but she doesn't seem to know much."

"I've never heard of her."

"Understood. But what about that man over there?" asked Lawrence, pointing to Frank Clarke.

"I should say I do. He's the man I told you to look out for when we last met. Frank is usually in The Rising Sun."

"Well, well. Miss Raven also pointed me in his direction, so I'd better give him the third degree."

"Then let's get to it."

Lonni grabbed his mug, and both men advanced towards the table. Frank Clarke looked up expectantly.

"May we join you?" asked Lawrence.

"And who might you be?"

"The name is Harpham. This is Mr Carpenter."

"It means nothing to me."

"No reason it should. But we are looking into the unsolved murder of Emily Dimmock. Will you help us?"

Clarke's eyes darkened and he glanced anxiously at his companion.

"Why? It's all done and dusted."

"How can it be when nobody was punished?"

Clarke shrugged. "The peelers are as thick as slurry. They don't solve every crime."

"I know. But this one's still fresh. She only died two years ago. It's a crying shame to leave her unavenged."

"You read too much," said Frank Clark's companion wryly.

"Will you help or not?" Lonni Carpenter, tired of cajoling, was on the offensive.

"Yes, if you're quick. We're here for a friendly drink, not an inquisition. And I'm thirsty," said Clarke. "My friend is too, as it happens."

"I'll go," said Lonni, heading for the bar.

Lawrence waited, engaging the two men in unanswered small talk until Lonni returned.

"Right. Let's get on with it," he said.

"What do you want to know?" Frank Clarke placed his chin on his hand resignedly.

"Let's start with a bit of background. What is your occupation, and where do you drink?"

"I'm a commercial clerk, among other things."

"What things?"

"An occasional agent for a private employer."

"Really?" Lawrence raised an eyebrow.

"Indeed. I arrange domestic staff on the side, you know, labourers, maids and the occasional artist model."

"You're a busy man."

"When the mood takes me."

"But not today."

"Not today." Clarke did not elaborate but took a long, deep draught from his pint.

"Were you surprised when the judge failed to convict Robert Wood?"

"Not at all."

"Why not?"

"I thought him no more than a convenient suspect. 'Twas the other Roberts that spent all his time with her."

"Robert Roberts?"

Clarke nodded, his friend aping his movements until they looked like a pair of nodding dogs.

"What did you see on the night of the murder?"

"Her, of course."

"Emily Dimmock."

"Phyllis. She called herself Phyllis."

"I know. Did you see her here?"

"No. I drank in The Rising Sun that night."

"We know that." Lonni Carpenter shot Lawrence an 'I told you so' expression.

"So, Emily. I mean, Phyllis was with Robert Roberts?"

"Eventually. He sat with me at first. We shared a couple of drinks. Then Phyllis came in about ten o'clock. I went off to relieve myself and when I returned, the two of them had pushed off to another table."

"What about Robert Wood?"

"He was there too. She spent the next half hour going between the two men like an Indian rubber ball. But Robert Roberts left with me that night. We lodged in the same building, him on the third floor and me on the second. I heard him banging around upstairs after I went to bed, so he didn't cut her blooming neck. It wasn't possible."

"Why are you so sure that Wood didn't do it then?"

Clarke shrugged. "He doesn't strike me as the violent type."

"Any man might hurt a woman in anger."

"The judge didn't think so."

Lawrence sighed. "Granted," he said.

"Now, what about another one?" Frank Clarke's friend held his empty tankard aloft.

"Your turn." Lonni Carpenter still nursed the dregs of his beer while listening quietly in the background.

Lawrence took the empty vessels and placed them in front of Lillian Raven. "Same again," he said.

"Don't fall for it." She cast a pitying look his way.

"Fall for what?"

"Clarke pleading poverty. He's got plenty of money, make no mistake. And his girls make a pretty penny, too."

"The domestic staff?"

"Get away with you. I mean the models. Rotten little tarts, every one of them. Who takes off their clothing for money? Only the lowest street harlot. Frank asked me if I'd do it once. The cheek of the man. I gave him short shrift, I can tell you."

"It sounds like an easy way to make money."

"If you've no morals."

Lawrence glanced over his shoulder at the two men sitting silently by Lonni.

"Shhh. He'll hear you."

"I couldn't care less. He should take his bony carcass back to The Rising Sun, where they're less picky."

"Right." Lawrence collected the drinks and returned to the table with Lillian Raven still in full flow.

"She doesn't approve," said Frank, having heard every word of the conversation.

"Apparently not."

"It's all very harmless. Most of my young ladies go into service. Domestic service, whatever she says. It's only the odd one or two who choose to pose. And not always unclothed whatever she thinks."

"Like Ruby Young?"

"Exactly like Ruby. I found her a couple of jobs. She loved it and even posed for that boyfriend of hers. He was an artist too."

"It sounds harmless," said Lonni, looking up from his introspection.

"So, you don't see Roberts or Wood as guilty?" asked Lawrence.

"No. Neither one. But don't ask me who committed the crime because I know about as much as the police did the day after the trial. A dead woman and nobody to blame."

"What about the others?"

"What others?"

"Dora Kiernicki and Esther Prager."

"Why bring them into it?"

"I think the same man killed them."

"Well I don't. You can't bind every murder together. It's ridiculous."

"They died in similar ways."

"I disagree."

"Alright. It was just a thought. Contact me if you remember anything else." Lawrence dropped a printed calling card onto the table. Frank crossed his arms and left it where it lay.

"Good day, gentlemen." Lawrence retreated to their original table by the window, Lonni following seconds behind. Frank Clarke scraped back his chair and swaggered towards the bar.

"Full of himself, that one," said Lawrence.

"For a duck."

"Sorry?"

"He waddles. Didn't you notice?"

"I do now." Lawrence grinned.

"He wasn't worth two pints of ale," said Lonni.

"No. I'm disappointed. Nothing is any clearer, and I'm running out of time."

"The coppers fared no better. Perhaps you should let it go."

"I may not have any choice in the matter. Look out those articles, Lonni, if you get a chance."

Lonni nodded. "I will. Give me a day or two."

Lawrence watched through the window as Lonni mounted his bike and set off up the road.

Five minutes later, he also left, ambling through Camden deep in thought, his mind so occupied he did not notice the faint tread of feet behind him.

Chapter Twenty-Seven

VERA CORRESPONDS

Friday, November 26, 1909

"Get the door, will you?" Violet put the finishing touches to her make-up as Lawrence adopted his favourite position by the window.

Lawrence scowled. "It's too early for company," he said. "Hurry up."

But it was too late. Whoever had disturbed them showed limited patience, taking the easier route of pushing a couple of letters under the door.

Lawrence scooped them up and handed them to Violet.

"This one's from Vera," she said, opening the first letter.

Netherwood, Bury St Edmunds

Dear Violet

Apologies that I haven't written sooner, but I have been settling in and getting accustomed to the ways of the household. Little Luna is a dear girl, and I am already fond of her. She is quite intelligent, you know, with an imagination far beyond her years. Luna tells me in all earnestness that she can walk through walls and cannot comprehend my reaction when I say it is impossible. At four years old, she should be playing with dolls and care nothing for the adult world. But she is a solemn little creature, shy and disinclined to befriend playmates of her own age, for all that Mrs Farrow tries to persuade her.

But you will be more interested in the actions of Mr Francis Farrow, and I have little to tell you. Aurora has revealed my mission to her husband, and though a little cross, he did not try to dissuade me from my plan. Truth to tell, he is rather relieved at the prospect of having an ally on the premises. Michael does not suspect his brother of any sinister intent, but when darkness falls, and the house settles and groans, he must wonder who he has allowed into his home. But Michael does not speak of such matters to me, and I can only speculate about his true feelings.

Mrs Farrow is another matter entirely. Aurora wears her anxiety like a mask. She restlessly wanders, her face pale and wan, eyes shifting this way and that. I hear her walking up and down the corridor at night, silently waiting by the bedroom door, never straying too far from her daughter's side. I fear she is ill and keeping it to herself. Aurora fainted at dinner on Thursday night and took to her bed. I woke early this morning and heard her crying in the bathroom, her sobs muffled as if she was suppressing a heart full of pent-up emotion. She came to breakfast with tear-stained eyes and drank half a cup of tea but would not eat. And she clutched her stomach as if she might vomit before retiring to her bedroom, where she remains as I write this letter. Fortunately, Luna is oblivious to her mother's pain and is under the care of a governess who visits daily throughout the week.

Aurora is not the only one who has taken to her bed. Although Francis Farrow can walk a little, he spends his time between his bedroom and the study. I have followed my brief to the letter and keep constant watch over him. Though this is difficult, he hasn't realised that wherever he goes, so do I.

As you know, I arrived here Wednesday evening, and they gave me a bedroom opposite Farrow's. This makes my job a lot easier and if I leave the door ajar and sleep on my left-hand side, I can see his bedroom door and know when he is on the move. But Farrow is clearly sick. He is all skin and bone, gaunt face, and sunken eyes. He lacks energy, and though he can walk, it is a chore. So, when I heard his door go in the early hours of Thursday morning, I put on my dressing gown and easily followed him to the study. He reached for the handle, but Michael had locked the door. A flicker of annoyance crossed his face and, just as quickly, died away. And he sat there, waiting on one of the wooden chairs by the buffet, watching the study door as if it might buckle under the weight of his concentration. Needless to say, it did not. Apart from that, I have seen nothing suspicious in Francis Farrow's behaviour. He is unfailingly polite and a witty raconteur. It would be easy to succumb to his charms were I not aware of his previous inexcusable behaviour. But nothing could tempt me to stray from the bounds of my contract.

Now, Violet. Please extend my regards to dear Lawrence and ask him if he would be so kind as to tell me how Cora is getting on in Cheltenham. I appreciate why you asked us not to contact one another, but we usually work as a pair, and I miss her.

I will continue to monitor Francis Farrow at all times, and I will ask Aurora to accompany me on a walk tomorrow. It will be good to have her full attention as I am more concerned about her than the child. But I do not think she will confide in me on the premises. I will, of course, insist that she brings Luna. I would fail in my duties if I left the child alone with Francis Farrow, even with Michael on the premises.

Enjoy your time in London, and please don't worry about anything. I will write again in two days, if not before, to keep you updated on my progress.

Yours

Vera Ponsonby

Chapter Twenty-Eight

A WOMAN ON THE EDGE

Saturday, November 27, 1909 - Netherwood

Dear Violet

My heart is broken, shattered into a million tiny shards of glass, each splinter piercing my soul like a poisoned dart. I kept a secret from you. From everyone I cared for, even Michael. And now, I have nothing and no one to share my terrible loss with. How will I go on?
Francis has caused this. Not directly, of course, for he is only a man, made frail by disease. But he brought fear into my home, created tension, and made me wary of my shadow. Can it only have been a week since he arrived?
I am sorry for the rhetorical question. It is unfair of me to presume you know what I know or that you might understand the dread within me. There is so much I haven't told you about my past. Not because I doubt your ability to empathise but because you are strong and I am weak. Pliable, cowardly, and terrified of my own shadow. I wish I had your stoicism and fearless ability to protect those you love.

I have tried, Violet. Luna sleeps with me every night, and I wait like a faithful hound by the bedroom door in the rare moments I can melt away from my domestic duties. Miss Ponsonby is a godsend. Her presence relieves me and instils a little calm. And though she would do it if I asked her, I cannot break away from the maternal need to guard my child myself. I care for Luna more than life itself and anything but my best is less than she deserves. But my sleep, already fitful, suffers greatly from my need to protect my girl. And butterflies dance through my breast at the thought of what might happen if I let my guard down for so much as a second. Michael says I am living on my nerves and it will destroy my health. Little does he know.

Francis often keeps to his room, but I have entered it several times since my last letter. On the surface, he leads a simple life, considering he was wealthy and ostentatious before he went abroad. A pair of trousers hangs in his closet with only two spare shirts, and his winter coat is threadbare. He travelled light, carrying a Gladstone bag, not yet fully unpacked. I left him in the study with Michael one day, giving me time to rummage inside and find the rest of his possessions. But they were truly paltry. Only a pen, an empty journal and a bound book of maps graced the bag. And I found a shaving kit and a few other personal items in his chest of drawers. I know from Michael that he took several expensive things to Mexico, so how he has lost it all is beyond my ken. Francis, though slow to walk, could have caught me rifling through his effects at any moment. Yet, being in his room and doing something productive made me feel better than I have since his arrival. I have not coped well with the uncertainty. Terror built inside me with every waking moment in the certain knowledge that something dark would happen – the lull before the storm.

Indeed, I felt it most on Thursday night. The weather was poor and the wind whipped itself into a frenzy. Francis and Michael were downstairs while Miss Ponsonby read a story to Luna. I busied myself by checking the windows, ensuring they were safe from the driving rain. Francis had left his on the latch and it rattled to the sway of the wind.

I firmly closed it before noting a sticky, glutinous substance the size of my palm on the outside of the window. I watched the rain pummelling against it, pitting the mass and making it shine. Then, to my disgust, gravity took its course, and the jelly-like mess slowly stretched down until, displaced by its weight, it flopped to the ground, leaving a kidney-shaped outline.

And suddenly, my mind's eye took me back to Duncryne, where Crossley had imprisoned me alone in the basement, lying torpid on the bed, cold, afraid, and too drugged to know my own mind. I recalled snatches of memories of travelling through the hills after dark in a racing carriage, being force-fed and compelled to relieve myself outside on command. I remembered the fuzziness of the drugs wearing off before waking on a tombstone surrounded by hooded men and burning torches.

It came to me in a waking nightmare right there in Francis Farrow's room. A pain shot through me like a bolt of lightning, and I felt a dampness at the top of my legs. At first, I thought I had wet myself in terror and visited the bathroom to clean myself up. Only then did I realise it was far worse. The child I was carrying, so dearly wanted, would never live to meet its father. Oh, Violet. I had not told Michael, for it was too soon, and my belly had not swollen enough to give my condition away. Naturally, I thought I had time, but I regret my complacency. Now Michael will never know.

I blame Francis Farrow. He did not lift a finger to hurt me, nor did he wish me ill. But the fear he instilled set my heart racing, and my body purged itself in terror. And now I suffer while he intrudes into my household like a cuckoo. There is no point in confiding in Michael now – no need for two hearts to bear the pain when mine is already broken. Keep my secret, dear Violet. I will stay close to Vera Ponsonby. She is all that keeps us safe.

Chapter Twenty-Nine

ANOTHER MURDER

Monday, November 29, 1909

"Oh, Violet. How dreadful. How unutterably awful. Poor Aurora. We should contact Michael. We cannot leave her to carry this burden alone."

Violet lowered the letter, her eyes shining with tears. "No, my dear. Aurora doesn't want Michael to know, and I must respect her wishes."

"But she's unwell. And Michael is her husband. He has a right to know. Anything could happen without proper medical aid."

"I know. I will telephone Vera immediately. She's had training in these matters. It is a betrayal of confidence, but one that Aurora might understand. Poor, poor girl."

"How many lives will Francis destroy?" Lawrence angrily strode towards the bedroom window and yanked it open before hurling an apple core into the distance."

"Be careful. You'll hit someone."

"If only," muttered Lawrence. "I would like nothing better than to crack Farrow's skull with it."

"That's not the way." Violet approached her husband and placed her head on his shoulder. Lawrence turned and kissed the top of her crown.

"I know it isn't," he admitted. "But enough is enough. Michael has placed his family in grave danger."

"It might seem so, but not necessarily."

"You've just read their news."

"But think rationally for a moment. Where was the intent to harm? Francis, for all his past wickedness, has not set out to damage Aurora. He is probably unaware of her fear. He would be responsible if he had caused physical injury, but we can't hold him accountable for her distress."

"Utter nonsense." Lawrence's eyes blazed with indignation. "Francis entered that house, knowing that Crossley had tormented Aurora. How could he share such a close friendship and not be aware? He must understand the impact his visit would have on a woman who had already suffered horrific abuse."

"You don't know that. Francis may not have known."

"Why are you protecting him?"

"Calm down, Lawrence."

"Answer my question."

"I will if you sit down and take a few deep breaths. You are too angry to think objectively."

Lawrence scowled and raised a cynical eyebrow but perched on the end of the bed where Violet joined him.

"Now," she said, taking his hand. She clasped it between her own, gently kissing the tips of his fingers. "We know Crossley has been abroad for a little while. But before that, he was in London, Scotland or on other well-documented travels around the world. Frank has kept us abreast of all Crossley's movements since we rescued Aurora in 1904. And we know Francis was in Mexico then. He was poorly when we met him, yet his skin still bore evidence of years of exposure to the sun. Francis is so ill that he is unlikely to have travelled for pleasure, and therefore, the two men must have lived on separate continents for at least five years. They would hardly have communicated during that time, and if they did, it's unlikely that Aurora was the subject of their conversation."

"So, you think we should give Farrow the benefit of the doubt?"

"No. Not while he's close and they are so vulnerable. But Vera won't let Francis hurt them, even if he was well enough to do so, and to the best of our knowledge, he hasn't tried. We must keep things in perspective, Lawrence. Aurora is terrified, and an overreaction from either of us can only add to her distress."

"You are right," sighed Lawrence. "And I trust Vera implicitly. In that case…"

But three sharp raps at the door interrupted Lawrence in full flow.

"Come in."

The door swung open to reveal a bell boy bearing a silver platter containing a folded note.

"Thank you," said Lawrence.

The bellboy paused.

"Ah. For you." Lawrence dropped a tip on the salver.

"Thank you, sir."

"Is the note for me?" asked Violet.

"No. Were you expecting one?"

"Not particularly. Walter said he might be in touch."

"It's been three days since you last saw your artist

chums. When you've finished pining, you might have time to spend with me again."

"How rude."

"Sorry. I was just stating facts."

"Then don't. I'm not pining. But I thought, I mean, I felt as if the artists had taken me under their wing. It was a tremendous privilege, and I learned a lot. And then, suddenly, nothing. I wonder if I have offended them.

"Did you look askance at one of their God-awful paintings?"

"Of course not. And don't be so disrespectful. They are talented men."

"Good Lord. It's from Lonni."

"How tiresome. What does he want?"

Lawrence whistled, then looked up, his face ashen.

"What is it, Lawrence?"

"A woman died last night – another murder. Come on, Violet. You've nothing better to do. Pretend you're still an investigator and help me track this monster down."

Chapter Thirty

THE NEXT TO DIE

Lonni was waiting for Lawrence in the hotel foyer. He sprang forward and lunged for Lawrence, extending his hand like a bayonet. Lawrence shook it.

"Lonni. This is my wife, Violet. Violet, Lonni Carpenter. He's helped me out of a few scrapes."

"Pleased to meet you." Violet sounded anything but, her features settling impassively. Lawrence glanced at her, hoping she would stay long enough to hear Lonni's story. He badly wanted the benefit of her calm, logical mind, but she had shown no interest in anything to do with the case.

"Tell me all about it," said Lawrence.

"Not here. Can we go somewhere private?" Lonni glanced furtively left and right.

"The snug," said Lawrence, leading the way to a small room at the back of the lobby. He glanced inside to see one person reading a book in the corner.

"Will this do?" asked Lawrence.

"I suppose so."

The reader looked up and tapped his nose as if sharing

a secret. "Don't worry. You can have your private business talk. I'm leaving now."

"Appreciated," said Lawrence, advancing to the loveseat by the fire, which crackled and spat as a flame took hold of the logs.

Lonni sat in an armchair to the side, removed a notebook and hunched over the low coffee table.

"Right. I shouldn't be here telling you this," he said. "I ought to be in the office writing my piece for the evening edition. But as I've been up since dawn getting this information, they can put up with my absence for a few hours. I'm dead on my feet and would have fallen asleep if I'd been at my desk."

"Understood," said Lawrence, impatient to know more and wishing Lonni would get on with it.

"The dead woman is Lily Templeton. She was thirty-seven, lived in Brixton, and made her money on her back. Sorry, ma'am." Lonni blushed as the coarse words escaped from his mouth.

"Please don't apologise," said Violet. "I'm quite unshockable."

"Jolly good. But it won't happen again."

"Brixton's a long way from the other murders," said Lawrence. "Are you sure they're connected?"

"You can be the judge of that when you hear how Lily died. She lived in Rushcroft Road, and that's only half an hour away by cab."

"Even so."

"Let him speak," said Violet, trying to move the conversation along.

"Yes. Let me speak." Lonni looked up from his notebook and pushed his chest forward and shoulders back, peacocking. "As I said, Lily Templeton died yesterday. They tipped us off last night, and I was up with the lark at Rushcroft House this morning, trying to keep ahead of the other newshounds. I got lucky, and one of the other occupants let me in. I saw Lily's room at sixes and sevens, blood still spattered everywhere. You'd have thought they'd have tried to clean up, but not at all."

"I should think not," said Violet. "The police can't do their job properly without a thorough understanding of the items in the room, not to mention the body. They must note the position of every object."

"They can't be doing with all that bother," said Lonni. "The murderer is probably on the run, and they ought to be in hot pursuit. You can't have them wasting time drawing pretty little pictures of unimportant details."

"I would if I were in charge," said Violet.

"She's very thorough," confirmed Lawrence.

"It doesn't work that way," Lonni blustered, seemingly offended at the prospect of the Metropolitan's finest producing large quantities of paperwork.

"Do go on." Violet pushed the conversation forward while trying and failing to read Lonni's writing.

"I will. I expect you'll be interested in the cause of death, Lawrence," said Lonni.

"Naturally. Although, I'll take a wild guess that it involved a cut throat. I doubt you'd be here otherwise."

"You're right, of course." Lonni regarded Lawrence with mild irritation, irked at having his limelight stolen. "Left to right or right to left, if you're so clever?"

"No idea," said Lawrence. "You're the expert. Tell us more."

Lonni flexed his fingers. The killer cut her throat so deeply that he nearly severed her head from her body. And he did it silently in the middle of the night. He slipped inside like a wraith, committed the crime and left unseen. At least, he thought so."

"What do you mean by that, Mr Carpenter?" Violet leaned forward, a glimmer of interest in her eyes.

"Call me Lonni. And I mean, Miss Templeton had a couple of dogs. One great big one and a second smaller one."

"Surely they would have barked the place down?"

"You would think so. Except that they didn't. And given the big dog's disposition, I can't help but wonder why. He was a fierce animal but uttered not a yip."

"That is odd," said Violet.

"Did you encounter any medical men at Rushcroft House?" asked Lawrence.

"Yes. I met a doctor when I arrived. He was tight-lipped, of course. But Miss Davies said she'd heard him speaking to his assistant and he thought the murder had occurred in the small hours around two o'clock."

"How much did you see?"

"More than I ever want to again. The blood was everywhere – all over the surfaces, reeking of iron and death. It was sickening." Lonni stopped talking, and a nervous tic below his eye visibly throbbed as a green-tinged pallor settled over his skin.

"Let me get you some water." Violet jumped up and left the room while Lawrence opened a nearby window.

"I'm alright. Don't fuss."

"You look as if you're about to pass out."

"I'm fine. It's just certain smells. They remind me of a slaughterhouse and a boyhood dare that went awry." Lonni staggered to his feet and hung out of the window, gulping deeply.

"Here," said Violet, reappearing and handing him a

tumbler of water. She carried a black and white postcard, which she slipped into her pocket. Lonni took a gulp, closed the window, and sat down again. "Sorry," he muttered.

"Don't worry. Let's move on. Can you remember anything else?"

Lonni consulted his notes. "Yes. Alma, I mean, Miss Davies, told me that Miss Templeton's day girl found her when she turned up for work."

"Day girl?" asked Violet.

"Her maid. Lily wasn't up, so the maid knocked on the bedroom door, walked through and opened the curtains to find her mistress lying in a pool of blood. She screamed and ran downstairs to fetch Miss Davies."

"Did they find a weapon?"

Lonni shook his head. "No. No knife, no razor, nothing. The murderer either brought his own blade or found one here and dumped it later on."

"I see. At the risk of upsetting you again, can you tell me more about the body? But don't make yourself ill." Lawrence aimed for tact and fell short.

Lonni angrily raised his eyes but kept his temper. "Can you read my writing?" he asked, passing Lawrence his notebook.

"More or less. Will you cope with the detail if I read aloud?"

Lonni nodded.

"Listen, Violet. Lily Templeton's body lay with her arm raised as if to ward off an attack. Blood covered the bed and floor, and her head lolled to the side, her throat severed from ear to ear. The bedclothes lay on the floor in a blood-soaked heap, with a bottle and glass nearby. Miss Davies said she smelled beer and noticed blood mixed into the liquid. She saw finger marks on the door, wallpaper, jug and basin, and a small dog waited by the dead body of its mistress."

Lawrence looked up. "Gruesome," he said. "Where was the other dog?"

"Locked in a bedroom."

"That suggests that the murderer was thinking on his feet," said Violet, pondering as she rested her chin on her hand.

"There's more," said Lonni.

Lawrence turned a page in the notebook. "Ah, so there is. Before entering the bedroom, the maid put a kettle on the scullery stove and laid breakfast out. After she alerted Miss Davies, she returned inside, noticing that Miss Templeton's auburn wig had fallen over. The bedclothes, drenched in blood, lay crumpled on the floor, and the bed had not been slept in, the pillow undisturbed. Close your ears, Lonni, there's more. The perpetrator had ripped a circular piece of flesh from her arm with a knife."

"I know. I wrote it. Fortunately, I didn't see that wound," said Lonni.

"Probably for the best. Luckily, the maid did."

"And Alma Davies too."

"How did the maid gain access?" asked Violet.

Lonni snatched his notebook from Lawrence and scanned the pages. "Damn. I didn't write it down, but I can remember. She pulled the bolt using a piece of string passed through the letter box."

"How extraordinary."

"Not at all. There was no lock. They rigged it up for all the occupants to enter that way."

"And how was Miss Templeton dressed?"

Lawrence watched Violet approvingly as she asked another pertinent question. He had hoped that involving her would spark a little interest in the investigation, and his plan appeared to be working.

"Again, no notes. But Miss Davies saw Lily Templeton sprawled across the bed, fully dressed except for her outdoor coat and hat. She noticed the throat wound immediately and the cut to her right arm, far worse than a flesh wound. Alma said someone had hacked the right arm through to the bone."

"What do you make of the injury?" asked Lawrence. Lonni hesitated, but Violet responded immediately.

"Was Miss Templeton right-handed?"

Lonni shrugged.

"Well, let's assume she was. Someone will know. If she was lying on the bed and the murderer was standing over her brandishing a knife, what would she do?"

"Try to protect herself, naturally."

"Exactly. Hence, the wound to the right arm. She would have raised it over her head to protect herself from the blade. The knife would have struck her arm, perhaps repeatedly, as the killer tried to slaughter her. I wonder why she didn't scream. Or did she?"

Lonni shook his head. "No. I spoke to several neighbours, none as well informed as Alma Davies, but nobody heard a sound. Not a scream, a bark, or the sound of the door closing. All very mysterious."

"Extremely." Violet stood up, approached the fire, and turned her back on it. She clasped her arms and vigorously rubbed them.

"I'll shut the window if you're feeling better, Lonni."

"Right as rain. Keep your good lady warm."

Lawrence pulled the window shut while Violet continued thinking aloud.

"Somebody should have heard something. There must

have been a struggle. Someone dislodged Miss Templeton's wig and the bedclothes didn't fall to the floor without help. The scene indicates signs of a struggle."

"Yet the evidence shows he was as cool as a cucumber."

"The murderer?"

"Yes. Miss Davies saw blood in the sink, and the doctor confirmed it. The killer took time to wash his hands before leaving, though blood must have covered his clothes."

"Not necessarily," said Violet. "If Lily Templeton died on the bed, he would have been standing above her, and his clothes may have remained perfectly clean."

"I wonder if it was a simple theft?" asked Lawrence. "Perhaps she caught a burglar in the act and he lashed out in shock."

"Definitely not," said Lonni firmly. "Miss Templeton owned a few pieces of jewellery which lay in plain sight. The maid accounted for everything, so you can rule robbery out."

"Then it's personal," said Violet.

"It must be, given the amount of blood. The murderer wasn't careful. There was no need to leave bloody handprints on the wall. Sheer carelessness."

"And yet, he washed his hands afterwards and took the knife away. It's more calculated than you think, Lawrence. Not opportunistic at all."

"Thank you, Violet. I value your opinion immensely. Is there anything else before we call it a day, Lonni? You look as if you need a swift drink."

"And I shall have one before I go. Perhaps you will join me in the bar. I hate drinking alone."

"I'll leave you gentlemen to it," said Violet.

"Wait, Violet. I should have mentioned a couple more things. Lily Templeton wasn't her real name."

"An alias, you mean?"

"Exactly. Lily's real name was Elizabeth Clarke, and she married a sportsman, then fell into bad ways when they separated."

"And the other thing?"

"Alma Davies would be worth talking to. She struck me as particularly observant, with a good eye for detail."

"I'm sure Lawrence will do the necessary."

"She may respond better to a woman."

Violet placed her hands on her hips. "You extracted plenty of information from her without any help from me. I'm sure Lawrence can manage too, as I won't be joining him. I have plans."

"No, you don't." Lawrence frowned.

Violet removed the postcard from her pocket and waved it triumphantly. "Look what just arrived. An invitation from dear Walter. I am afraid I will be otherwise occupied."

Chapter Thirty-One

FALLING OUT

Lawrence escorted Lonni from the hotel and returned to find Violet at the foot of the hotel stairs.

"Ah, there you are," she said. "I must leave at once to reach Mornington Crescent on time."

"When has Sickert summoned you?"

"Eleven o'clock."

"Impossible. You'll never get there."

"I will if I hurry."

"Violet. It's after half past ten. And I don't care how well-known Walter Sickert is in the art world; he can't demand your attendance halfway across town at the drop of a hat and expect you to go running. It's ridiculous."

Violet frowned and looked at the postcard again. Her features brightened.

"Oh, silly me. Walter doesn't want me in Camden today, after all. I misread the card. He says that some of his group are working on their pieces in Fitzrovia today, and we can get together at eleven o'clock on Wednesday instead. That's much better timing."

"Good. Then you can come with me when I drop in on Roslyn D'Onston before visiting Miss Davies."

"I'd rather not."

"Come on. I know it's a bore, but I'd value your help?"

"You know how I feel about workhouses. They bring back such awful memories."

"I understand. Forget D'Onston and help me with Miss Davies then?"

"You go, Lawrence. It's your case."

Lawrence sighed. "Very well. What will you do?"

"Take a walk."

"Where?"

"Fitzrovia, perhaps."

"You intend to visit the workshops, don't you?"

"What of it?"

"Oh, come now, Violet. Were you invited?"

"Not exactly. But Walter didn't need to mention Fitzrovia. He clearly wanted me to know."

"I'm sure Mr Sickert meant exactly what he said. The gathering at Mornington Crescent is tomorrow because they are busy today. It is not a carefully disguised invitation."

Violet turned, hands on hips and glared at Lawrence. "What do you find so threatening about my interest in art?"

He shook his head, taken aback by her barely controlled anger. "Nothing. But, Violet, I'm worried. I don't trust Sickert. He's a peculiar man."

"I know what you did to get your injury. You were poking around the personal property of a man I am proud to call my friend. How dare you, Lawrence? Don't you trust me?"

"Implicitly. More than you could ever know. But you see the best in everyone, Violet. And Sickert is not safe. His paintings are twisted, disgusting things. God only knows the depths of his depravity. They are sick and wrong, and you should stay away."

Lawrence trembled with the effort of trying to contain his loathing for Walter Sickert and his fear for Violet's safety. Sickert had bothered him for days. He had tried to stem his worry after breaking into his studio and attempted to see the best in the man, for Violet's sake. But her need to act on Sickert's every whim and be there whenever he called both grated on his nerves and alarmed him in equal measure. He opened his mouth to speak again, but Violet beat him to it.

"I'm going upstairs to collect my art bag, and when I come down, I will visit my friends in Fitzroy Street whether or not you like it. I cannot understand your distasteful show of jealousy, Lawrence. It is unbecoming. I love you, but I will make friends of my choosing. If you can't accept that, we've reached a sad state of affairs."

"Violet. You are overreacting."

"I want you to make an effort with my friends."

"I have. I walked all the way to Camden with young Covington."

"Good. Then you will appreciate Leonard is a very nice young man."

"Covington doesn't worry me. Nor does Freddy Gore and the other young man who looks like he needs a good meal. I forget his name."

"Maxwell Lightfoot."

"Yes, him. Watch them all day long if you are so inclined. But not Sickert. He bothers me, and he ought to bother you."

"He doesn't. I find Walter perfectly charming and I hope he will be there with the others when I call by in…"

Violet checked her watch. "In the next twenty minutes. I will see you at dinner."

"But Violet, what about...?"

But Lawrence's words were lost as Violet swished up the stairs, her head an unholy combination of excited anticipation of new painting techniques and annoyance at her unreasonable husband. Lawrence made to follow her, then paused. Violet was not herself. She had always been independent, but her recent behaviour bordered on foolhardy. She was headstrong, throwing all caution to the wind, embroiled with people who worried him for good reason. Or was he the fool? Was he making too much of Sickert's interest in the darker side of London life? What else could he expect from an artist? Perhaps he should go upstairs and apologise to her. But Violet was too angry to accept any words of regret. Instead, Lawrence secreted himself at a small table by the front of the hotel with a bird's-eye view of the door.

Chapter Thirty-Two

FOLLY IN FITZROVIA

Lawrence's first instinct when he saw Violet stagger through the door, weighed down with a heavy bag and a canvas tucked beneath her arm, was to rush to her aid. But that would have given the game away, so he settled for a slow walk just far enough behind that she did not notice his presence.

She squeezed past several enthusiastic shoppers blocking the pathway, nearly losing the corner of her artwork to a passing cab, as she wobbled across the road. But once off Warren Street, Violet slipped into the quieter alleys, and Lawrence trailed her without detection to the familiar bounds of Fitzroy Street. Violet stopped, opened her purse, and withdrew a piece of paper before proceeding towards Sickert's studio, where she pressed the doorbell and waited. She was still waiting expectantly with her canvas resting against her shins some five minutes later, before realising Sickert wasn't there. He wouldn't be admitting her to impart valuable words of artistic advice. Sighing, Violet consulted her piece of paper before turning left and continuing up the street. She tried one door and another before finally arriving outside a rundown end-of-terrace property with an entrance wide open to the elements. Tentatively, Violet went inside.

Lawrence jogged towards the property, up a short flight of steps to the door, popping his head inside and removing it just as quickly, hearing voices from farther within. He couldn't risk Violet's wrath by going inside, so he ducked down a narrow alley by the property until he reached a spot halfway down where the wall had crumbled. Glancing left and right, Lawrence hurdled over, landing with a thud on the other side. Grimacing, he rubbed his left hand as it angrily throbbed. Lawrence had spent many years strengthening the old injury and making the most of his damaged hand. But any exertion was always painful and his hand would always be weak. Lawrence reached the rear, found another open door, and crept inside. Whoever painted here had an unhealthy attitude toward fresh air. Keeping doors and windows open in the summer might be good for the soul, but not in the middle of a harsh November winter. Lawrence imagined an artist impeded by frozen fingers too rigid with cold to paint, assuming the occupant didn't succumb from exposure to the elements. As Lawrence mused, he noticed the silence and wondered where the resident artist had gone. More to the point, where was Violet?

The door led to a rear lobby, which opened into a dining room with an extensive cooking range by another open door. The range lay unlit, cold, and unloved. Lawrence shivered even harder as he passed the unwelcoming blackened plates. But as he reached the door, he heard the faint murmur of a female voice. He listened again, relieved that it was Violet's. Lawrence entered the door, traversed the hallway, and followed the sound up a flight of stairs. As he reached the last step and the wood violently squeaked, Lawrence darted into an empty bedroom, fearing the sound would alert them to his presence. But it did not. Clutching his beating heart, Lawrence advanced towards the open door and peered inside to see Violet kneeling beside young Maxwell Lightfoot. His bile rose as she reached for his hand, and he clapped his hand over his mouth to stifle the urge to stop them. Then Lawrence realised that the young man was crying and felt a flood of empathy. He crouched by the door, watching through a gap near the hinge, and listened.

"It's outstanding, quite unbelievable," said Violet, gesturing towards the large pencil drawing on the easel. "Why are you so upset? Maxwell, it's a masterpiece. Anyone would be proud."

"You don't understand," he muttered.

"I know. I'm not an artist and have no formal training. But the sheer force of the emotion in your drawing is breathtaking. You must surely know the extent of your talent?"

Maxwell did not reply but piteously groaned, clasping his forehead as his shoulders shook. Lawrence shuffled to a better vantage point by the opening and stared at the picture. Violet was right. The young painter was as skilled an artist as Lawrence had ever seen. The sketch of a young girl on a bed, clutching her head in anguish, showed every detail of her emotional breakdown, a descent into lunacy, the beginning of the end. It was a magnificent work and deeply disturbing. Lawrence wondered how much of himself Maxwell had poured into the picture.

"Why are you so upset?" Violet asked.

"It's no good. I can't take it."

"Of course, you can. This work of art would captivate

your peers, not to mention Walter. You must have taken months to produce a piece of this quality."

"Ten hours," said Lightfoot. "That's all, yet it feels like a lifetime."

"Please show Walter as soon as possible. You can't keep something this powerful to yourself. Take it to him and show it off to the world."

"He's seen similar sketches. This is no better than my previous efforts. It isn't ready." Maxwell pouted like a recalcitrant child.

"Then bring it when the time is right. Oh, Maxwell. We will all be in for a treat if the others are working on paintings like this."

"You are right. My friends are working like dogs. You won't see them for days."

"What about tomorrow's gathering?"

"Which one?"

"This." Violet removed the postcard from her purse. Lightfoot took it, scanned the text, and handed it back.

"I dare say Ethel will be there and some of her cronies. I may not, and I can't be sure you'll see the others. When the muse is upon us, we must work."

"I've brought a canvas to show Walter. I thought he might be in his workshop."

"He isn't, and I don't expect to see him today. Another time, perhaps?"

"Shall I wait here until you feel better? I could fetch you a drink and something to eat."

"I am better left alone."

"I understand. Then I'll call on Freddy, perhaps, or Leonard if I can find his studio."

"Don't. Leave them be. Time is not on our side, and we must strike while the urge is strong."

"I didn't realise Walter was such a stickler. Surely he can defer the exhibition."

"It's not that. We must paint while the images are clear in our head."

"How I wish I understood true artistic talent. To know when the time is right and to persevere while the muse is strong. I have never felt these things. I cannot call myself a painter."

"Don't say that, Mrs Harpham. You show great promise. The difference between you and me is one of necessity. You paint because you want to. I paint because I must."

"You are right, of course. My artwork lacks a sense of urgency."

"Which it more than makes up for in other ways. Do not despair. There is nothing wrong with painting for the joy of it."

"Thank you. I'll leave you to it."

"Good day, Mrs Harpham."

"Good day, Maxwell."

Lawrence watched as the young artist doffed his hat before realising that Violet was on the move and he was still visible. He scrambled to his feet as Violet strode towards him and stepped backwards into a box room as she turned the door handle. Lawrence closed the door in the nick of time and anxiously listened as Violet powered downstairs. Had he been there officially, Lawrence would have told her she had been in such a hurry she'd forgotten to pick up her canvas. But walking into a large spider web, now stuck to his temple, had preoccupied his thoughts. Resisting the urge to flee the unlit, coffin-like space, Lawrence rubbed his sleeve against his head, trying in vain to dislodge it. By the time he had succeeded, silence reigned. Lawrence pushed the door ajar and peered ahead. Nothing impeded his line of vision, yet he hadn't heard Lightfoot descend the stairs. Lawrence cautiously tiptoed forward and looked into Maxwell's workroom again. He was wrong. The room was not empty. Maxwell Lightfoot was inside but not standing as before. The young painter had retreated to the corner of the room, sitting with his legs in front like a child and staring towards the window as he rocked to and fro. Tears poured down his ashen face as his mouth moved wordlessly, an expression of unendurable pain etched across his features. Lawrence shuddered as he wondered what had evoked such unutterable despair in a young man with his whole life ahead of him.

Chapter Thirty-Three

FORGING RELATIONSHIPS

It was a day for sickness of the mind. First, Maxwell Lightfoot and his display of unadulterated anguish, followed by a visit to the High Hill infirmary where Roslyn D'Onston endured what could only be described as a bad day. A mad, bad day. Lawrence found him in the same ward, but this time lying silently in a bed at the top of the room.

"We moved him near a window to cheer him up," said the ward nurse. "For all the good it did. If anything, he is worse."

"Is he up to visitors?"

"Physically, yes. But whether you will get anything sensible from my patient is a different matter."

"May I try?"

The nurse checked her fob watch. "You have fifteen minutes. Not a second more. Mr D'Onston tires easily."

Lawrence approached the bed where Roslyn D'Onston stared fixedly ahead.

"Good day."

D'Onston's eyes did not flicker, nor did his expression

change. He reclined against a raft of pillows, overcome by lassitude and extreme indifference to the world.

"I bring news," said Lawrence.

D'Onston sighed and moved his head resignedly.

"Another woman has died."

"I know." D'Onston slowly spoke as if talking at half his usual speed. His grizzled moustache drooped and he looked for all the world like a melancholic sea lion.

"He cut her throat."

"So I heard."

"Using the same method."

"I daresay."

"Have I come at a bad time?"

"There are no good times, just poor and damned awful."

"Can I get you anything?"

"A large bottle of scotch if you can get it past matron."

"I don't know about that."

"I was being facetious. It would do me the power of good but the old harridan would whip it away as soon as look at you. We are not here to enjoy life and I have never felt it more keenly than while stuck inside this hellhole."

"You asked me to keep you updated."

"Thank you for your efforts. As you can see from my demeanour, I couldn't care less and must warn you that my apathy could last for some time."

D'Onston closed his eyes and sank back into the pillows, his face relaxing momentarily.

Lawrence waited, hoping D'Onston would show some enthusiasm, but he remained motionless, barely breathing.

Lawrence cleared his throat. "About Lily Templeton..."

D'Onston's eyelids flicked open and he stared angrily, his head still on the pillow. "Not now. Another day, old man."

"Time is of the essence. I'm returning to Cheltenham in a week."

"So be it."

"I thought you wanted to help."

"I'm a sick man, Harpham. You must pick your moments."

"Very well. I'll leave you in peace. Goodbye."

Lawrence angrily spun around, cross at his wasted time. But D'Onston raised a lethargic eyebrow. "Have you spoken to Inspector Ward yet?"

"Who?"

"Alfred Ward. He's in charge."

"How do you know?"

"I can still read when I have the inclination."

"But the woman only died yesterday. There's no mention of a policeman in my press copy." Lawrence unfurled the newspaper he had purchased on the way to High Hill and double-checked the page. "No, nothing here."

"Take my word or don't," said D'Onston, "It's all the same to me. I know Ward. He listens. I'd speak to him if I were you. It can only help."

"Where is he?"

"The usual place," said D'Onston. "Leave me now. I am too tired to continue."

"Right. I'll be back."

"As you will."

Lawrence arrived at the handsome square building on the corner of Gresham Road and advanced to the noticeboard to one side. A quick look confirmed he had been right to ignore D'Onston's assumption that Ward might be in the Metropolitan police building on The Embankment. After many years of inactivity, his natural instinct had been up to scratch. Ward was working from Brixton Police Station, as Lawrence would have elected to do in the same situation. He advanced through the central door and spoke to a bearded police constable behind the reception desk.

"Is Inspector Ward in the building?"

"Who wants to know?"

"Lawrence Harpham."

"Tell me more."

"Ex-inspector Lawrence Harpham."

"Is the gov'nor expecting you?"

"No."

"That explains why he's not back from the stores yet," said the officer.

"When are you expecting him?"

"I don't know. Sarge, when's the gov'nor back?" the police constable bellowed towards a sandy-haired man with greying temples kneeling on the floor. He scrabbled around, trying to pick up a pile of tiny brown bud-like objects. A small envelope with a large hole lay beside them.

"Can I help?" asked Lawrence.

"Not really. I've had a spillage. And the hole in my trouser pocket has hardly helped."

"Do you need something to put them in?"

"Yes, if you would be so kind."

Lawrence returned to the desk and helped himself to a manilla envelope without asking. The constable glared but did not object.

"Here." Lawrence handed the envelope over and squatted down, helping to transfer the objects, which he could now see were seeds, into their new home.

"Thank you," said the man, getting to his feet. He extended his hand and Lawrence noted three chevrons on his uniform.

"You're welcome, Sergeant…?"

"Hawkins."

"He wants to know when Inspector Ward is back in the station," said the police constable, looking up disinterestedly.

"Don't shout, Foster. We're not barrow boys."

Lawrence noticed the bad-tempered glare from Foster to his sergeant as Hawkins turned back around.

"You're out of luck, I'm afraid. I don't expect to see the inspector until this evening. Can I help?"

"I hope so," said Lawrence.

"What do you want?"

"I've just come from High Hill infirmary."

"Grim. Who would be an inmate there?"

"Roslyn D'Onston," said Lawrence.

Hawkin's eyes widened. "Come to my office," he said. "It's Inspector Ward's office, strictly speaking, and a bit more private."

Lawrence followed him down a short corridor into a plain, square room with a large patch of paint peeling from the ceiling.

"Water damage," said Hawkins, following Lawrence's eyeline.

"Really. I could swear there are another two floors above this one."

"It's a long story," said Hawkins. "I'm sure you have better things to think about than the state of our plumbing. Tell me about D'Onston. How is he?"

"In poor health. His neurasthenia has got the better of him."

"Not to mention the alcohol addiction, I daresay. I'll pass it on to Ward. I only know D'Onston by reputation, but the inspector has a curious regard for him. Frankly, I can't imagine why." Hawkins paused and cocked his head. "I hope that hasn't offended you."

"Not at all," said Lawrence. "Roslyn D'Onston is an odd fish, make no mistake. But he knows a lot of information and seems to have unlimited useful contacts."

"Inspector Ward being one of them. I believe they had an information-sharing arrangement in D'Onston's journalist days."

"I'm sure. It's a pity that your inspector isn't here now. D'Onston pointed me in his direction for a reason but didn't elaborate."

"On what matter?"

"Lily Templeton's murder."

"Oh, I see." Sergeant Hawkins stroked his chin and considered a suitable response.

"Do sit down," he said, gesturing to a chair.

Lawrence sat, crossing his long legs at the ankle.

"What is your interest in this?" asked Hawkins.

"The correlation between the Templeton murder and three others."

"Emily Dimmock and Esther Prager, no doubt. And the third?"

"Dora Kiernicki."

"Ah, I see. We are aware, you know. But we've no real evidence."

"Only if you are overlooking the circumstantial similarities of the crime."

"But there are differences too. We haven't ruled out that the murderer may have killed two or more women, but that is not our primary focus. Nor will it be. You must understand that women of that class expose themselves to danger, earning their living by such reckless means."

"They are not expendable." Lawrence's eyes flashed angrily.

"No implication intended," said Hawkins reasonably. "I'm simply stating facts."

"And public opinion, no doubt. Yet those women are often the most vulnerable, as evidenced by the spate of crimes against them."

"I'm not unsympathetic to your argument. But I cannot pursue a course of action my inspector has no interest in following. We must act as one in this regard."

"And I must act as an interested party, determined to hunt down this man and take him off the streets."

"Our finest officers have failed to make any headway. We have worked every clue and talked to every witness. What makes you think you can do better?"

"My sympathies lie with the victims regardless of their chosen profession. They deserve justice. And I believe that the evidence points to one killer, not four."

"Why?"

"Because it is statistically unlikely that four killers with similar profiles would operate so close to each other. At least two women regularly walked Southampton Row. They could have known each other, or the killer could have found them there."

"You don't subscribe to the notion that Robert Wood fooled the court and killed Emily Dimmock after all?"

Lawrence shook his head. "I don't know enough to say, but every witness I have spoken to without exception believed in his innocence."

"We found that too. Odd, isn't it? I could have sworn he

would go down for murder. But then Wood had an excellent barrister."

"Mr Marshall Hall was a worthy defence, undoubtedly. But his talent alone could not have secured Wood's release. The prosecution must have failed to produce sufficient proof of his guilt."

"We thought it was good enough, but the judge did not. He practically instructed the jury to acquit. Months of investigation down the drain in one fell swoop."

"But worthwhile if the defendant was innocent."

Sergeant Hawkins raised a brow. "If," he said.

"I heard the evidence was purely circumstantial."

"Mostly."

"As is your objection to my theory of a multiple murderer."

"We are dancing around in circles," complained Hawkins.

"My apologies. I don't mean to offend, and I would appreciate any help you're prepared to give."

"I can't officially offer any."

"Then unofficially…?"

Hawkins sighed. "I didn't tell you this, although if you read tomorrow's newspaper account and compare it to the other cases, you will see one notable similarity."

"Which is?"

"One moment." Hawkins opened his desk drawer and withdrew a small pile of papers. "Here we go," he said. "Now, a witness saw a man outside Miss Templeton's flat on the night of the murder. We subsequently received two separate statements about his appearance, both corroborating the other."

"Go on."

"The man in question was in his early thirties, about five feet seven or eight in height, with a pale complexion and a dark brown moustache turned up at the ends. He was otherwise clean-shaven. The suspect, of medium build, dressed in dark overcoat and trousers with tight-fitting legs, a white collar and a black, hard, felt hat. He walked with a distinct swing."

"That description sounds familiar."

"It should. This man, with minor variations to the description, was seen near both the Dimmock and Prager murders around the time of their deaths. I'm not sure about the Kiernicki killing. I'll need to check. But it's something to be getting on with, don't you think?"

"I do. And I'm very grateful for the tip," said Lawrence.

"Keep it to yourself, please."

"I will."

"What will you do next?"

"Visit Lily Templeton's flat. I hear Miss Davies is an excellent witness."

"She is. I spoke with her myself this morning. But don't get in our way, will you? We can only turn a blind eye to amateurs so far."

"I'm hardly an amateur."

"You're a retired inspector. I heard you tell my constable earlier. But retired is the operative word here. You have no legal right to interfere. Ward and I are open to suggestions as long as we're kept well out of it. One misstep from you, and we will have no choice but to come down heavily."

"You won't need to. Would you like me to keep you informed of my progress?"

"Very much so," said Hawkins. "Telephone me here any time. Tell them it's a cuckoo call, and they'll put you straight through."

"Ah. A code."

"Yes. We all have them, but I rather like our version. A little window of lightness on an otherwise dark business."

"Indeed. Well, I'll head off now, but I'll let you know if anything arises. And I do appreciate your open-mindedness in this matter. It's a refreshing change."

"You are welcome. This must not become the fourth unsolved murder in as many years. I will take any help if it secures a conviction."

"Good man." Lawrence warmly smiled as he left the room, pleased, and genuinely astonished at the sergeant's willingness to collaborate. If only all serving police officers were as cooperative with private detectives, unsolved crimes might be a thing of the past. But his good mood did not last for long. Having called into the local victualler for directions to Rushcroft House, he had not noticed the freshly white-washed front wall. A faint smell of ammonia alerted him to trouble as he leaned against it while removing and examining a bottle of the finest ale for his supper. Lawrence glanced over his shoulder to see that his once black overcoat now resembled an explosion in a flour mill, which no amount of chemicals would ever remove. Feeling ridiculous and having no time to change, Lawrence advanced to Rushcroft House, ignoring the stares of amused bystanders behind him.

Chapter Thirty-Four

ALMA DAVIES

Alma Davies was in residence when Lawrence arrived. She answered the door and invited him into her flat as if she were the most trusting girl in London.

Lawrence passed her his card. She nodded, glanced, and quickly returned it.

"I don't need that."

"You must be careful."

"Lightning doesn't strike twice."

"I'm not so sure. I don't mean to frighten you, but please don't let strangers into your home without knowing who they are."

"I knew you were alright the moment I saw you."

"Murderers appear perfectly normal most of the time."

"Yes. But they don't go around dressed like zebras."

"Ah. A little carelessness against a whitewashed wall. How did you know? You can't see my back from here?"

"No. But I could as you walked past my window. No killer in their right mind would walk through Brixton so conspicuously. Now come in, my darling, and take the weight off your feet."

Lawrence did as she asked, taken aback by her disarming charm and overfamiliarity. He made to sit down on a small wooden chair by the fire.

"Not that one. Use the comfy chair. It's padded. You can take your shoes off if you like."

"Thank you," said Lawrence, relocating to the easy chair. "I'll keep them on if it's all the same to you."

"Suit yourself." Alma shrugged, then planted herself down and turned the chair to face Lawrence. "I suppose you're here about Lilly?"

Lawrence nodded. "Yes. And you seem curiously unaffected by her death."

Alma's face dropped, and her eyes pricked with tears before she blinked them away. "You only see what I want you to see," she said. "Lily is dead. I liked her. She was my friend. But I can't bring her back to life. Nobody can."

"I know. Not everyone is as pragmatic as you. Most go through a period of mourning lasting hours or years. We are all so very different."

Lawrence drifted back in time and saw himself sitting broken and alone in the charred remains of his Bury St Edmunds home. He brushed the image of his dead wife and daughter away and concentrated on matters at hand. Once again, he had defeated the circling black dog quickly. He must take full advantage of his clear mental state. "Tell me about Lily," he said.

"Tell you what?"

"Anything. Just talk about her."

"Well. We were great friends. We talked a lot, sometimes about personal matters. Did you know she was married?"

Lawrence nodded. "Her real name was Elizabeth Clarke."

"Yes, it was. I bet you didn't know that her husband was a professional footballer."

"Really. You do surprise me. Yet they didn't live together?"

"No. They have been apart for many years. I don't know why the marriage broke down. Lily didn't say, and I didn't ask."

"Go on."

"Lily moved into the upstairs flat about five or six months ago. I first met her in the hallway, trying to drag a large trunk up the stairs. Silly girl. It could have crushed her. So, I took one end and Lily the other, and together, we made quite the team. She unpacked and called into my flat for a cup of tea. And that was that. We saw a lot of each other. We even went out on the town from time to time."

"How old was Miss Templeton?"

"In her thirties, I suppose. I asked her once, but I can't remember what she said."

"And you?"

Alma laughed. "A good thing I'm not easily offended. Don't you know you shouldn't ask a woman her age?"

"I hope you understand facts take priority over manners when murder is involved."

"Of course I do. And I'm twenty-five next birthday, so a good deal younger. But age didn't matter, and we got along famously."

"When did you last see Miss Templeton."

"That depends whether you mean in person or by sight? She dropped in to borrow some notepaper a few days ago. She said she wanted to write a letter. Did you know they found it ripped open? That nice police constable said there were finger marks on it. He thought they might be able to identify them. Have you ever heard of such a thing?"

"Why yes. Dactyloscopy is a fascinating science. Very new, of course, but reliable. The police solved a high-profile case in 1905 with the aid of fingerprints against two brothers accused of a double murder in Deptford, later convicted at the Central Criminal Court. They found a distinct print on a cash box, compared it to Alfred Stratton's thumbprint and proved his guilt beyond doubt. It was the talk of my club for a while." Lawrence's eyes shone with interest as he remembered the case.

"So, they should be able to catch Lily's killer?" Alma asked eagerly, encouraged by Lawrence's enthusiasm.

"It depends. The print might belong to Lily, her maid, or another unconnected person. And they must be able to collect the print and photograph it. I suppose that's how it works now. I haven't kept up with the process."

"Why?"

Lawrence shook his head sadly, momentarily regretting his retreat from current events. Science bored and fascinated him in equal measure. But the advent of investigative processes had held his interest in the earlier years. Realising that he was four years behind the times provoked unexpected resentment. He would try to correct his ignorance when he had time to spare.

"I stopped reading newspapers," he said frankly.

"I don't blame you, darling," said Alma. "Horrid things full of unpleasant stories. I never touch them myself."

"Did you see Lily Templeton after she borrowed the notepaper?"

"Yes. On the last night of her life. She left with two of the girls shortly after half past eight."

"Where did they go?"

"Annie Waltham said they had some money to spare, so they went shopping."

"So, no shortage of funds. How did Lily make her living?"

Alma hesitated. "I don't know. We didn't talk about it."

"I thought you were friends?"

"Which is why I didn't ask. But there were rumours. Some of the girls, well, you know. They talked."

"Did you see Lily walking out with men?"

"She had male friends and female friends too."

"Was she close to the other residents?"

"Yes. Mrs Waltham, in particular. But also, to Olga."

"I should probably speak to them."

"You'll need to come another time. Annie has gone away for a few days, and Olga has little English."

"Do you know anything about that night?"

"Yes. Annie told me and anyone else who would listen. The police have a full account."

"And where did they go?"

Alma nodded. "First to The Penny Bazaar under Brixton station and then to the Empress Music Hall on the Brixton Road. Annie said they ended up at The Prince of Wales Hotel, quite the worse for wear. It was a jolly night."

"And the ladies returned together?"

"No. Annie left Lily with Olga. But she said she saw Olga return home first."

"So, Lily remained alone?"

"With friends, apparently."

"Does Lily have children?"

"Funny you should say that. She only told me a few months ago she has a son born of her marriage to the Woolwich footballer. But the boy was sick from birth and resided in Wimbledon under the care of a doctor. It is very sad."

"Poor woman," said Lawrence, thinking of Daisy. A rush of longing to see her almost choked him.

"I know. But having a picture helped."

"Did she show you a photograph?"

"No. A watercolour made from a photograph taken in a portrait studio. Lily and her husband were estranged, as you know, but he let her borrow a picture and she had it copied."

"Small comfort," said Lawrence.

"It made her feel better and that's all that matters. Being apart from her boy would have broken her heart but for the dogs."

"Ah, yes. I meant to mention them. Were they always quiet and well-behaved?"

"Not so much the larger dog, but Daisy was a sweet girl. She never barked but followed Lily around like a little shadow."

"My daughter's called Daisy."

"It's a lovely name and not right for an animal. I don't think people should use real names for dogs. It's confusing."

Lawrence laughed. "I agree. When I get a dog, and I will one day, I shall call him Rex or Rover."

"Rex is a real name."

"Rover then. Rover or Shep."

"I approve."

"Glad to hear it." Lawrence shifted around in the chair. "Well, thank you for your insight. I must speak to Mrs Waltham to learn more."

"About what?"

"The person Miss Templeton concluded the evening with on the night before she died."

"Oh, but I know. Hanna saw her."

"Who is Hanna?"

"She shares a basement flat with Olga. Hanna came to London from Budapest and had very little English. But I was with her when the police questioned her, and they brought someone who understood Hungarian. Lily met a man that night: a short, well-dressed man wearing a bowler hat. He was quite ordinary, she said. Except for the way he walked with an odd swinging gait."

Chapter Thirty-Five

PLANNING

I slip inside the empty room, quiet and unoccupied as I knew it would be. It was all too easy to gain access; only a matter of waiting until someone distracted the receptionist, allowing me time to sidle to the board and collect the key. I had already discovered the room number from patient research.

I listen at the door before turning the service fob to read, 'Do not enter'. An interruption would be risky, although I am a cool enough character to talk my way out of any difficulty.

I assess the room. It is large and comfortable. The window overlooks Warren Street, a disappointing view, though suitable for watching people bustling towards Tottenham Court Road. But I care nothing for the outside. I must contextualize my surroundings and conclude whether they will fit my purpose. Will they inspire and sate my lust? My heart quickens at the thought and excitement snakes through my body. But I pause and marshal my thoughts. I must not allow that side of me to take over from the matter at hand. I am here for a reason, a single-minded purpose, not to enjoy the kill. Murder is a means to an end. It is unimportant except to provide the backdrop to the main event. Could this be the right location?

I pull the mantle chain and watch as the room illuminates. It is daylight outside but I must test the atmospheric potential. The well-furnished room is also utilitarian. A typical hotel room, functional but not homely. And far too clean. Yet as I go from sconce to sconce, turning on the wall lights, shadows flicker across the harsh white walls, taking on an orange glow. Thank God the ugly new electric lighting hasn't yet infected the building. I stand back, appreciating the ambience. That works, but the rest of the room is too pristine.

I advance to the bed, take the counterpane, and draw it back before disturbing the pillows and tossing them randomly over the sheets. Then I lie on the bed, turning this way and that, before getting to my feet and surveying the rumpled mess. I see a nightdress, laundered and starched. It is too clean. I toss it under the bed. What next? A telephone on the buffet unit catches my eye, squatting there incongruously and alien to my tableau. I retrieve the nightdress and lay it over the instrument. Out of sight, out of mind. But an unopened letter lies beside it, addressed in long, cursive strokes. It might work in my scene and I toss it on the bed.

The wardrobe naturally contains both male and female garments. But I am creating a backdrop for a lady. I take a scarf and a stole, arranging them over the bed. One upturned shoe completes the montage. I stand back and visualise a recumbent, lifeless body, feeling satisfied with my work.

If the scene in my head is possible, then it will be a departure from anything I have attempted before. But needs must. The usual method has failed. What worked before has served only to sate the beast that grew from the savagery. But the primary objective has eluded me several times. I must change my ways if I am to succeed again.

Casting one long look at the scene before me, I try to remember every detail. My work is complete for now. Feeling accomplished, I remove the nightdress from the telephone and start the long process of tidying up.

Chapter Thirty-Six

AN UNEXPECTED CALLER

Wednesday, December 1, 1909

"Not again," said Lawrence, slamming his journal shut and hurling it skittering across the desk.

"Yes, again, but this is the last time I will leave you. I know we have spent little time together and must return to Cheltenham by the end of the week."

"Good. I'll be glad to leave this godforsaken city behind. Too much of London always leaves me feeling tainted."

"I'm glad to hear it. I thought you might object, given your passion for these unsolved murders. Now you can leave it to the police."

"If I do that, they will remain unsolved."

"That, my dear husband, is not your problem."

Lawrence signed, retrieved his notebook, and stared at the page as if the answer was an earnest glance away.

"I've let them down," he said.

"Who?"

"The dead women, their friends. Everyone."

"This was never your case. Don't feel bad. You did as much as one man could in a few short weeks."

"Which amounted to nothing. I'd leave it with D'Onston, but he's still wallowing in apathy."

"Or seriously unwell, as we humans like to call it."

"His illness manifests itself in lassitude."

"That's no reason to demean it."

"Sorry."

"Accepted. Now, I'll say my goodbyes to Walter today as planned."

"Where?"

"Mornington Crescent. He is having another event."

"How delightful."

"It will be. Several of the Camden group artists are giving talks on their techniques. I should learn a great deal."

"I'm surprised Sickert's massive ego will make way for anyone else to speak."

"I beg your pardon?"

"I said I hope you enjoy the talk."

Violet regarded her husband, considered a reprimand, and concluded she had better things to do with her day.

"What time are you leaving?" he asked.

"Eleven o'clock."

"You'd better get a move on. It's nearly half past nine."

"I know. I'll go as soon as I've brushed my teeth. Oh, and Lawrence…" Violet glanced towards her husband, head cocked to one side.

"Yes?"

"Did you tidy up earlier this week?"

"No. I may have straightened the odd ornament. Nothing more. Why do you ask?"

"Only I crossed paths with the hotel maid, bringing up a letter the other day. She said she would leave it in the room.

It wasn't there when I returned and I thought no more about it. But I've just remembered. Did you move it?"

"I haven't seen a letter to move. Who wrote it?"

"I don't know. She carried it on a salver. Silly idea, isn't it? That bearing mail on a tray somehow elevates the experience. Don't worry. I'll ask her where she put it. Perhaps it fell down the back of the buffet."

"I'll check." Lawrence inched the heavy unit away from the wall and stared behind before grimacing. "Nothing here except spiders."

"Good. They keep the flies away."

"Neither have any place inside a hotel room," said Lawrence firmly. "I say. The letter wasn't from Cora, was it?"

"No. Stop worrying. I called Cora last night. They are still resident at The Ladies College, and Daisy is having a fine time of it."

"Did you speak to her?"

"Yes. For ten minutes while you were propping up the bar."

"I had one small brandy, Violet. It took all of ten minutes to drink."

"It wasn't a criticism. Now, what will you do while I visit Walter?"

"Catch up with Lonni, I suppose. I've got one or two ideas. Might take one last toss of the dice."

"Doing what?"

"I'll talk to Alma Davies again."

"Why?"

"To find out more about the dogs."

"To what end?"

"I'd like to know why they didn't bark."

Violet sighed, then stood behind Lawrence, who had

reoccupied his seat by the desk. "You won't get very far unless you speak animal," she said.

"Very funny."

"If time is short and your resources are low, then you must apply logic."

"That's all I've done. What do you suggest?"

Violet leaned over Lawrence and stared at the journal, flicked a page or two, then moved her finger across the page while muttering below her breath. "Hmmm, interesting," she said.

"What is?"

"That description. Who is it?"

"A man spotted near three of the four victims the night before they died."

"I see."

"I don't. It could apply to thousands of Londoners. He has no redeeming features."

"But he does."

"What?"

"You've written about a swinging gait."

"Oh, I know. But I ignored it. I don't know what it's supposed to mean."

"Yet several people described an unusual walk. What do you think they were getting at?"

"A casual stroll, a swagger. I don't know."

"That's a pity. It seems significant to me."

Lawrence opened his mouth to speak, but a sudden knock at the hotel room door cut him off.

"Come in," he said, but no one entered.

"I'll get it." Violet advanced to the door.

"Hang on a minute."

"Don't worry. I'll get it."

"Not that. I mean, I know someone who walks with a peculiar gait."

"Luna. What on earth are you doing here?"

Violet stepped back before kneeling and embracing the little girl standing by the door. Behind her, a tall woman was arguing with an angry-looking hotel staff member.

"I tried to stop her," said the woman, her jowls quivering.

"Vera. Why are you here?"

"Can we come in?"

"Of course. This way."

"I'm sorry for the intrusion. It won't happen again." The hotel worker wrung her hands in abject apology.

"They are friends of ours," said Violet. "You can go now."

The woman pursed her lips and strode away.

Lawrence jumped up as Vera entered the room. "What on earth?"

"Didn't you get my letter?" asked Vera.

"No," said Violet. "We know there was one, but it went missing. Do sit down. Have you come from the station?"

Vera nodded. "Yes. Straight here by cab. It was all I could think of on the spur of the moment."

"You did the right thing. I'll ring for some tea. What would you like, Luna?"

The little girl glanced up, her eyes round and fearful. She held her hands to her mouth and said nothing.

"She'll drink milk," said Vera, placing an awkward arm around the child.

"I still don't understand." Lawrence, who had finally recognised a potentially important clue, now struggled to rationalise the intrusion into his sleuthing.

"Aurora asked me to take Luna away. She believes Francis Farrow is plotting something dangerous."

"She may be right," said Lawrence. "But the last time I saw Farrow, he was too ill to be a physical threat to anyone."

"Be that as it may, she has convinced herself."

"I'm surprised Michael was so ready to let Luna go."

Vera paused. "Why don't you take Teddy and play with him on the bed," she said. "See if you can tuck him in. I thought I saw him yawning. He's a very tired little bear."

Luna clutched the toy and clambered onto the bed. She placed the bear on the pillow and sat beside him, sucking her thumb.

"Michael doesn't know," whispered Vera.

"Dear God."

"Don't blaspheme," said Violet. "You'll only make it worse." She turned to Vera. "I don't know what to say. Michael is my friend, our friend. We've known him for years, and if it comes to a question of loyalty, we must choose Michael over Aurora."

"I thought you might say that." Vera walked towards the door, opened it, and beckoned them down the corridor. "Stay here, Luna dear," she said. "We'll be outside. Knock on the door if you are worried, but you'll be able to hear us. Sing Teddy a little song."

She shut the hotel room door and leaned against it while Lawrence and Violet arranged themselves on the opposite wall.

"I know she's only four, but Luna mustn't hear us talking about her parents like this. It might do long-term harm. Fortunately, she's still quite immature with a poorly developed memory. But let's not take chances."

"Did you not think to ask Michael first?" asked Violet, irked at the position she now found herself in.

"Of course I thought about it. But Michael's duty to his brother has hindered his objectivity. He cannot see that Francis might be dangerous."

"Nobody dislikes Francis Farrow as I do," said Lawrence. "But even I recognise his feebleness. What could he possibly do?"

"Anything," said Vera. "He has already caused trouble, and if I hadn't seen it myself, I wouldn't have believed Aurora."

"What happened?"

"Someone opened the secret room."

"Wasn't it nailed shut?"

"Yes."

"Then how did he open it?"

"I don't know."

"Is Francis strong enough?"

"Again, I don't know."

"What did Michael say?"

"That Aurora has an overactive imagination. He told her to lie down, as she was evidently unwell."

"I don't understand." Lawrence snapped the words before following them up with a gruff apology.

"Let me explain. We tried to show Michael the open door, but by the time he returned, we found it nailed shut again. With the same nails in the same holes."

Lawrence raised his eyes heavenward. "I could just about accept Francis opening the door in his fragile condition but not fussing around, lining up existing nails to holes. It's ridiculous. Michael is right. Aurora must have imagined it."

"Except that she didn't. I saw it myself. Michael took a trip to Ipswich two days ago and stayed for most of the day. Naturally, I remained with Aurora, so she wasn't alone with

Francis. Michael had only been gone for an hour, and Francis was sitting outside on the lawn in an overcoat with a blanket over his knees while reading the newspaper."

"In the middle of winter?" Violet raised an eyebrow.

"Yes. Anyway, I was in the nursery with Luna when I heard Aurora scream. We found her by the study door, shaking like a leaf at the foot of the stairs. I asked Aurora to stay with Luna while I explored alone. There is a room at the top."

"We know," said Lawrence, his mouth set grimly.

"Someone had been inside and chalked a circle on the floor, and I found recent wax deposits."

"Oh, no." Violet shivered as she clapped a hand to her mouth.

"What did you do?"

"I took Aurora and Luna back upstairs and tried to settle them. But Aurora visibly shook with terror, and Luna cowered at the sight of her stricken mother. I distracted Luna for an hour with toys in the nursery until she tired and dropped off in my arms. When I returned to Aurora's bedroom, I found her staring at the wall. We talked while Luna slept, and she first mentioned the idea of taking her away. I refused and said we must tell Michael about the door. And eventually, she conceded. It must have been one o'clock by the time we went downstairs. Francis was eating lunch in the dining room."

"So, there were others in the house?"

"Yes. One of Michael's guards and the cook."

"I thought they didn't keep domestics?"

"Not living in. Cook and a housemaid come in once a day from Bury."

"Francis was eating downstairs," repeated Violet, trying to keep the conversation on track. "What happened next?"

"I passed the study and saw the door nailed shut."

"So, you are asking us to believe this happened in the few short hours you were upstairs?"

"Yes."

"And you heard nothing?"

"No."

"Are you sure?"

"Quite certain. We told Michael anyway, and although he was doubtful, he did at least accompany us to the study. He conceded the door was remarkably dust-free but could not see any evidence of foul play. There were no obvious marks on the wooden planks, and he refused to take them apart to check beneath."

"Did Michael speak to Francis about it?"

"Yes. But Francis appeared nonplussed and upset at the implication. So, here we are now."

"I'm sorry we put you in this position," said Violet, softening her tone.

"Don't worry. It's part of the job."

"It's above and beyond your duty. We are grateful, and I understand the tough choice you made." Lawrence patted Vera on the shoulder. She moved away from his touch.

"Appreciated. But what do we do about the child?"

"What do you think?" Lawrence turned to Violet, hoping she would offer a sensible solution.

"Why don't you take her to Cheltenham for a few days?" said Violet. "Just until we know a little more. We'll join you on Friday. In the meantime, I will write to Michael and tell him Luna is safe."

"He'll know exactly where to find her," said Vera.

"Of course. But he is her father and has a right to know. Luna will be safe if she is away from Francis. I will invite

Michael to our home, and we can talk there. Will you stay with Luna for a few more nights?"

"I will," said Vera. "Cora and I can return to London together.

"Have a hot meal, and I will arrange a cab to the station," said Lawrence. "Will that do?"

"In the short term." Vera closed her eyes wearily. "But something is very wrong at Netherwood. Something dark is on the horizon. It is only a matter of time."

Chapter Thirty-Seven

PADDINGTON STATION

Lawrence hailed two cabs. One for Vera and another for Violet, who had left it too late to get to Mornington Crescent by foot. He helped Violet into the cab, planting a kiss on her cheek as she fussed over her bag of art supplies, checking she'd packed everything.

"I do hate rushing," she said. "Now, Lawrence. Will you accompany Vera to the station?"

"Is it necessary?"

"I think so. Better safe than sorry."

"Then of course I will go. How long will you be?"

"A good few hours. Walter is hosting a workshop. We will paint and display."

"Right. Well, enjoy yourself. I'll see you later."

Lawrence nodded to the driver, who twitched the reins before ferrying Violet away.

When Lawrence opened the door and stepped inside, Vera and Luna were already in the carriage.

"Are you joining us?" asked Vera.

"Only as far as the station. I'll see you safely on the train."

"That's kind but unnecessary."

"Do you mind?"

"Not at all. As long as we are not wasting your time."

Lawrence smiled and slipped into silence as the swaying cab created its usual soporific effect. He was half asleep by the time they arrived at Paddington station. And little Luna was out for the count with her head in Vera Ponsonby's lap.

"I'll take her," Lawrence whispered, picking up the little girl and snuggling her into his shoulder.

Vera purchased a ticket, and they advanced to the platform to find the train already in the station. Vera sat, and Lawrence settled the sleeping child back in her lap.

"I telephoned The Ladies College before we left. Cora is expecting you," he said.

"Thank you."

"Take this." Lawrence passed her an envelope.

"What is it?"

"Your fee. And a little more besides. We are so very grateful."

"Appreciated. What will you do now?"

"I don't know. We are leaving soon ourselves. I was working a case and I've all but given up."

"That's a shame. But you can't win them all."

"Actually, Violet said something earlier which has given me food for thought."

"Tell me about it."

Lawrence began to articulate, but a harsh whistle called time on their conversation.

"You'd better get off," said Vera.

Lawrence jumped down just in time as the train pulled away. He stood waving until they were out of sight, then returned to the concourse, watching the clock as it ticked down the minutes. Violet's talk of the swinging gait had provoked a memory of a man in a public house walking towards the bar. Or waddling, as Lonni called it. A man whom the police had questioned about Emily Dimmock's death. But other than his odd walk and proximity to the Camden victim on the night of the murder, Lawrence had no reason to suspect Frank Clarke of being anything more than arrogant and unpleasant. Still, he had limited choices of suspects, and time was short. He could visit Alma Davies as intended or have a few more words with Frank Clarke instead. And Violet had attached far more importance to the unusual gait mentioned in the police description than he had. Lawrence contemplated the old days, working as a pair with Violet, employing fierce logic to solve their cases while he relied on instinct. He closed his eyes. Instinct was telling him to trust Violet. She might have drifted away from investigating, but her intellect was as sharp as ever. He would speak to Frank Clarke again, which meant revisiting Camden, hoping to find Clarke in The Eagle. Lawrence stood, purchased a ticket, and headed towards the underground station.

Chapter Thirty-Eight

IF IT WALKS LIKE A DUCK

Lawrence departed the train at Mornington Crescent on the spur of the moment. He should have alighted a few stops later, but the thought of passing close to Violet without seeing her disturbed him so much he decided to walk to The Eagle instead. And as he left the underground, with its pristine red oxblood tiles, he considered his next course of action. It was only right to tell Violet he was nearby, and she could join him for lunch if she wished. Better still, they could travel back together when her workshop was over. Crossing the road, he strolled towards Mornington Crescent, briefly hesitating when he reached number six. He stood on the doorstep, about to ring the bell, when he noticed the door was ajar. Lawrence pushed it open and went inside to find the building full of the same familiar faces he had seen during his last visit. It took moments to locate Violet chatting with Walter Sickert in a large reception room as he held court before the dozen artists surrounding him. Lawrence spotted Freddy Gore, Maxwell Lightfoot, and Leonard Covington, all too busy talking to notice him. Lawrence lurked uncomfortably for a while, waiting for a gap in proceedings. And when none came, he advanced towards the group. Walter Sickert saw him first.

"Ah. You didn't tell me your husband was coming," he said, reaching to shake Lawrence's hand.

Violet flashed her husband an angry glare. "I didn't know."

"Well, you're very welcome," said Sickert, raising a smile that did not reach his eyes.

"Sorry to interrupt. I just wanted a few words with Violet."

"Of course. Go ahead." Sickert melted away while Leonard Covington smiled and tipped his forelock before following Sickert.

"Why are you here?" asked Violet. "Is Luna alright?"

"Yes. She's fine. Can we speak for a moment? Not here."

They left the building, hovering near the front while an irritated Violet wiped her nose with a lace handkerchief.

"Have you got a cold, old girl?"

"Never mind that. Don't close it." Violet shot an anxious look towards the door. "It's not on the latch. I don't want to get locked out and have to interrupt them. Now, why have you come? Walter is about to speak, and I don't want to miss it."

"You won't. I'll be quick. I wanted to let you know I'll be in Camden for the next few hours."

"Right. Why?"

Lawrence stopped and cocked his head.

"What was that?"

"I didn't hear anything."

"Sorry. Must have been my imagination."

"You were about to tell me why you were in Camden."

"Because Frank Clarke has an unusual walk."

Violet pondered for a moment. "Describe him."

"Dark hair, medium height, pale complexion and a moustache."

"Then you should make further enquiries."

"But apart from his appearance, I have little reason to suspect him."

"Why did you meet him in the first place?"

"He saw Emily Dimmock the evening she died."

"He was a witness?"

"Yes."

"Well, you are here now. It can't do any harm to meet up with him again."

"Good. I'll head off to The Eagle. Shall we travel back to the hotel together afterwards?"

"I don't know when I'll finish. Let's not tie ourselves down."

A sharp rap from an upstairs window interrupted their conversation. Freddy Gore stood above them, pointing to his watch.

"I must go," said Violet.

"I'll see you later." Lawrence reached for a kiss, but Violet had turned her back and hurried inside. Sighing, he set off for Camden.

Chapter Thirty-Nine

RETURN TO THE EAGLE

"You again?" asked Lillian Raven as Lawrence approached the bar at The Eagle. The public house was once again unusually quiet. He gazed around the empty room to the highly polished bar where Lillian had been hard at work. The counter gleamed and the glasses sparkled, ready for a lunchtime influx of customers. He hoped they would soon arrive and reward her diligence.

"Me again," he confirmed.

"Another half a pint?" she asked, emphasising the half in sarcastic tones. Lillian still bore a grudge for his earlier misdemeanour of under-ordering.

"A pint and a pie," Lawrence replied.

"Right you are." Lillian's tone softened as she set about her task, handing him a beer.

Lawrence took a long draught. "That's good," he said, licking his lips.

Lillian briefly disappeared into a back room. "Your food will be along in a minute or two," she said on her return.

"It's quiet today," Lawrence replied conversationally.

"Won't be for long." Lillian glanced at the wall clock. "The regulars will be along any minute now."

"Does that include Frank Clarke?"

"Maybe. You'll have to wait and see. It depends how busy he is."

"I thought his job was casual."

"It depends on what line of work you believe in. Frank Clarke calls himself a commercial clerk, but he doesn't do much writing."

"Sorry, I'm confused. I thought he found employment for young ladies."

Lillian snorted. "In his head, I'm sure he does. In the real world, he knows some women down on their luck who will do anything necessary to earn their keep. So, yes. You could say he encourages them into positions, but by and large, it's not respectable work."

"I heard he places them in domestic situations."

Lillian picked up a glass and began polishing. "Perhaps one or two by chance. He knows people and matches their needs. That's about the size of it."

"I wonder why he lied to me."

"You wouldn't ask that if you knew him. If Frank Clarke said it was raining, I'd check outside."

"He's not to be trusted?"

Lillian put the sparkling glass on the counter and sighed. "I told you that on your last visit. I thought you understood how things were. This is not some fine establishment in Westminster," she continued. "What clientele do you think we have when the likes of Frank Clarke are rubbing shoulders with the Emily Dimmock's of this world?"

"I'm not sure what you mean."

"Night ladies drink here. It gives them a place to hawk their wares. God knows being a barmaid isn't much of a way to live, but at least I'm respectable. They are not. And men like Clarke are worse."

A bell rang in the distance. "Back in a minute," said Lillian.

Good to her word, she returned bearing a steaming pie in the centre of a bowl covered in a thick, brown gravy.

Lawrence armed himself and dug in.

"What's so bad about Clarke?" he asked, huffing his cheeks out to avoid burning his mouth on the molten pie filling.

"He's a thief," said Lillian frankly.

Lawrence looked up. "Really? That's a world away from being a commercial clerk."

"As I said, Frank is a liar."

"What did he do?"

Lillian leaned forward and placed her chin on her hand. "I shouldn't be tattling," she said.

"It's not tattling when you're helping an investigation."

"Give over. You're not police."

"I know. Neither am I following the route they took. That would be pointless. I realise you didn't know Miss Dimmock well, but you must have heard the story about Robert Wood."

"Of course. He got off, as well he should."

"The police pursued several lines of enquiry according to the newspaper articles I've read. None were fruitful, so I'm largely ignoring their work. Nor am I wasting time trying to chase down Scotch Bob, Jack Crabtree, or any other suspects named in their reports. If I am to succeed where they failed, it must be with a fresh approach."

"It's too late. Emily is dead and buried. What's the point anyway?"

"The murderer is still out there. Still at large. Don't you read the papers?"

"No."

"But you must have heard about Lily Templeton. It's all over the front pages."

"What's that got to do with it?"

"I believe the same man killed her."

Lillian Raven stepped back. Her eyes widened, and she clapped a hand to her mouth. "No," she said.

Lawrence took a forkful of pie and masticated thoughtfully. "I'm afraid so."

"Nobody here has connected the two crimes."

"Why would they?"

"It's a pub. Gossip is rife."

"If they haven't, they will. And if I'm right, Lily is the killer's fourth victim."

"My namesake," said Lillian.

"No. Lily was a nomme de plume. Her real name was Elizabeth Clarke."

"Like Frank?" Lillian chewed her lip anxiously.

"Yes. But don't worry. Lily Templeton was married to a professional footballer. I doubt Clarke ever achieved that kind of glory."

"Not bloody likely. Look, I'll tell you whatever you want to know. Frank and I don't get on. He's a lowlife, and I don't pander to him like some of the other girls do. But though I don't know him especially well, I know all about him, if you see what I mean."

Lawrence nodded.

"Well, it's like this. Earlier this year, they arrested Frank for stealing overcoats and gloves."

"From a shop?"

"No. Houses in Houghton Street. And somewhere in Russell Square too."

"Break-ins?"

Lillian nodded. "And though they couldn't prove it, I heard a rumour that Frank was in the frame for many more."

"Thefts?"

"Yes. All women's overcoats. Forty or more went missing from houses in the neighbourhood."

"Only women's overcoats?"

"Exactly. What do you think of that?"

Lawrence cleared the last of the pie from his plate. "So, Frank Clarke has a history of breaking into women's properties and stealing clothing, presumably to sell?"

"Yes. And now you put it like that, he would have a reason to break into Emily Dimmock's place. She wasn't short of money and her garments were of decent quality."

"Did he serve time?"

"Six months in Wormwood Scrubs," said Lillian. "They've only just released him."

"Well, thank you. That changes everything."

"Good. Now, I'll leave you to it. It's busying up in here."

Lawrence ordered another pint and nursed it for an hour, scrutinising the door for signs of Clarke, who never appeared despite his watchful gaze. As the public house filled with customers, the noise and chatter increased while Lawrence's mind mulled over the new information. Eventually, Lillian rejoined him.

"You're wasting your time," she said. "If Clarke were coming, he'd have arrived by now. Why don't you return this evening or try The Rising Sun?"

"Noted," said Lawrence. "But time is not on my side. I'll head for The Rising Sun now."

Chapter Forty

AND ON TO THE RISING SUN

After several pints and a large pie, Lawrence knew he ought to walk it off but hailed a cab to Euston Road instead. He had hoped to collect Violet on the way but if finding Frank Clarke during his last few days in London was remotely possible, he must forego the pleasure. And given the unpleasantness of Clarke's character, he preferred not to expose Violet to any unnecessary danger.

Lawrence mulled as he travelled. Walter Sickert was not his cup of tea. Not at all. And finding the revolting paintings in his warehouse had not endeared him to Lawrence. But Violet was undoubtedly safer there in the company of artists than with a convicted criminal. Lawrence had not made firm arrangements with her and if he did not appear before she was ready to leave, Violet would find a safe route back to the hotel. Yes. His decision was sound.

Lawrence pushed open the door of The Rising Sun, casting a glance at the now familiar bar. Sid and Bet were both behind it, busily pulling pints. He waited behind a group of men, their jackets dusty with the fruits of hard labour. The men, in good spirits, joked with each other as they jostled for position at the busy counter.

"Hold your horses," cried Bet good-humouredly. "I've only got one pair of hands."

"Then hurry them up," said an Irishman, winking as he spoke.

"Mind your mouth, Connor, or you'll go straight to the back of the queue."

Sid wiped a hand over his glowing brow, and Lawrence wondered why he was so warm on a chilly November day in a barely heated pub. The fading fire glowed feebly in the corner, requiring new coals and a sharp poke to revive its fortunes. Lawrence waited momentarily, then advanced to a free seat near the fire. It would take a moment or two to reach the counter, and he dutifully prodded the embers while he waited. Once finished, he leaned back against the wooden chair, watching the window while briefly closing his eyes.

"Don't I know you?"

Lawrence woke to the feel of a hand on his shoulder, gently rousing him from sleep.

He stared bleary-eyed into Sid's face.

"Sorry. I only closed my eyes for a moment."

"I know. I saw you. Don't worry. You were only out for five minutes. Just long enough for the bar to clear. I do know you. We spoke the other day. You're the private detective."

"I am."

Sid drew up a chair opposite Lawrence. "Any news?" he whispered.

"Have you heard about the Brixton murder?"

"Sid nodded. Oh yes. And it seems very similar to me."

"It is," said Lawrence. "Worryingly so."

"Do you think it was the same man?"

"Probably."

"Then what are you going to do about it?"

"As much as I can in the short time I have left in London."

"Are you going away?" Sid's face fell.

"I must go home. My time here was always limited."

Sid sighed. "God help us all if they cannot find him."

"Did Lily Templeton drink here?"

"She may have done. I can't say. We know our regulars, but people drop in and out, and we can't remember every face."

"You know Frank Clarke though?"

Sid nodded. "Yes, he's a regular alright, and knows all the girls. Are you going to ask him about Lily?"

"That's why I'm here. I hoped to find him. He wasn't at The Eagle."

"No, I daresay. He spends more time here and usually drops by for a lunchtime pint."

"Usually? I thought he had been away."

"You know about that? Yes, he has. But he's been back for a few weeks and calls in most days."

"Good. I shall wait for a while."

"It's past his usual time though," said Sid, pulling a battered fob watch from his pocket.

"Damn. I counted on seeing him today. Do you know where he lives?"

"No. But Bet might. I say, you remember me mentioning Esther Prager?"

"Of course. She's the poor girl who died last year."

"Yes. But did you know they questioned Frank Clarke about her murder?"

"I did not. Why?"

"Because he lived there."

"Where?"

"At the same lodgings."

"Frank Clarke lived with Esther Prager?"

"No. He moved out just before Esther died. But he was familiar with the place."

"So, Clarke lived in the same building but not with the girl?"

"That's right. He had a room at the house and Esther had another. They must have known one another, at least in passing."

"Then I must speak with him at once."

"Bet," Sid hollered across the crowded room. Silence briefly descended and Bet momentarily stopped halfway through filling a tankard.

"What?" she yelled.

"Come over here when you've got a second."

"Or you could shut your sauce box, get back behind the bar and give me a hand."

"Bet, it's important."

Three pairs of eyes glanced angrily towards Sid, and a tall man spoke. "We're back to work in a minute. Give us our ale, or we'll help ourselves."

"Calm down," said Bet. "I'm going nowhere." She wiped her hands on a dirty apron, took one tankard, then another, expertly pulling pints while bantering with the men.

"Don't worry. Bet will come over when she can," said Sid.

"I don't want to cause any bother."

"Cause as much as you like if it helps our cause. I am still losing sleep about Emily. You know that."

"I do."

They sat in silence for a moment, watching Bet work as the queue of men melted away. The three rowdy workers took their beer and settled by the window while others propped up the bar. When Bet was satisfied that no drinking vessel remained empty, she approached them.

"You're limping," said Sid.

"I tripped over in the cellar. Don't fuss."

"Thank you for coming over," said Lawrence. "I didn't mean to make things awkward."

"Don't worry about them," said Bet, nodding towards the seated men. "They're half rats anyway."

Lawerence cocked his head.

"She means under the influence," said Sid, noting his puzzled expression.

"Not going back to work then?"

"Maybe. But not this side of the hour. And not with clear heads either. Don't listen to pub talk. They're all trying to sell you a dog."

Lawrence looked blankly towards her again.

"She means they tell lies, " translated Sid.

"Yes. I'm beginning to notice." Lawrence scratched his head as he tried to regain control of the conversation. "Frank Clarke's address," he said. "Do you know it?"

Bet nodded. "He intended to return to his parent's home in Hendon," she said. "And maybe he will. But for now, he's in lodgings off Russell Square, north of the cab stand. Look for him there if you can stomach it."

Lawrence grimaced. "What do you mean?"

"You'll see when you get there. When you're low on funds, you can't be too choosy. And Frank likes to spend what he has on drinks. But you'll have to be quick. Frank was flashing his money purse around the last time I saw him. Seems he's come into a bob or two and will doubtless be on the move."

Lawrence thanked them both and said his goodbyes. Then he steeled himself for a short walk to what sounded like a thoroughly unpleasant destination.

Chapter Forty-One

DEN OF INIQUITY

Lawrence approached the tall, red brick building with trepidation. It loomed above him, and he counted the levels. As far as he could see, it was six storeys high, including the basement. The building was old, the brickwork crumbling, the windows small and barred. He approached the front door and tried it, but the lock stood firm. He would need to find another way.

A narrow alley ran down the side of the structure, descending lower the farther along he went. The smell of damp assailed his nostrils and brought something worse: a pervading odour suspiciously like human waste with a dash of ammonia. Lawrence retrieved a handkerchief and held it to his mouth with a sense of dread. London's hygiene had improved beyond measure with the highly efficient sewerage system. He expected a building in the heart of the city to smell better.

Lawrence advanced to the rear, past a locked and bolted side door to a patch of rough ground behind, soon discovering the source of the smell. Several roughly constructed shelters covered the area, one occupied by a sleeping man. Lawrence looked and looked again, initially unsure whether the man was alive. But a rumbling snore and twitching foot confirmed he was in a deep sleep. The other three shacks bore evidence of recent use. A smouldering metal box contained a filthy, unwashed pan, while an empty bottle lay beside it next to a small pile of animal bones of an undetermined nature. Lawrence did not dwell on the species of unfortunate creature that had given up its life to feed the destitute men. But he marvelled at their hardiness for living outside despite the fierce November cold. Lawrence spared a fleeting thought about where they might be. Hopefully scavenging a distance away as they would doubtless resent the intrusion into their territory.

Lawrence soldiered on, creeping through the yard, and circumnavigating the property via a second alleyway on the other side of the building. The smell was less offensive here, and a small window overlooked an ivy-clad wall. He peered inside, squinting as he tried to comprehend the layout of the dark room. It was no use. The only natural light was coming from the window now blocked by his body.

Lawrence reconsidered his options. He only wanted to speak with Frank Clarke, a legitimate action that did not require subterfuge. Sneaking around alleyways was hardly necessary. Clarke had been amenable to a discussion in The Eagle, and there was no reason to suppose he would object now, especially if Lawrence made it worth his while. Breaking in was unnecessary, and after his years of retirement, it surprised him that the idea of illegally entering had been his first thought. He should knock on the door until gaining admittance. How hard could it be?

Lawrence finished his loop of the building's exterior and advanced to the front door for the second time. For a moment, he stared nonplussed. Something vital was missing. The only piece of door furniture was a round brass doorknob – no knocker in sight. Lawrence rapped the door with his knuckles and waited. Nothing. He slammed the wood again with the heel of his palm, once, twice, three times – still no movement from inside. Frustrated, Lawrence grabbed the doorknob and yanked it several times. Something gave inside, and the door opened into a mould-infested porch. Clasping his handkerchief over his mouth, Lawrence entered and quickly checked the door. It remained unfastened, there being no lock. But it had still impeded his progress because the door had swollen into the jamb, requiring a hefty thump to gain entry. The trick was in the knowing. He pushed the door and advanced to the stairwell, passing a pair of peeling, unloved doors along the way.

Lawrence prepared to descend the stairs. Bet had mentioned that Frank had a basement room, and given the symmetrical structure of the building, it could only be one of two. But as Lawrence set foot on the disconcertingly sticky tread, a door opened to reveal a large-bosomed woman who eyed him suspiciously.

"Who are you?" she barked.

"A friend of Frank's." Lawrence nodded to the basement.

"Him down there?"

"That's right."

"Well, mind you, don't stay for long. I won't have guests on the premises. It's against the rules."

"Is this your building?"

She crossed her arms over her chest and nodded.

"Very good. I'll only need a few minutes with Mr Clarke, then I'll be off."

"Best you do. There are too many strangers around today for my liking. I'll be watching you."

With one long, lingering look, she slammed the door.

"Charming," muttered Lawrence, making his way downstairs to an overwhelming smell of dampness. Mildew coated the once-white walls, interspersed with black mould patches. Frank Clarke must have been down on his luck to have resorted to such lowly dwellings. And with parents living in Hendon, Lawrence wondered why he had sacrificed more comfortable accommodation to dwell in the city. Why was it necessary?

The stairs opened into a narrow hallway with the same two-door configuration as the level above. A plank lay over one door, nailing it shut, leaving the other unhindered. Finding Frank's room would be easy. Lawrence approached the second door and rapped sharply on the wood. Something moved inside, but the door did not open. He knocked again and waited, listening for sounds of life. Once again, he heard a shuffle and an unnerving noise like a low moan. Lawrence tugged the door handle, but it did not give.

"Frank, are you there?"

The room fell silent.

"It's Lawrence Harpham. We met in The Eagle a few days ago. I need to speak to you. Will you let me in?"

Lawrence placed his ear to the door, hearing more muttering and a dragging sound, followed by a thud.

"Damnation." The expletive hissed from Clarke's mouth, leaving Lawrence sure he was inside.

"What's wrong?"

"Never you mind. I need help." Clarke's voice rose and fell as if speaking was an effort.

"What? How?"

"I can't open the door. You'll need to unlock it."

"Where's the key?"

"On the lintel. Hurry now."

Lawrence raised his hand above the architrave, immediately feeling a metallic object beneath his fingertips. He grasped the key, unlocked the door, and went inside.

Chapter Forty-Two

A BROKEN MAN

Lawrence opened the door into a room too dimly lit to see. He grimaced as a terrible smell assailed his nostrils, rank with dampness and the odour of unwashed linen. A chink of light escaped from a curtain, flapping over itself, the hook hanging forlornly from the tattered fabric.

"Where are you?" asked Lawrence, stumbling over an item that appeared to be a leather boot. He kicked it aside.

"Watch out, you bloomin' fool."

Frank's voice came from the corner of the room. Lawrence advanced to the curtains and pulled them open. Several more hooks clattered on the floor.

"Look what you've done now. Why do you think I keep it dark? I'm not a bloody owl."

"Dear God, what's wrong with you, man?"

"Never you mind. Help me up."

Lawrence approached Frank Clarke, squinting to see. A wall only feet from the window allowed little light despite the open curtains, but it was enough to note that the man before him was in a poor state. Clarke peered at Lawrence through puffy, slitted eyes with the beginnings of bruising around the orbits. Smeared blood coated his face and forehead, and his swollen lips parted as he tried to speak.

"Help me up or go away."

"What happened?"

"Mind your own business."

Lawrence ignored his rudeness and held out a hand. Frank grasped it, his bloody, dirt-encrusted nails digging into Lawrence's arm.

"Pull harder," said Frank. "I've no strength."

Lawrence yanked again, but Frank let out a strangled cry and clutched his hand to his belly.

"You're making it worse," he muttered.

"Give me both your hands."

Frank's eyes fluttered as if he would pass out, but he clenched his jaw and offered his hands like a child. Lawrence took both, feeling the familiar weakness in his scarred left hand, and pulled for all he was worth. Frank leaned forward, resting his head against Lawrence's shoulder as he caught his breath. But moving him was more manageable now that he was away from the wall. Lawrence placed his hands beneath Clarke's armpits and wrestled him onto the bed. The stricken man moaned, held his arms around his shoulders, and then passed out on the mattress.

Lawrence searched the room for a light source, found a gas lamp and lit the wick. Then he placed it on the corner of a bedside table and loosened Frank's collar, touching pale, clammy skin. Lawrence rested his head against Frank Clarke's chest, his breathing laboured and shallow. Then he held two fingers to Frank's neck, feeling for a pulse, and counted to sixty. Satisfied with the firm, regular beat, he unbuttoned Frank's jacket. But something was awry. The worst of Frank's injuries appeared on his face, yet the garment was sticky with blood. And although shabbier than it appeared in the pub, Lawrence noticed a disconcerting cut in the fabric he would have seen had it been there when they last met. Lawrence loosened the final two buttons and opened the jacket, surveying the bloody mess before him.

Frank's soft grey shirt turned scarlet halfway down his body, one side of his suspenders frayed and about to split from a cut that ran into the shirt. Lawrence paused, his heart thumping, bile rising in his throat in anticipation of the wound. Then he waited until the queasiness passed, mentally cataloguing his surroundings while he marshalled his thoughts. Frank's room, which initially appeared self-contained, had, on closer inspection, a gap where a door once stood into what looked like another area. Lawrence checked Frank's breathing. His pallor was poor, but the colour was returning. Lawrence could do little more to help without water. He got to his feet, and the nausea returned, the room seemingly closing in on him. The metallic smell of blood made his mouth water. He retched and ran towards the window, throwing it open and breathing in the city air, thanking his lucky stars that Frank's room was on the side of the building, not used as a human toilet.

The fresh air did the trick, and Lawrence hastened towards the door gap, leading to a tiny room half the size of the bedroom but with a small cooking range and a large bowl of water. A pitcher and washbasin stood beside it. Lawrence filled the jug and scanned the kitchen, finding several rags in a bucket in the corner. He grabbed one, recoiling at the fetid, stained cloth likely used for cleaning the floor, and decided he would do more harm with it than without. With a resigned sigh, Lawrence removed the monogrammed silk handkerchief Violet had given him for Christmas from his top pocket.

By the time he returned to the bed, Frank Clarke was stirring. He moved, groaning pitifully before his eyes fluttered open.

"Are you still here?" he muttered.

"Yes. And if you stay still, I'll clean you up. Unless you would prefer a doctor?"

"No. No doctor," snapped Frank. "I don't want anyone to see me."

"I thought you might say that," said Lawrence, "given the state of your belly. A knife, was it?"

Frank nodded.

"Should be a police matter."

"Not on your nelly. I've only just got out of chokey."

"Well, you didn't stab yourself, so you're hardly going back for the crime of being injured."

"It's not that simple."

"I'll clean your wound while you tell me all about it. Have you any bandages?"

"Yes. Boxes of them."

"No need for sarcasm. Let's sit you up."

"Let's not. Just get on with it."

"Very well." Lawrence took the collarless shirt and yanked it apart. Frank Clarke yelped.

"That was my Sunday best."

"Well, it's covered in blood. Say goodbye. You'll never wear it again. Oh dear, that wound is quite a mess. Only one cut though, and you'll be glad to know your guts are intact. It's a flesh wound but needs stitches."

"I'm not going to the hospital. Patch me up. I know a woman with a bit of medical knowledge. She'll do the necessary."

Lawrence nodded. "Any alcohol?"

Frank pointed a grimy finger towards a wardrobe. "In there."

"Hold this over your wound." Lawrence handed him the now damp handkerchief and opened the wardrobe. Two bottles of an unlabelled brown substance lurked in the corner beneath a shabby jacket and two shirts. Lawrence took a bottle and pulled another shirt from the hanger.

"What are you doing with that?" asked Frank suspiciously.

"More bandages."

"No. I need it intact. I've only one left, and I'm not made of money."

"If you can afford to drink in The Eagle, you can buy new clothes. I heard you were flashing your cash around last week. And newly out of jail too. What's going on?"

"I had a few coins and then I lost them," said Frank.

"Careless of you. Now, this may hurt." Lawrence took the handkerchief, sniffed the bottle, and doused the cloth with alcohol. He cleaned the area around the wound and held the dressing over a deep gash.

"Jesus Christ and all the angels," grimaced Frank, his fists clenched. "That hurts like a bitch."

"Manners. I'm trying to help."

"Nobody made you."

Lawrence ignored him, took the shirt, and ripped it into several pieces, which he tied around Frank's middle. "You'll need to see your lady friend today," he said. "Or you'll suffer an infection. This wound is deep, and it won't heal without intervention. Do you understand?"

"Yes. You can go now. Thank you."

Lawrence crossed his arms and remained seated on the bed.

"I don't need you anymore."

"I came here for a reason," said Lawrence. "I want answers to some questions. And the least you can do is tell me why I found you bleeding out on the floor of your room."

"I can't," said Frank, his face a mask of panic.

"Then I'll call a doctor."

"You wouldn't."

"In a heartbeat. Tell me."

"He'll kill me."

"Not if you're in prison."

"I'll be safer there."

"Then I'll call a policeman."

"Why are you so interested in my wellbeing? It's none of your business."

"I'm investigating Emily Dimmock's murder, as you very well know. And I think you have had more to do with it than you told the police. Although I hear they spoke to you about Esther Prager too."

Frank's eyes widened. "Who told you that?"

"Is it true?"

"Yes. And they let me go again. It was only talk, information. That's all."

"Tell me where you were when Dora Kiernicki died."

Frank pulled himself up, winced, and crossed his arms, an expression of smugness settling over his face. "I wasn't even in London. It had nothing to do with me. Nothing, I tell you."

Lawrence watched his earnest expression and allowed his instinct free range. "I believe you," he said. "How about Lily Templeton?"

Frank Clarke looked away, his eyes darting around the room, anywhere but near Lawrence's face, not lingering for a second.

"You'd never make a poker player," said Lawrence. "Did you kill her?"

"Of course, I bloody well didn't. Good God, man. I am many things, but I am not a killer. Never that."

"But you know something?"

"I can't tell you."

"You could if you tried. At the risk of repeating myself, I will leave and call a doctor and the nearest police constable in that order." Lawrence glanced at his watch. "I'm a busy man. It's now or never. You have precisely one minute to start talking."

Chapter Forty-Three

HOW IT ALL BEGAN

"Alright. Calm down. I can't tell you much anyway. A man can't reveal what he doesn't know."

Lawrence shot him a warning glance. "Don't make excuses."

"I'm not. God knows I've better things to do than waste my time talking to you. But you should know I can't give you what you want to hear."

"That being?"

"Phyllis Dimmock's murderer."

"My expectations weren't that high. But I suspected you were involved, and now I'm certain."

"Bully for you."

"So, why don't you start at the beginning?"

Frank Clarke took a deep, unsteady breath. He clutched his hand over his mouth and rested it there, watching Lawrence through anxious eyes. He hesitated, saying nothing.

"I'm waiting, and I'll sit here all day if you don't get on with it."

"Promise me you're not the law."

"I'm not a serving policeman."

"Because I'm not going back inside."

"Frank. I'm looking for information. That's all. Unless you are directly responsible for Miss Dimmock's death, you have nothing to fear from me."

"Well, that's the thing."

"I don't understand."

"A man can be responsible for something without realising it."

Lawrence glanced at his watch. "You're speaking in riddles. Any more procrastination from you and I'm off to find the nearest bobby."

"Look. I didn't cause anyone to die, but I might have been the means to their end."

"Go on."

"First, pour me a drink."

"Glasses?"

"Over there."

Frank pointed a shaky hand towards the entrance to the second room.

Lawrence stood, advanced towards him, and spun around at the sound of movement from the bed.

"Don't worry. I'm only shifting position," said Frank, clutching his stomach.

Lawrence reversed towards the room, watching Frank through cynical eyes.

"You've nothing to fear. I'm too badly injured."

"Or you'd have been off like a startled whippet. I don't trust you an inch."

"Charming. Just get me a drink if you want me to talk."

Lawrence collected a couple of chipped, stained glasses and strode back to the injured man's bedside. Frank wouldn't have stood a chance in a fair race against Lawrence's rangy, athletic frame, but any attempt to escape, however futile, would waste precious time. And Lawrence was heartily sick of Frank Clarke's procrastination. He grabbed the bottle and carelessly sloshed an inch of the unappetising liquid into the glasses.

"Cheers," he said.

Frank ignored him, gulped the brandy down, and slammed the glass on the bedside table.

"Another."

"No."

"I said another."

Lawrence took the bottle and placed it back in the wardrobe. "You can have more when I'm satisfied with your story."

"I won't forget this." Frank scowled at Lawrence with an expression of pure hatred.

"Right. Now to business," said Lawrence. "Dora Kiernicki. You didn't know her?"

"No. I told you that."

"And you know nothing about her murder?"

"Not a damned thing."

"But you were acquainted with Esther Prager?"

Frank nodded.

"Knew her well?"

"Tolerably."

"Did you have anything to do with her death?"

"I left the lodgings before Esther died."

"That's not what I asked."

"I got her a job."

"Really?"

"Yes. I told you I did a bit of matchmaking on the side."

"Domestic work?"

Frank chewed his lip.

"Something else?"

"Anyone can find domestic work. I specialised."

"Let me guess. You took advantage of desperate women."

"Not exactly."

"Why don't you explain?"

"Well, it works like this. I hear of a particular need and find a girl willing to supply it."

"Such as?"

"Something innocent much of the time. Like the artist's models. Nice girls aren't in a hurry to strip off in front of men they don't know. But my girls will lie on their backs for as long as it takes to paint them warts and all for a few shillings. It's easy work."

"Nothing wrong with that between consenting adults," said Lawrence. "But why the secrecy? There must be more."

"There is. You see, the dolly mops will do almost anything for gin and a bed for the night. But they like it quick if you know what I mean. A fumble up the alley, lots of trade in a short time. Other customers want more. Something specialist, if you take my drift."

Frank winked lasciviously. Lawrence scowled, his searching eyes never leaving Frank's face. "What do you mean?" he asked coldly.

"Anything out of the ordinary. You know, some men like it rough."

"And you procure this service?"

"Yes. I'm a fixer. A broker, if you like."

"I don't. You should be ashamed of yourself."

"Well, I'm not. It pays well. A man must take work where he can."

"Honest work, yes. But this is inhuman."

"Fine. If you don't like it, bugger off. Nobody made you my judge and jury."

"Keep talking, Clarke. So, Esther Prager. Did you fix her up?"

"I did."

"With whom?"

"I don't know. He asked me to find a girl. I found one."

"And that girl was Esther?"

"I don't know why you're banging on about Esther Prager. I thought you were interested in Phyllis, and she came first."

Lawrence flipped his notebook open. "Ah, yes. Emily Dimmock, or Phyllis as you insist on calling her, died in 1907, Miss Prager in 1908 and Miss Templeton a few days ago. Are you responsible for all these deaths?"

"I keep telling you. It's not me. Look. Let's talk about Phyllis. It's easier to explain."

"Go ahead."

"Back then, most of my jobs involved modelling, and I gave a lot of them to a girl called Ruby Young."

"Robert Wood's sweetheart. I've met her. She said she'd been an artist's model, but I assumed she sat for Mr Wood."

"No. Ruby gave Wood an entirely different service," said Frank wolfishly.

"Continue."

"So, I dished out a few jobs to Ruby and one or two other girls, and they liked it. I mean, it was simple work, like I said. Now, Phyllis wasn't short of a bob or two. She had a man at home, and he kept her well. But Phyllis was a good-time girl with a past. And old habits die hard. She wasn't averse to some extra while her man was away. The poor chump had a job on the railways, and Phyllis spent most of her nights alone. So, she did what she wanted with no interference from him. And what she wanted was readily available. And that, I think, was the problem. I wouldn't say that Phyllis liked a bit of rough, but she wasn't fussy either. I put her in touch with one or two men with that sort of taste. They paid well, and she seemed happy. Job's a good 'un. Now, the year before, a man had approached me outside The Eagle and asked me if I was interested in earning some extra money. Naturally, I said yes, and he asked me to find him a girl who was happy to provide a certain service in the comfort of her own home. He was very particular in that regard. No knee-tremblers in the streets for him. I agreed, and we shook on it."

"What did this man look like?"

"I don't know. He wore a cloth over his face, kept it hidden like."

"Could you recognise him again?"

Clarke shook his head. "Not possible. His scarf, hat, and cloak covered all identifying features."

"He sounds like a pantomime villain."

"Probably didn't want some smart Alec private detective asking silly questions."

"What happened next?"

"We tussled over payment. I would only give him a name and address once he'd paid me, and he refused to hand over the coins without the information. It nearly scotched the deal. And then he agreed to pay half in advance and half after he got what he wanted."

"Which was?"

"An audience with the young lady."

"Emily?"

"Eventually. But Esther was first, and another couple of girls before her who came to no harm."

Lawrence leaned forward, waving his finger.

"Let me get this straight. This stranger paid you half a fee, you gave him a name, and he visited the girls. How did you get the rest of the money?"

"He would meet me outside their houses. They'd put a light on the windowsill, so he knew they were expecting him, and I got paid after he left."

"And that worked every time?"

"Until Phyllis."

"Emily."

"Fine, Emily. Then things became trickier. I lived in the Temperance Lodge then and the landlady locked us in after a certain hour. It wasn't easy to get out. But I've done a bit of housebreaking in my time, and if you can get in, you can sure as hell get out again if the will is there."

"Did you facilitate Miss Dimmock's death?"

"Away with your fancy words. If I did, it was unknowingly. My contact had never done a thing to upset any of the other girls. Didn't hurt them at all. He paid for a service he barely used. I had no reason to suppose a problem at that point. I hadn't considered he might have hurt anyone. Not seriously."

"Yet you didn't bother telling the police about him. No wonder you believed in Robert Wood's innocence. You knew damned well he couldn't have done it."

"That's not true. Just because my chap was there didn't mean he killed the girl. And don't forget, someone had made a proper mess of her postcard album. Wood had good reason not to want his card found. The night was long, and Phyllis had many male friends. Who's to say she didn't have others over?"

"That's ridiculous."

"But is it? I felt bloody awful when I first heard about Phyllis, like I was the responsible one and had put my hands around her throat and done her in. But the postcard collection stopped me in my tracks. Why would my chap waste vital time sorting through her things? He wouldn't, would he?"

"Unless he was trying to create an alibi."

Frank Clarke's jaw fell open, and silence descended. He chewed his lip as his mind worked through Lawrence's words. "He didn't need one. I wouldn't have told anybody."

"Did he know that?"

"Not then. But he must have trusted me because he came back again."

"After her death?"

"Not immediately. A good few months later, by which time Robert Wood was on trial. I hoped he was guilty, although I didn't think so deep down. But there was enough room for doubt to overlook the matter."

"What about Esther the previous year?"

"Ah, Esther. It was the usual pattern. He paid over the odds for another couple of girls, but when I spoke to them later, he'd been a perfect gentleman with no fornication involved. It was almost as if he had been rehearsing."

"Did they see his face?"

"Never. That was their only concern. Both found it sinister. He didn't cover his entire face, just the lower half, with a neckerchief."

"And Esther herself?"

"I gave him her address and turned up at her flat after dark. I should have been more careful. A nosy neighbour saw me and ratted me out to the police. Their description was of me, not him."

"How do you know he didn't look like you if you've never seen his face?"

"The height was all wrong. That chap towered over me

when we met. He was a good several inches taller. And his hair was lighter. I caught glimpses of that. In fact, I took a fistful of it earlier when the rascal came to do for me."

"We'll come to that," said Lawrence, eyeing Clarke's bandaged torso. Blood was slowly seeping through, not at an alarming rate, but enough that their conversation would need to end soon. But Lawrence meant to extract every detail in the short time they had remaining.

"Did this man kill Esther Prager?" Lawrence demanded.

"Perhaps. I don't know."

"He was there that night. You led him to her?"

"I didn't see him. He paid half upfront. I saw the light in her window. He was supposed to meet me, but he didn't show."

"Did you get the other half?"

"Yes."

"How."

"An errand boy delivered it to me."

"Where?"

"In The Rising Sun."

"Not The Eagle?"

"No."

"How did he know where to find you?"

"I'm usually in one place or the other. All my acquaintances know that."

"And how long did you wait for the second half of your fee?"

"A few days."

"So, you can safely assume it was for services rendered."

Frank Clarke shrugged. "Probably."

"So, your man killed Esther Prager. You might as well have tied a bow around her and handed him a knife."

"It wasn't certain. Someone else could have done it."

"No. You caused her death as surely as if you had killed her. And if you carried on providing girls after that, their blood is entirely on your hands."

Clarke narrowed his eyes and glared at Lawrence without a flicker of remorse. "What are you going to do about it then? Grass me to the law? Because there is no proof. Not a bar of it."

"Did you procure Lily Templeton?"

"No."

"I don't believe you."

"That's your lookout."

Lawrence darted forward, took the remains of Frank's shirt, and twisted his hands around the fabric, pulling Frank from the bed. Lawrence thrust his face towards Frank's until their noses were almost touching. "If you don't tell me the truth, so help me God, I'll finish what he started."

Frank Clarke curled his lip. "The hell you will."

Releasing one hand, Lawrence took two fingers and jabbed them into the bandaged wound. Frank shrieked in pain. Lawrence moved his hand as if to strike again.

"Don't do it," yelled Frank. "You make that hole any bigger, and my guts will fall out."

"It couldn't happen to a nicer guy," Lawrence snarled.

"No point in patching me up only to half kill me."

Lawrence raised two fingers to Clarke and positioned them over his voice box. "I'll take that chance," he whispered. "Now, answer my question. Did you offer Lily Templeton to this maniac?"

"No, I never."

"Then why does the police description match you again?"

"God. Tell me it doesn't."

"I'd be lying. It's the same as the other three."

"Not three. I had nothing to do with Dora Kiernicki."

"But you did with Miss Templeton?"

"Only in so far as I had already spotted her as a prospect. I mentioned it to him sometime before, but we never shook on it, like. No money changed hands."

"But she agreed to see him."

"In principle, but we didn't arrange it. Maybe the dogs put him off."

"Then why were you there?"

"Don't jump to conclusions. That description matches half the men in London."

Frank Clarke flinched as Lawrence's fist cracked into his face. "I told you not to mess me around."

"Christ almighty. You nearly broke my jaw, you savage."

"Why were you outside Lily Templeton's flat?"

Frank rubbed his chin and examined his fingers, now damp with blood. "I'd give you what for if I weren't laid up."

"I'm sure. Now answer my question. Why were you there?"

"Because I wanted to check on her."

"You're on dangerous ground, Clarke. Tell me something that makes sense."

"I mean it. He followed me home last week. I was about to enter when I felt a hand on my shoulder, and he was standing there, masked up as usual. I hadn't seen him since I got out of chokey, which suited me – with Phyllis dying, then Esther. Look, deep down, I knew he could have killed them. There, I've said it. He could have done it, and I didn't want to get involved further. And I didn't intend to hand over another girl. Fortunately, he didn't request one but asked me if Margaret Dooley and Lily Templeton were still interested in some well-paid work. I told him that Margaret had long moved away, so he asked about Lily and whether she still lived in Brixton. I didn't see the harm in confirming it because he already knew. I'd given the game away long ago. I rarely give addresses before seeing the money in case I don't get my dues, but I let it out by mistake. He asked if I could fix a time for him to see her and I said no. I wasn't in that game anymore and didn't like what had happened to the others. And he said I should keep my mouth shut as I was as involved as him. I told him to sling his hook, but he laughed at me. Said he'd manage without me this time, but I should watch my back."

"Is that why he visited you earlier today?"

Clarke shook his head. "I shouldn't think so. Trying his luck outside the flat in the dark would have been easier. No one would have seen him. He had a clear run. This morning's visit was far riskier."

"What did he say to you? And how did he gain access?"

"He knocked on the door mid-morning. Just as well I was home, as it's not always the case. I asked who it was and heard nothing but another knock. So, I got up and opened the door. He barged in and threw me on the bed, holding a knife to my throat. And not just holding it but slicing my skin."

Clarke placed a hand over a slim cut on his thorax, faintly crusted with drying blood.

"What did he say?"

"That if I didn't stop squealing, he'd stick me like the pig I am."

"Have you been talking?"

"Of course not. Who would I tell?"

"A drinking companion? A lady friend? Some lowlife you could brag to. I don't know."

"Well, I didn't, and I wouldn't. God knows I don't need

the peelers banging on my door. I've been in enough trouble recently."

"Why did he stab you then?"

"To teach me a lesson so I wouldn't say anything else."

"Why did he think you'd been loose-lipped?"

"No idea. Perhaps it's your fault for poking around in business that doesn't concern you."

Lawrence stopped, looked up and pondered Frank's words, his mind rewinding to recent conversations. "Barely anyone knew I was coming here. Unless. Oh no. Surely not?"

"What?"

"Describe your assailant."

"A couple of inches taller than me, similar build, sandy coloured hair, and like I keep saying, wearing a bloody kerchief, so I can't tell you any more than that."

"Wait." Lawrence gestured for Clarke to be quiet. He clicked his fingers while his brain whirred.

"What colour was it?"

"Sandy, like I said."

"Not the hair. The neckerchief."

"Ah. That. Yes, a big red patterned monstrosity tied around his face."

Lawrence froze. "Did this man ever express an interest in art?"

"Of course. I told you. The first few girls were models."

"Oh my God."

"What is it?"

"I last saw a red neckerchief in Walter Sickert's studio. And my wife is with him as we speak."

Chapter Forty-Four

ESCAPE

I run through London town, still bearing traces of Frank Clarke's blood, red and sticky on my hands. I stare at it, almost hypnotically. Scarlet blends to a crimson crust against a fleshy background, creating a natural masterpiece. I wonder if I can replicate it on canvas. I stop momentarily, lost in admiration, until I almost run into a woman ahead, bumping her shoulder as I pass. She shoots me an intolerant glare, sees my bloody palm, claps a hand to her mouth and rushes on, keen to put some distance between us. Her actions bring me back to earth, and I consider the foolhardiness of roaming the city with another man's lifeblood so readily displayed. I duck into a back alley and find a water trough where I wash my hands. The water is cold, almost set to freeze in the wicked November chill. But I don't care. A man should suffer for his art. I dry my hands on my coat and check my watch. I must return, and soon, before my absence excites any chatter. After all, my contribution is significant. I have much to teach, and they know it. They rely on me, holding me in high regard. Their expectations drive me onward to new and dangerous territory, like my earlier assault on Frank Clarke.

I have left him alive and now I regret it. If I had more time, I could have used him to my advantage and disposed of the problem in one fell swoop. But time was my enemy. God knows, but for a chance remark, I would never have known the interfering detective had found a connection with the man who procured my models. But luck came my way and delivered a chance to correct my error. Clarke may have kept his mouth shut this time, but he'd dropped the odd word in the wrong place before. Fortunately, he was too deeply entrenched to risk divulging details of our arrangement to the law. But in the presence of a busybody investigator fixated on a series of unsolved murders, I had no confidence in his silence. He might have said something seemingly innocent to another, but not to a man intent on righting past wrongs. I could not take the chance, nor did I. But needs must, and I extricated myself from my obligations swiftly and without fuss, arriving at Clarke's house with plenty of time to spare, knowing that it would take many hours for Clarke's pursuer to find his address. With collar up and scarf affixed, I inveigled my way into the house I had seen Clarke enter a few days before and made my way to his disgusting rooms.

He did not expect me and his eyes started in fear as I entered, brandishing a knife. I grabbed Clarke by the arm, twisting it around so I was behind him, holding the blade against his scrawny neck. He trembled beneath my grip, filling me with a power that surged from my belly to my heart. It coiled around me like a warm blanket, nourishing, feeding, and rousing me to greater heights. I nicked his throat because I could. And because I desired to see the blood welling beneath the cut. But for all my might, I remained restrained, cutting only skin deep, unlike the women. It was enough to sate the blood lust and prove I could control myself. I was there to warn Clarke not to kill him. I have never killed without a creative purpose.

I pushed Clarke to the bed while ensuring my scarf stayed full on my face. If he was to live, he could not know me. And I explained again that our acquaintanceship must remain private and that if he ever revealed any details of our dealings, he would end his days in the morgue. He laughed in my face like the fool that he is. So, I plunged my knife into his belly to show him I meant business. Blood spurted from his abdomen and welled in pools around my hand. His face whitened, and his head fell back on his pillow almost in a faint. I could not tear my eyes from the scarlet pool, transfixed by its beauty, imagining the myriad colours on my palette. For a moment, I lost myself in an exquisite world of resplendent hues, seduced by the power of the flowing liquid, almost sentient in its form, until Frank Clarke roused himself and kicked me in the shoulder. The vision disappeared. I jumped up, grabbed his arm, and hurled him from the bed, kicking him into the corner of the room, where he flopped in a heap on the floor. I picked up the knife and kicked Clarke's recumbent body over with my foot. A cursory glance told me that his life was not in immediate danger. He would rally and get help should he choose to do so. I was sufficiently familiar with human anatomy to be sure of that. Job done, warning delivered, I left.

And here I am, navigating the streets with clean hands on my way back. The adrenaline rush has subsided, and tiredness overwhelms me. But it does not displace the urge that burgeons in my belly at the memory of the red. I want and need it, and I shall have it again. My plans are in place. I will enact them soon.

I hail a cab for the final mile, conserving my energy for what will soon follow. A passing carriage slows to a halt. The driver doffs his hat as his ebony horse swishes its tail while steam rises from flaring nostrils. He lowers his whip and jumps down, holding the door open for me to enter.

I mutter my thanks as he slams the door shut, and I sit on the fading green leather.

"Where to gov'nor?" he asks.

"Number six Mornington Crescent," I reply.

Chapter Forty-Five

TEARING THROUGH LONDON

Lawrence Harpham slammed the door and raced full pelt from Frank Clarke's slum dwelling. Taking the stairs two at a time, he stormed down the hallway, barging past a man dressed like a vagrant who fell against the wall at the weight of Lawrence's frame.

"Oi, what the hell do you think you are doing?" screamed the man, but Lawrence did not stop. He kept going through the door, down the alley, back onto Tottenham Court Road, weaving between people going about their business, attracting angry comments, raised fists and a missile thrown in his direction by an angry stallholder. Still, he continued. After a mile, Lawrence slowed, breathless, from sprinting towards Violet. But at the rate he was going, he wouldn't get there. He needed to calm down and deal with the situation logically. Running wouldn't cut it. He needed a cab or, better still, an automobile. Lawrence slowed and reached out his hand, striding along the roadside, left arm outstretched, while looking fixedly ahead. Someone would slow, and then he would negotiate a fee. He walked twenty yards. Twenty yards became fifty. Nobody stopped and his arm grew numb and cold. And just as he thought he must find a better way, he heard the crunch of tyres on stones, and a car pulled up beside him. He glanced to his left, seeing only a private vehicle, and his heart momentarily fell until he heard a familiar voice.

"Lawrence. I thought it was you. Good timing. We need to talk."

"Lonni. Thank God. Can you give me a ride?"

Lonni turned towards his companion. "Gregory, what do you think?"

Lawrence peered through the side window to see a large man sporting a handlebar moustache gesture to Lonni. "I'd really rather not. We're running late as it is."

"It's urgent," said Lawrence. "I'll pay you whatever it takes."

"What's wrong?" Lonni peered sympathetically. He had noticed Lawrence's pained expression.

"Violet. She's in trouble."

"Where?"

"Mornington Crescent."

"That's miles away from the meeting," groaned the moustached man, his grizzled face relaxing into something resembling a walrus.

"You could stretch a point though?" Lonni sported his most winsome smile.

"I'll get the sack."

"Come on. Ginger values you too much for that. I know this man. If he says he needs help, then he needs it badly."

"For God's sake. Either help me or don't," spat Lawrence. "My wife's life is at stake."

"Get in then," snapped Walrus face.

Lawrence hurled open the rear door and flung himself inside.

"Mornington Crescent," he repeated.

"Right. I'm on my way."

The car moved briskly onwards, stopping occasionally for passing horses and careless foot traffic. Lawrence sighed and put his head in his hands each time it slowed.

"What's going on?" asked Lonni.

"My wife is in the presence of a maniac. A cold-blooded killer."

"What are you talking about?"

"The Camden Killer. Emily Dimmock, Esther Prager, Lily Templeton. Even Dora Kiernicki, perhaps. He killed them all."

"Who?"

"Walter Sickert, the man currently hosting my wife. Thank God she is with other people."

"Thank God," echoed Lonni Carpenter. "When did she get there?"

Lawrence glanced at his watch. The colour drained from his face as he looked up at Lonni in horror. "I hadn't realised the time. She's been there for hours. Everyone else could be long gone."

Chapter Forty-Six

WALTER SICKERT

The car drew up at the junction of Mornington Crescent and Hampstead Road. "Out you get," said Walrus face.

Lonni turned to Lawrence.

"I'll come with you. Wait here, Monty."

"No can do. I'm in a rush, as you well know. And you should be with me."

"I can't leave a friend in need. Lawrence, do you...?" But his words trailed away as Lawrence wrenched open the car door and pelted down the street.

"I'll see you later," said Lonni, following behind.

Lawrence reached 6 Mornington Crescent first, pulling and pushing the door as he tried to gain access. The door stood firm. He backtracked and stood appraising the building, trying to decide how best to gain access. He hadn't time to search for a rear door, assuming one existed. And the ground-floor windows were too badly situated to reach without risking harm.

"Bloody hell," he spat, casting an exasperated glance towards Lonni. Lawrence gritted his teeth before vaulting over the iron railing and landing beside a locked basement door. One futile attempt to open it was as much time as Lawrence was willing to waste. He glanced by the door, noticed the boot scraper was in poor repair and kicked for all he was worth. The most damaged side snapped easily away, but it took a few more attempts for the second side to cleave from its support, by which time Lonni was by his side.

"Try to stay lawful," Lonni pleaded as Lawrence grasped the scraper in his hand. But it was too late. Lawrence wielded it like a weapon, smashing it through the basement window as shards of glass splintered onto the tiled floor beyond. Lawrence reached into his pocket and slid his hands into leather gloves before pushing the remaining glass pieces through to create a safe access point. Then he hoisted himself onto the window ledge and entered the basement.

"Wait for me," said Lonni.

"Hurry."

"I will, but there's safety in numbers."

The two men pressed on, powering through the lower floor, opening doors, peering inside, and trying to keep silent despite the noise of their entry. Lawrence worked carelessly, his worry for Violet transcending due caution. But Lonni remained hopeful that Sickert wouldn't have heard the commotion if occupied on the upper levels of the house. The basement cleared, the two men ascended to the ground floor, treading lightly as the wooden stairs creaked their disapproval.

The silent drawing room confirmed Lawrence's worst fears. The meeting was over, with the artists long gone. And judging by the tidy interior they had left some time ago, all traces cleared away by a diligent cleaner or possibly Sickert himself. Lawrence's spirits plummeted. "Where the hell has he got to?" he asked. "And where is Violet?"

"Probably back at the hotel," said Lonni reasonably. "You should have started there."

"Don't think I didn't consider it," said Lawrence. "But I couldn't risk wasting time and leaving her here. And I must stop Sickert at all costs. He's a triple murderer, for God's sake. Possibly worse."

"But not at home, I fancy. We should go."

"Not yet. Not until we've searched every corner of this damned building," said Lawrence. "I must be sure Violet isn't here. And if Sickert is absent, I will try his workshop. So help me, I will hunt this monster down."

Lonni shook his head resignedly. "Very well. Onwards."

They quickly checked the rest of the floor and proceeded upwards. "Just another two floors to go," sighed Lonni.

"Leave if it's bothering you."

"There's no need for that, old man. I know you are worried, and I'm right behind you."

"Thank you. I apologise."

Lonni clapped Lawrence on the shoulder, saying nothing further and letting the gesture speak for itself. Then he followed behind as Lawrence led the way, stopping suddenly at the top of the stairs.

"What's that?" hissed Lawrence.

"I don't know."

Lonni cocked his head. Lawrence waited. The noise started again, a rhythmic creaking sound coming from farther down the corridor.

Lawrence pointed his finger and gestured. Lonni nodded. They silently picked their way down the landing, past the large front room Sickert used for his gatherings and listened outside the door to the rear room.

"Not there," said Lonni, pointing upstairs. "It's higher."

"So it is." Lawrence climbed the third set of stairs. The creaking grew louder, started, stopped, and began once again. They approached the closest room, Lawrence in front of the door, Lonni behind him.

"Ready?" asked Lawrence.

Lonni nodded.

Seconds later, the door crashed open and bounced against the wall as Lawrence and Lonni powered inside. Lawrence spotted a tennis racket propped against the wall, grabbed it, and held it aloft, towering over Sickert and his recumbent partner.

"What the hell?" yelled Sickert, covering his manhood as he darted from the bed. The woman turned away, burrowing her head into the pillow. But even without a full view of her face, Lawrence could see it wasn't Violet.

"Get dressed and go," said Lawrence coldly.

"How dare you?" Sickert, who had swiftly slipped into a smoking jacket, confronted Lawrence, his face contorted, cheeks glowing red with rage.

Lawrence ignored him. "Here," he said, handing the woman garments neatly piled on a wooden chair. "We'll leave you to it, madam. Mr Sickert, follow me."

"I will not."

Lawrence brandished the tennis racket again. "You will if you know what's good for you."

"You had better go, Sally. We'll speak tomorrow. I am sorry for this intrusion."

"As well you might be." The occupant of the bed had found her voice. The shock had subsided, and she sat up, arms crossed over her full, mature breasts, no hint of shame.

Lawrence looked away, opened the door, and gestured. "I'll be right behind you," he said as Sickert left the room, scowling.

"That way." Lawrence pointed downstairs as Lonni slipped ahead of Sickert, who looked even angrier, sandwiched between the two men. Lonni stopped abruptly outside the front room. "Will this do?"

"Perfect."

They stepped inside; Lonni lit the mantle, then four more wall lights, glancing outside as the insipid afternoon sun faded. The room still contained easels, all now empty. The small lectern from which Sickert earlier pontificated had been moved to one corner and covered with a sheet.

"Sit," said Lawrence, pointing to a small settee.

"You'd better have a good explanation for this madness," snapped Sickert, his handsome face a mask of hostility.

"My sentiments entirely," said Lawrence, pulling up a wooden chair. He sat directly before Sickert, and Lonni naturally gravitated to Sickert's side without being asked – a loyal and instinctive henchman.

"What do you mean?"

"That you had better have a bloody good reason for your actions. Not that there could be any justification for killing women."

"What are you talking about?"

"I haven't time for this," said Lawrence.

"Then make it. You barge into my house, interrupt my lovemaking, and order me around as if you own the place. How dare you. I made you and your wife welcome in my home, and I deserve better treatment."

"Talking of Violet, where is she?"

"I don't know."

"You must. She was with you only a few hours ago."

"And then she left with the others. Probably returned to your hotel, but I'm not her keeper, and she didn't confide in me."

"Who did she leave with?"

"Freddy, I think. Possibly Maxwell too. Oh, and Leonard, I assume. They intended to paint at the Fitzrovia workshops, near your hotel."

"Did they go by vehicle or on foot?"

Sickert cast his eyes heavenward and thought for a moment. "Foot," he said confidently. "I saw them strolling up the street."

Lawrence emitted a deep sigh and put his head in his hands. "Thank God," he said.

Lonni chewed his lip. "If you believe him."

"Are you sure, Sickert? God help you if you've misled me."

"You are off your chump, Harpham? Why this sudden hostility? I wouldn't harm Mrs Harpham. Unlike you, she is a charming, dignified woman who I greatly esteem. God knows why she tolerates a man like you."

"Be quiet. Let me think." Lawrence crossed his legs, placing the racket over his knees. Silence fell. Sickert fidgeted.

"No, I bloody well won't be quiet. This is my house, and I demand an explanation."

Lawrence raised his head and looked up, his eyes boring into Sickert's. "Dora Kiernicki, Emily Dimmock, Esther Prager, Lily Templeton," he said, exaggerating each syllable.

"I know who they are." Sickert looked back, a flicker of interest in his grey eyes.

"As well you might."

"What's that supposed to mean?"

"Murder," said Lawrence. "Cold-blooded murder. And if I hadn't got to Clarke in time, you would have increased your total by another."

"You're mad," said Sickert, his eyes anxiously darting around the room as if genuinely fearful of potential lunatic behaviour.

"Not me, you," said Lawrence.

"I don't know what you are talking about."

"Do you deny knowing Frank Clarke?"

"Who?"

"Frank Clarke. A career criminal and general lowlife with an interesting sideline in finding unusual sexual partners for those in need."

"Do you think I need any help in that department?" Sickert sat up, chest thrust out, peacocking.

"He has a point," said Lonni.

Lawrence ignored him. "If Frank Clarke doesn't get himself patched up today, he will probably die from his injuries," said Lawrence. "Though why you didn't finish him off is a mystery. It would relieve the world of another selfish, undeserving waste of air."

"Shut up," said Sickert. "You're talking rot. I don't know this man. I have never met him before in my life, and I have no intention of ever crossing paths with him. You are mistaken."

"Did you solicit him to find models?"

"No."

"Have you ever done so?"

"Never."

"Did you ask him to find you a woman prepared to indulge in intercourse under unusual conditions?"

"What do you mean by that?"

Lawrence shifted awkwardly. "I'm not entirely sure. Roughly, I suppose. Intercourse with violence."

"Non-consensual?"

"No. With an agreement for a fee."

"I do not use prostitutes."

"These women were more than that. At least they took their clients home."

"I do not need such women. I have been married and had more than my fair share of lovers."

"Then why did you assault Frank Clarke?"

"I did not. For the last time, I've never met the man."

"Where were you mid-morning?"

"Here. You saw me and I did not leave."

"Can you prove it?"

"Of course. You need only ask Mrs Harpham, who was here the entire time."

"And when did this meeting of yours finish?"

"Around midday, possibly a few moments later."

Lawrence raised his hand to his temple and considered the matter. "That would be too late. Clarke said his attacker appeared in the morning. And he'd been bleeding out for some time. The blood was drying."

"Then Sickert couldn't have attacked him." Lonni stood, briefly paced the room, and returned to his starting position.

"I told you," said Sickert, smugly. "Now leave my house before I call the police."

"I haven't finished," said Lawrence coldly. "I had good reason to assume you had attacked Clarke."

"Do tell." Sickert adopted an indulgent, sarcastic tone.

"Many of Clarke's girls were artists' models."

Sickert sneered. "London is full of painters. It means nothing."

"And the man who attacked Clarke wore a red neckerchief. Frank Clarke never saw him without it."

"I admit to owning one which I frequently wear in my studio." Sickert momentarily lost his composure and a worried frown crossed his face. "But I am not alone in that regard. They have all taken to doing it. Flattering their mentor, I like to think."

"Who?"

"Freddy, Maxwell and Leonard of course."

"But they were all here earlier today."

Sickert leaned forward, put his head in his hands and took a sharp intake of breath."

"What is it?" Lawrence snapped the question, sensing a change in the atmosphere.

"They all popped out at one time or another," said Sickert. "It wasn't a formal meeting. My guests come and go."

Lawrence paled. "How well do you know these men?"

"Like brothers," said Sickert.

"Are they capable of murder?"

"No. Of course not."

"Then why do you look so fearful?"

"It's nothing. I'm sure they couldn't hurt anyone. They are admirable men who will do anything for their art. But murder is a different matter.

"I've heard enough," said Lawrence. "They had the opportunity, if not the motive. I must find them."

"Indeed, you must," said Sickert. "As much as I trust their integrity, the last time I saw them, they were leaving with your wife."

Chapter Forty-Seven

PLANNING THE NEXT KILL

I see her leaving as I return, breathless and sated from my emergency foray into London town. I had not planned my morning that way, but a chance conversation turned my day upside down. Fortunately, my able acquaintances stepped in at short notice, my absence barely registering for the bare hour it took to perform my task. I am back at the house, but there is little point in entering, especially as she is on the doorstep saying her goodbyes. I join the others, chat for a moment and we all set off in different directions. Then, I run ahead and conceal myself behind a bush, crouch, and wait. Five minutes later, she passes by.

My quarry walks quickly, soon lost in the crowd of pedestrians milling along the pavements, this way and that. She passes a boy bearing a newspaper board, a man shining shoes on the corner, a flower girl, and a woman whose sunken eyes and pockmarked face are familiar to me. Not personally, but as one of the night creatures I often pass, desperate, diseased, and willing to sell all for a bottle of gin. Still, my prey moves along, bustling ahead with a clear purpose.

Any moment now, I expect her to stop and hail a cab or board a tram. Perhaps even hire an automobile. She carries several bags, unlike most women of her class who typically travel comfortably. But not her.

This lady strides forward, determined to use her legs. She is physically fit for a reason.

The Hampstead Road shop hoardings fade away into residential housing, some properties in good condition, others poorly maintained. She scurries by, but my eye alights on the architecture beside me. I take in the regularity of the stucco fronts, the symmetry of iron railings, and the beauty of variations in the red brick, each a balm to my soul. They briefly distract me from my task.

But then she stops and takes a moment to look around. She drops her bags to the floor and turns three hundred and sixty degrees. I slip into an alleyway, my heart thumping. Has she seen me? I must wait it out, but not for too long. Or she will move away, and I will not catch her in the crowd. This is the most opportune moment I can hope to get while she is alone and away from familiar things. But the most challenging part is yet to come. I cannot approach her outside, so I have planned my move to the finest detail. I could not easily influence the timing, which up to now has been troubling. Had fate not stepped in, I would have lured her partner away. But this won't be necessary if I take care now. Decisive action is the order of the day.

I check my watch. An entire minute has passed, and I crane my neck around the alleyway to see if she has moved. She has left my sight and I must find her immediately.

I hasten along the street, hoping she is still on the Hampstead Road. It is long enough, and given that I know her likely destination, she has little reason to deviate from it. But she might enter a shop on a whim or pause to inspect an interesting landmark. I must not lose her.

My body stiffens as I approach the gates of the Temperance Hospital. It looms tall and domineering, its facade scarred by external stairs that have no place at the front of a building. And if that wasn't bad enough, someone thoughtlessly built an ugly extension to the front and subdivided it into square shops. They squat there like unwelcome intruders, one selling medical supplies, another groceries. Two are unused and in danger of dereliction. As much as I dislike the structure,

I linger by the fifth building, now selling tobacco and other sundry products. My eyes alight on a row of shiny smoking pipes, bringing a surge of disturbing memories of hospitals. My brother George was a smoker and he died in a ward.

Medical establishments are there to provide aid and save lives. But in my experience, once you're in, you're more likely to come out in a box, just like George. He did not die in this hospital, but another one like it – a hospital for cholera patients. George became ill in the 1890 epidemic, tearing our family apart and breaking my mother's heart. Not for long, for she soon succumbed to the same disease. Tears prick my eyes at the memory. I involuntarily shiver, dig my nails into my palms, and swiftly move along.

I fear I have lost my quarry as I glance down the road to a sea of heads, none of which looks like her. But I continue along, hoping against hope that our paths will cross again. And just when I am about to give up, I see her emerge from a baker's, cake in hand. Weak with relief, I watch with heightened imagination. I cannot see her bite through the bun nor witness the pleasure on her face as she tastes the sweet treat. But I know she eats it on the move, for she soon deposits the empty brown paper bag in a metal bin by the side of the road.

She moves onwards, oblivious to my presence, sashaying along London's busy streets. We are close to our destination now and my heart quickens in anticipation of what I must do before I can indulge in the fruits of my labour. I must not allow myself to gain enjoyment. It is a task, not a pleasure. But a flicker of fierce anticipation burns inside me and for a moment, the swell of excitement makes me ashamed. I push my feelings away, deep into my soul, with my unacknowledged desire for the deed I am about to commit.

She approaches the entrance to the hotel and I linger far behind. Following her is no longer a priority. I thought she might come here, but it's all about the timing. Other people limit my opportunities. Her husband may return at any moment, compelling me to abort the plan. He is currently elsewhere, but for how long, I cannot say. So, time is of the essence, yet I must be careful not to draw attention to myself. I must be a spirit, a wraith, a spectral presence lingering on the periphery, a tactic that has served me well until now. Nobody has ever seen me nor knows I exist in the context of my crimes. Descriptions arrive aplenty, but they are of another man, not me. I have played the game well.

I lurk for another five minutes and cast an eye to check that no other interested parties have followed behind. The coast is clear, and having rehearsed before, I know where I must go to enter unseen. I will knock at the door and she will have no reason to deny me access. My presence may surprise her, but it will not excite suspicion. And then I will strike.

It is time. Destiny calls. I must do my duty.

Chapter Forty-Eight

TOO LITTLE TOO LATE

Lawrence left Mornington Crescent, running south down Hampstead Road, his only thought to reach Violet as soon as possible. He sprinted onwards, easily outrunning Lonni Carpenter with long, rangy strides. He had run half a mile before a horse and cart pulled up beside him, and a familiar voice yelled. "Wait."

Lonni was sitting astride an ironmonger's cart pulled by a sweating pony. "Get in," Lonni commanded.

Lawrence pulled up and doubled over as he fought to recover his breath.

"Good plan," he whispered, panting hard. He vaulted into the cart and sat on a dirty, upturned box. The driver nodded to Lonni.

"Carry on," he replied.

"Speed up," hissed Lawrence.

"Don't worry, I will," the driver replied. "As long as there's something in it for me." He cracked his whip, and the horse galloped on, careering towards London with little regard for the traffic.

"I'd never have kept up," explained Lonni. "I'm too old and unfit. But I ran into this chap, slipped him a few shillings and Bob's your uncle."

"Well done," gasped Lawrence, still fighting to catch his breath. "I'll see you right." He reached into his pocket, but Lonni held his arm.

"No need," he said firmly. "Let's find Violet. Though I'm sure she'll be perfectly safe."

"I'm not," said Lawrence. "Whoever roughed up Frank Clarke is capable of anything."

"But they had a reason to hurt him," said Lonni. "He sounds like a man who can't keep his mouth shut. Violet has hurt no one."

"Neither did Emily Dimmock or the other women."

Lonni chewed his lip, struggled for a suitable response, and gave up. The cart rocked from side to side, and the men gripped rough wooden struts to stay balanced. Every pothole, every bump in the road disturbed them and, worse still, slowed things down. But it was not for want of trying. The driver leaned forward, pushing his horse ever onward while Lawrence closed his eyes and tried to banish dark thoughts of not arriving in time.

They screeched to a halt at the front of the hotel, Lawrence jumping from the cart before it had fully stopped. He raced into the foyer and took the stairs two at a time. Lonni lingered, paid the driver a few more coins, and followed Lawrence upstairs. By the time he arrived, Lawrence was trying to insert his room key with shaking hands.

"Is your wife inside?" asked Lonni.

"I don't know. She didn't answer the door or reply to my knock."

"Let me." Lonni tried to take the key, but Lawrence

refused. "I can do it," he growled, finally inserting it into the hole and opening the door. He paused for a moment before peering inside.

Lawrence blinked as his eyes grew accustomed to the dark room, light restricted by the heavy velvet drapes. But he knew something was wrong before he strode over and pulled the curtains open. It was late afternoon and dark, but feeble daylight illuminated the room, revealing rumpled bedding and an upturned chair.

"Oh Lord. What is this?" Lawrence pointed to a large, red stain on the rug and another by the bathroom door. Blood trails led in two directions, and a red neckerchief lay on the floor. Lawrence picked it up and gasped.

Lonni placed a hand on Lawrence's shoulder. "Steady on, old man."

"Where is Violet?"

"I don't know."

Lawrence strode towards the window, hauled it open, and retched. But the minimal food he had eaten while traversing London remained inside.

"We'd better call the police," said Lonni.

Lawrence nodded, momentarily paralysed into inaction.

"I'll go."

The door closed as Lonni left, and Lawrence switched from terrified husband to intelligent detective. The blood stains ran towards the entrance but also beyond. He paced towards the bathroom and tried the door. It didn't move. He tried it again. The door wasn't stuck but locked from the other side. Relief coursed over Lawrence. Violet must be there. He banged on the door. Silence. "It's me, Violet. Open up."

Another volley of raps. Nobody moved. Then, without further hesitation, Lawrence shouldered the door, splintering the wood. He tried several more times, and finally, the lock gave. Lawrence pushed the door open. It hit something soft and stopped.

Violet lay in a pool of blood on the tiled floor. Lawrence gasped, got to his knees, and turned her over. Her head flopped backwards, her face as pale as a marble statue. Lawrence placed his fingers on her neck – barely a pulse. Choking back tears, Lawrence lifted his injured wife, his face close to hers as he carried her to the bed. "Hang on, my darling girl. We'll fix you up in no time. Tears rolled down his cheeks as he stroked her hair. He unbuttoned Violet's jacket to see a jagged tear across her breast, wet blood matting her new navy dress. The wound was deep but away from her vital organs. Yet the blood spill was immense and Violet would die if she lost any more. Kissing her greying lips, Lawrence ran towards the door, almost crashing into Lonni, the hotel manager, and a young receptionist along the way. "Help me," he said.

"Have you found her?" Lonni stared at Lawrence's bloodstained hands.

"In the bathroom. She must have locked herself in before passing out."

"Get a doctor," said the manager, and the girl retreated down the corridor.

The three men dashed towards the room. Lawrence pushed past and sat on the edge of the bed beside his wife. Violet's eyes momentarily flickered open. Just for a second, Lawrence thought everything would be alright. Then her eyelids fluttered, her head lolled back, eyes rolling into the back of her head as a breath rattled in her throat. Lawrence clutched her hand and prayed.

Chapter Forty-Nine

LIFE OR DEATH

Lawrence hated the smell of hospitals. Antiseptic mingled with death with a dash of hopelessness. He'd almost forgotten how much he disliked being in medical establishments, as his last few visits had been just that. Fact-finding exercises with no confinement for him or anyone he cared for. Hospitals were alright if you could come and go as you pleased. But if stuck on a ward with the black dog circling or, worse still, being powerless to help in the treatment of a loved one, hospitals were hell on earth.

And here he was again in his own version of Hades, stuck in a waiting room with Lonni Carpenter, who had stopped trying to say the right thing as no words could help while Violet fought for her life.

They sat silently, Lawrence with his head in his hands, Lonni watching passersby through the dusty paned window. The wall clock ticked loudly. Lonni crossed and uncrossed his legs, wiggled his shoulders, and stood, flexing one leg after another before walking towards the window. He leaned against it, stared for a moment, then approached Lawrence.

"Can I get you anything?"

"No."

"I'm sure one of the nurses will rustle up a cup of tea."

"Thank you, but no."

"Very well." Lonni loitered awkwardly.

"No need for you to stay," said Lawrence. "You've done more than enough."

"I can't leave you like this. Not until we know."

"It could take hours. Please go."

"What about the killer?"

"It can wait."

"I'll meet you at the hotel tomorrow. Unless you're still intent on Fitzrovia."

Lawrence grunted, barely raising his head. The door closed with a creak, and Lonni was gone. Alone in the waiting room, Lawrence felt the weight of hopelessness upon him. The black dog circled, and a rising tide of anxiety threatened to overwhelm him. But Lawrence knew the signs of old. Clenching his jaw, he mentally drove it away, rising above the temptation to sink into a paralysing gloom. He was no use to Violet if he succumbed to depression.

The door opened again, and a pair of metal heels clicked over the floor, presenting themselves in front of Lawrence. He looked up.

"Mr Harpham?"

"Yes."

The man extended his hand. "The name's Lawton. I have just operated on your wife."

"How is she?" Lawrence asked breathlessly, his heart thudding in his chest.

"Comfortable for now. She suffered two deep knife

wounds, both of which caused significant blood loss, but fortunately, did not damage her vital organs."

"Oh, thank God. I hoped that was the case."

"Mrs Harpham must remain here until she has fully recovered."

"Can I see her?"

"Not until tomorrow."

"Please. I must."

"Very well. But for five minutes only. I must insist she has proper rest. And you are required in the lobby."

"Why?"

"The hotel staff naturally reported the assault to the police. They want to question you."

"Very well. But not until I've seen my wife."

"Follow me."

Dr Lawton strode from the room, heading north, then east along the hospital corridor. Lawrence followed, his mind racing.

"Wait," said Lawton as he approached the ward reception desk. "Nurse Jones. I'm permitting Mr Harpham five minutes with his wife. Please ensure that you escort him away when the time has passed."

"I will," said the nurse.

"Where is she?" Lawrence spoke to Lawton's back as the busy doctor sped away.

"At the far end of the ward," said the nurse.

Lawrence strode towards the window, peering behind a curtain. Violet lay there, pale and delicate beneath the half-lit wall lamps.

He took her hand and sat beside her, stroking the back of her hand with his thumb. Her eyes fluttered open.

"Lawrence," she said weakly.

"I'm here, my darling."

"What happened?"

"I hoped you might tell me that."

"I can't remember." Violet raised a hand to her head, closed her eyes, and tried to conjure the memory.

"It doesn't matter. Don't tax yourself."

She shifted uncomfortably in the bed, gingerly touching her bandages, then frowned as clarity crept through the shadows. "There was a man in our room. He went for me with a knife. He must have slipped inside while I was in the bathroom. I came out, and he lunged at me from his hiding place."

"Who was it?"

"I don't know. I couldn't see his face. He wore a red mask."

Lawrence reached into his pocket. "This one."

Violet shrank back into the pillows. "Yes."

"And it covered his face?"

"The lower half. There was something familiar about his eyes, but everything happened so quickly. The mask must have fallen when I fought back, but I didn't see it. I wrestled the knife away and plunged it into his side. But he was bigger than me, pinned me down and took it back again. He stabbed me twice, I think, but I bit him, distracting him long enough to get into the bathroom. I locked the door, and he couldn't get in. I can't remember what happened after that."

Lawrence fought back tears. He leaned over and kissed Violet's forehead. "You fought like a tiger," he said. "And I would expect nothing less from you."

"Was it the same man who killed the other women?"

"Yes," said Lawrence.

"Why me?"

"Because you know him."

"Are you sure? I couldn't see his face. Who was it?"

"One of your artist friends."

Violet's hand flew to her mouth. "Surely not. You must be mistaken."

"The nurse will soon make me leave, but tell me this first. Did Walter Sickert leave his house at any time this morning?"

Violet licked her lip in contemplation. "No. Not for a moment."

"Then he told the truth. It was not him."

"Then who else?"

"One of the others. They all wear red neckerchiefs when they paint."

"How do you know?"

"Sickert told me. Can you remember anything else that might help?"

Violet's face fell and she nodded, looking like a small child, lost and alone.

"What is it?"

"I didn't think about it until now. But I distinctly smelled turpentine on his clothes. You are on the right track, Lawrence. I thought they were my friends, but one of the Camden artists tried to kill me."

Chapter Fifty

CATCHING A KILLER

Lawrence did not give the nurse the satisfaction of ejecting him from the ward. He spied her moving towards him through a chink in the curtains and squeezed Violet's hand.

"See you tomorrow, old girl," he said. "Sleep tight."

"Be careful, Lawrence."

"I will."

Lawrence doffed his hat as he passed the nurse, negotiated the hospital corridors and made for the entrance. He stood outside, marshalling his thoughts, his coat fastened against the November chill. The night was calm, the evening crisply cold. He glanced at his watch. It was only half past seven. The natural light would have long gone, but the Camden artists had been working on a project. They might still be there, daubing oils on canvas, lost to their cause. And one of them was going to get what was coming to him.

Lawrence set off, striding briskly down a still-busy street, his mind a mile ahead, imagining how he might deliver retribution and which man he would punish. He ground his teeth, jaw unnaturally set as he tried to keep his temper in check. But for her bravery, Violet might have died. She had done nothing to deserve the attack. God knows, she had tried in vain to keep her distance from his investigation, almost as if she had known it might prove disastrous. But he now knew without a doubt that unveiling the Camden killer was in his grasp.

The winter air was biting now, and Lawrence raised his collar. He strode forward, breaking into a slow run as he shoved his hands in his pockets to keep the cold from his scarred hand. No time for gloves, no time for comfort. Onwards, panting, small curls of breath rising in the air. Lawrence slowed as he approached Fitzroy Street, walking more carefully now, footsteps measured. He advanced slowly and scanned the buildings, searching for signs of occupation. Cheerful flames blazed from the gas lamps, masking the weaker light behind curtains, window shutters, and dirty panes. But not so much that careful examination could not reveal life inside.

Darkness bathed Freddy Gore's workshop. No one was at home. Numbers 8 and 21 also stood unlit and unloved, but a weak glow emanated from 19 Fitzroy Street. Someone was at home and about to get an unexpected visitor.

Lawrence had already accessed a studio once through a helpfully left key in the basement door. And he knew the artists shared number 19. He crossed his fingers and hoped to enjoy the same fortune tonight. He was heartily sick of breaking and entering. It all seemed a bit too dramatic, and now that Violet was safe and well in the hospital, time was on his side. He descended the steps, felt for the door lock, and knew he'd been lucky. His hands closed over the key, and he used it. Lawrence entered the house without a light. He could have opened his trusty tin and reached for a candle. But he wanted to maintain the element of surprise. He would slink through the house like an alley cat, feeling his way forward until his nocturnal vision sharpened. He passed through the kitchen, using a glint of light here and there to pick his way through. And by the time he reached the stairs, he knew there was more than one occupant in the house. Voices rose and fell in earnest discussion. Lawrence placed a foot on the tread and cautiously moved, one step at a time. The wood surrendered to his weight, groaning a little now and then, but he ascended with the minimum of noise and made his way towards a chink of light under the nearest door. The door was ajar. Lawrence gave a little push and peered inside.

Three shadows loomed against the far wall, each boxed in by a tall square object, which Lawrence soon realised were easels. They stood there, frowning in concentration, frenziedly painting as if it were the last night of their lives. Covington stepped back, stared earnestly at his painting, and shook his head.

"No," he grunted. "That's not it. Not the same standard at all. Damn, these hands. There will never be another masterpiece."

Gore stopped and looked up, a flash of irritation in his eyes. He moved away from his canvas and stared over Covington's shoulder. "The colours are remarkable," he said. "Quite up to scratch. You are your own worst critic."

"No." Covington pursed his lips. "It's not good enough. I can only paint when inspired and lost in the moment. It didn't happen tonight. It should have. God knows I couldn't have tried any harder."

Lightfoot slammed his brush on a nearby table, knocking a jar of spirits to the floor. "Damn your noise, Len. I cannot paint with all this talking. This is not how our sessions should be. Still your pessimism and let us get on with it. We might yet seize victory from our self-prophetic defeat."

"I cannot." Covington flopped on a settee in the corner of the room and looked glumly towards the window. Lawrence drew back and watched quietly in the background while listening intently.

"You're sweating like a pig," said Freddy Gore.

"Charming."

"Seriously, old man. Are you ill?"

Covington shot him a withering look. "When I want an opinion on my health, I'll ask for one. And it will be from a doctor, not a second-rate artist."

"Take that back." Gore spat the words syllable by syllable.

"I do. I'm sorry. You are a fine artist. I am just frustrated by my talentless offering. Forgive me." Covington looked earnestly before wiping his brow with the back of his hand.

"Granted," said Gore unenthusiastically.

"Shall we call it a night?" Maxwell Lightfoot parked his palette on a nearby table and wiped his hands. "I can't paint in this atmosphere."

"Sorry it hasn't worked out," said Covington.

"It has for me. I'm rather pleased with this. Take a look, Maxwell." Freddy Gore beamed with pride at his canvas as Lightfoot advanced towards him and scrutinised every inch of the picture.

"This has the makings of a fine piece of work. Really, it does. Walter will be proud."

"I think he might be."

Lawrence had heard enough. The artist's self-congratulations were making him nauseous. He coughed and entered the room.

"Good evening, gentlemen."

Lightfoot started, and Gore stared beneath a furrowed brow, but Covington stood, walked towards Lawrence, and offered his hand.

"What on earth are you doing here?"

"Passing by. I saw a light and thought I might look in." Lawrence spoke calmly, toying with them for a moment before revealing his true intentions.

"Sadly, we are about to leave. Our business is concluded for the night."

"It's late for a workshop. You are painting by gas light. Doesn't that have a detrimental effect on your work?"

"It depends on what you are painting." Freddy picked up his palette and dabbed his brush in a swirl of pale blue oils. He placed a carefully considered daub on the canvas. "A dash of light here, another there, do you see?"

Lawrence nodded. "Yes. That's smart. It's lifted the shape and given it contrast."

"Warm light, cool shadows," said Gore, knowledgeably, but Lawrence had moved on, his feigned interest in art techniques already waning.

"I'm not here for a painting lesson," he said.

"I rather thought not." Covington gave a friendly smile, but Lawrence did not return it.

He turned to Freddy Gore. "Where were you this morning?"

"In Mornington Crescent."

"You left."

"Briefly, yes, not that it's any of your business."

"Indulge me for a moment," said Lawrence. "I saw your

mentor several hours ago. He told me where to find you and that you had all been absent from Mornington Crescent this morning. Once again, please tell me where you were."

Gore's eyes blazed angrily. "Not unless you give me a damn good reason for your impertinent question?"

"I'll tell you when you cooperate."

"I went for a pie if you must know. I was hungry. It was almost lunchtime and I had missed my breakfast helping Walter prepare. He did not need my full participation. Satisfied?"

"And you, Mr Lightfoot?"

Maxwell Lightfoot stared at Lawrence like a rabbit in headlights. "M-me?" he stuttered.

"Yes, you."

"I didn't leave the building at all."

"I heard otherwise."

"I see. I left the room, not the house. I needed a lie-down. My nerves got the better of me. It happens a lot."

Lawrence watched the pale young man, insipid, gangly, and far too thin for his height. He could readily believe that Lightfoot lived on his nerves.

"And you, Leonard."

"I went home to fetch a canvas."

"Did you return with it?"

"He did," said Freddy. "We all saw him. Now you promised an explanation. Get to it."

"My wife is in hospital."

The three men exchanged glances. Covington spoke. "Good lord. How is she?"

"Alive, by the grace of God."

"What happened?" This time, Gore responded, his eyes wide with compassion.

"Someone attacked her."

"London is a hellhole. Safe for no man." Gore shook his head.

"A lady should feel secure inside her hotel room," Lawrence spoke calmly, watching each man in turn. All three looked up questioningly.

"I don't understand." Maxwell Lightfoot frowned, a flash of fear crossing his face.

"A man entered my wife's room earlier today and attacked her with a knife."

"Oh, my God. Why would anyone hurt Violet?" Lightfoot was trembling, wringing his hands, eyes darting from side to side.

"Calm down," said Leonard, advancing slowly towards him. He placed an arm around the young man's shoulder and drew him towards the couch.

"Sit down, there's a good chap. There's nothing to worry about. I'm sure Mrs Harpham is perfectly safe."

"No thanks to one of you." Lawrence stood before them, drawing himself to his full height, staring steely-eyed, the picture of authority.

"Don't be ridiculous." Gore returned his gaze.

"One of you tried to kill Violet. And succeeded in murdering at least four other women."

"Are you out of your mind?" Gore scowled, hands on hips, enraged.

"No. I am merely stating facts, which should be easy to prove in Violet's case. The man who attacked my wife sustained injuries of his own. She bravely fought back, causing a wound to his side and a large puddle of blood on the hotel room carpet. And now, you can unbutton your shirts if you don't mind so we can settle the matter."

"No," said Gore firmly. "I simply will not tolerate this. I'm sorry Violet is injured, but it has nothing to do with me, and I will not indulge your whims by publicly undressing."

"You will," said Lawrence, standing in the doorway, hands on each side of the doorframe.

"Or you will make us?" Lightfoot shrank back, his face ashen.

"That's correct, gentlemen. I will force you if necessary."

"You've gone too far this time," said Leonard Covington, still slumped on the couch with his arm around Maxwell. I understand why, but you must see we cannot agree to such an unreasonable request."

"You can and you will."

"Oh, for God's sake." Freddy tore off his jacket, flung it to the floor and unbuttoned his shirt. He raised it to his chest, the pale grey fabric bunched below his arms. Gore was young and lithe, his stomach flat with a faint dusting of dark hairs on the lower part of his belly. But his sides were clear. No wound, no bruises, no signs of a struggle. Lawrence nodded.

"You may go."

"How very generous of you," spat Gore. He allowed his shirt to drop and collected the fallen jacket. Lawrence stepped aside, and Freddy Gore left the room.

"Just you two chaps," said Lawrence, facing the settee.

"Not going to happen, old man," said Leonard.

"Why ever not if you've nothing to hide?"

"I have my pride."

"Not good enough. Shirts up, the pair of you, then we can all go home to bed."

Leonard Covington sighed, slowly stood up and advanced towards Lawrence. He unbuttoned his artist's smock and inched it over his head, revealing a dark brown jacket below.

"Keep going," said Lawrence.

"Well, if you're going to do it, I shall too," said Lightfoot. He stood on Covington's other side, swiftly unbuttoning his jacket and letting it fall open.

Lawrence crossed his arms and watched.

Lightfoot placed his hands on the bottom of his shirt, and Covington fiddled with a button. And then, as quick as a flash, Leonard Covington reached into his trouser pocket. A handwritten envelope fell to the floor as he pulled out a knife. A sharp-bladed, wickedly curved knife encrusted with blood. He raised it in front of him, pointing towards Lawrence. "You'll get out of my way if you know what's good for you.

Chapter Fifty-One

EXECUTION

Lawrence raised his arms but did not move.

"Step away now." Covington barked his orders, lip curled, eyes angry slits in his face. He wiped his brow with the back of his hand.

"Looks like the beginning of a fever," said Lawrence. "An infected wound, perhaps? Violet must have hurt you badly earlier. Good for her."

"What's going on?" stuttered Lightfoot, his eyes wide, pale hand clasped to his throat.

Covington sneered and pushed him away, opening his mouth to speak. But Lawrence got there first.

"Go," he commanded.

Lightfoot looked from one man to the other, torn by indecision.

"I said go." Lawrence boomed the order and Maxwell Lightfoot ran from the room as if the hounds of hell were baying for his blood.

"That's a little more even," said Lawrence, keeping a safe distance from the knife.

"Not really. I have a weapon and you do not." Covington waved the knife menacingly.

"I'm glad you think so."

"What? You're bluffing."

Lawrence slid his hand into his trouser pocket and removed a blunt penknife.

"You couldn't cut paper with that."

"Try me." Lawrence advanced towards Covington, brandishing his weapon, but the other man was quicker, thrusting his knife forward, the blade zipping through Lawrence's sleeve. He jumped back and placed an arm over the area. No pain, no blood.

"You owe me a coat," growled Lawrence.

"Shut up." Covington lunged forward, his knife pointing directly towards Lawrence's throat. Lawrence twisted his head, slammed his arm towards Covington's chest and pushed him away. Covington staggered back, clutching his side. He backed towards the couch as Lawrence followed sensing triumph, but Covington was one step ahead. He reached to the side and seized a brass table lamp, waving it forward in one hand while wielding the knife in the other. "Now we'll see who has the upper hand," he roared.

Lawrence ducked, avoided the lamp, but turned the wrong way. Covington thrust the knife towards him, ramming it into his shoulder blade.

Lawrence howled, turned pale, sickened with pain. He backed towards the door, clutching the knife now stuck in his wound. Blood seeped through his fingers as he seized the handle and pulled it out in one gut-wrenching move.

Covington laughed. "You shouldn't have done that. Now you'll bleed to death."

"Not from a superficial wound, I won't," Lawrence said with false bravado. "And now I have two knives while you have none." Lawrence seized the opportunity, moving forward, a knife in each hand. He jabbed the large blade, now coated with his blood, towards Covington, who easily dodged it and jumped back. Lawrence thrust again, but Covington was ready. As Lawrence lunged, he held the lamp over his head and brought it crashing down on Lawrence's skull, felling him to the ground.

Leonard Covington grinned, reached for the knife and knelt by Lawrence, pointing the blade over his heart. Lawrence lay on his side, head spinning, staring ahead, immobilised.

"Ha." Covington gloated as he edged his foot towards Lawrence's groin. Lawrence flinched but didn't overtly react, preoccupied with the envelope he could see directly ahead. An envelope addressed to Felix Crossley. The same envelope, which moments earlier, had fallen from Covington's pocket. Lawrence blanched, dread washing over him in waves.

"How shall I kill you?" asked Covington.

Lawrence placed a hand on the floor and attempted to sit up, but his head swam.

"Stay on the floor like the dog that you are," said Covington.

"Why, Leonard. Why?"

"You wouldn't understand."

"Try me."

Covington adjusted his stance, clutched his side, and eased himself to the floor.

"Sit on your hands," he commanded.

Lawrence ignored the swaying room and the lump on his head, knowing that any position was better than being recumbent on the floor. Groaning, he arranged himself appropriately and tucked his hands beneath his buttocks.

Covington faced him, knife held in front within an inch of Lawrence's face. He smiled insincerely. "One wrong move and you'll lose an eye."

Lawrence ignored the threat. "If you're going to kill me, then at least tell me why."

"There's no if about it, Harpham. I will kill you tonight. And it may be the bloodiest yet."

"It makes no sense."

"That's because you don't have an artistic bone in your body. No appreciation of form and colour, light and texture. You're all facts and figures."

"What has that to do with murder?"

"You've heard of my masterpiece, *Sunset over Primrose Hill*?"

"On more than one occasion."

Covington jabbed the knife towards him, kissing the blade against his cheek. "Show more respect," he snarled.

"Yes, I have heard of it."

"I painted my magnum opus the night I killed Dora Kiernicki," said Covington. "She was my muse, my inspiration. The blood, the thrill. She galvanised me in ways I could never have imagined."

"You killed her for your art?"

"Of course not. I killed her by accident. It should never have happened."

"Then how did it?"

Covington's lids flickered closed as he sought the memories, then opened them abruptly, eyes glinting with pleasure. "It was a winter's evening, not dissimilar to this," he said. "I was in my studio in Fitzroy Street with an old acquaintance. The other artists were still celebrating the yuletide festivities, but my family did not live in London, and I had no desire to travel to the countryside. So, I remained in town, happily practising my art and accepting the odd visitor.

But whether alone or in company, a man has certain urges. And when I locked up late one night, I saw a young lady heading past my door. I recognised her as a member of the unfortunate class, and my friend Felix suggested I might find a use for her. He left while I pursued Miss Kiernicki to a public house. We talked, agreed terms, and I accompanied her home to her room in Whitfield Street, only a short distance away. The night was eventful in ways I had not imagined, for in the height of our lovemaking, an urge came upon me to put my hands around her neck. I had intended to kill her from the off but thought I might stop myself despite my fantasies. But an earlier conversation with Crossley had fired me to unrestrainable heights. He had gained satisfaction before under similar circumstances and I could not forget the look on his face as he described them.

But Dora objected and screamed, and I could only shut her up with my pocketknife. One slash, and she met her maker. I jumped off the bed and prepared to leave, but a glance at the blood spewing from her neck stopped me midflow. The wound gaped open, and the scarlet tide flowed onto her bodice and the bed sheets. Mr Harpham, you cannot understand the effect such a sight has on the creative mind – the exquisite pleasure gained from watching a living river of vibrant reds dancing to a symphony of pulsating rhythms. My greatest masterpiece lay there unpainted. And all I could do was capture the memory in my mind's eye. I ran to my studio and painted through the night, producing my greatest work, my triumph. Oh, if I could only relive that night again."

"A woman died for the sake of your occupation."

"How dare you. My art is not a job of work. It is my life, my soul."

"And let me guess, you have spent the last few years trying to replicate your early success."

"Naturally."

"Have you ever considered that her death and the quality of your painting were mere coincidences?"

"No. And I never will."

"So, you intend to spend the rest of your life searching for victims, hoping to create another masterpiece."

"I will do whatever it takes."

Lawrence frowned. "Did you plan to kill my wife?"

"In graphic detail. Sadly, she did not cooperate."

"How did you know she would be alone?"

Covington laughed, a bitter sound more like a bark. "Mrs Harpham is always alone. She seems to prefer the company of other men."

Lawrence flinched and tried to hide his reaction to the hurtful remark, but Covington grinned, knowing he had inflicted a wound. "You are dull. Violet appreciates art. You should try it, you know. You might win her back. Oh, silly me. You can't. You have an appointment with my little knife." Covington stroked the blade with his thumb.

Lawrence shuffled. His head had cleared, and now would be the right time to make a move before he lost the opportunity. But there were still questions to ask, many questions. "Did you slash Frank Clarke earlier today?"

"Of course," said Covington calmly. "I must thank you for the tip-off. But for your loud rendition of your proposed afternoon's activities to Mrs Harpham in Mornington Crescent, I would not have realised you were so close to tracking me down. I visited Clarke to shut him up."

"It didn't work. You should have killed him."

"On that, we can both agree. I was unnecessarily merciful, but I will put it right later. Still, Clarke doesn't know my identity. I have always been meticulous in that regard."

"So, Clarke procured the women, and you murdered them."

"That was the arrangement."

"So you could paint them after death."

"Always."

"Was Sickert a part of this?"

"Walter? Of course not." Covington laughed hollowly. "Walter Sickert is a talker, not a doer. He had an unhealthy fascination with the man they called Jack the Ripper. I wonder if that makes me the Camden Ripper. But I care not for titles. No, Sickert followed all the newspaper reports, even canvassing the police occasionally. He spared no effort in learning about his fixation, but he would never wield a knife. He hasn't got it in him."

"And yet all the time, he was rubbing shoulders with a multiple murderer."

"I did enjoy that," said Covington, a smile playing over his handsome face. "I persuaded Walter to paint that awful depiction of Miss Dimmock from the pictures in the penny dreadfuls to set him up as a suspect, should the need arise. But let me tell you this. His work bore no resemblance to the beauty of the original scene, lovingly arranged by my fair hand. His skill is not up to it."

"Nor yours lately," said Lawrence.

Covington leaned forward. "I should cut out your tongue," he said conversationally. "But that will distract me from the task at hand. And my skill is not up for discussion by you. I mentor my friends as well as Sickert, if not better."

Lawrence craned his neck and took a slow, deliberate

side look at Covington's canvas. "Then why is your picture markedly inferior to Lightfoot's and Gore's."

Covington's features scrunched into a mask of fury. He thrust the knife forward directly towards Lawrence's face. But with his hands still firmly below his backside, Lawrence hurled himself sideways, rolled free and darted towards the doorway. Covington followed, staggering as the pain glowed red in his side. Lawrence stood in the entrance as Covington thundered forward. Ignoring his pain and the weakness in his maimed left hand, Lawrence used the doorframe to support his upper body as he kicked out towards Covington. The knife flew from his hand as he crashed backwards onto the carpet. Winded, Covington gasped for breath. Lawrence seized his chance and sat on top, landing a blow on the wounded man's side. Covington's face turned red, his eyes watering. After a heart-stopping moment, he drew a wheezy, deep breath.

"Good. I thought I had lost you for a moment. Death is far too good for you. But a visit to the gallows will be just the ticket."

"It will never happen," said Covington.

"I'll make sure of it."

"No. I have something to barter with."

"What? Your relationship with Felix Crossley?"

Covington stared open-mouthed. "Do you know Felix? I wouldn't have thought you moved in the same circles."

"More to the point, how do you know him?"

Covington stared mutely. Lawrence gave a carefully positioned punch to his kidney, generating a high-pitched scream from the man beneath him. "I'll ask again. How do you know Felix Crossley?"

"I was a member of the order."

"Why am I not surprised? Well, Crossley can't help you,

I'm afraid. He's cooking up some nonsense in the Algerian desert."

"Yes, he was. But he's en route home again to Blighty after a minor health problem. My letter should reach him at his club by the weekend once I've dealt with you and posted it."

Lawrence paled. The weekend was rapidly approaching. They must be far away from London when Crossley returned. Lawrence would need to make urgent arrangements to take Violet home. She could not remain vulnerable in a medical establishment right on his doorstep.

"You're coming with me," said Lawrence, still astride his prisoner.

"Not if you want to know my little secret."

"Get up now."

"The hell I will."

Lawrence swung his fist into Covington's jaw and his head flopped to the floor. He stood for a moment, admiring his work.

Good shot. Now, what can I use to tie him up?

A glance at the floor revealed Covington's discarded smock. Lawrence tore it into three long strips, double binding Covington's hands behind his back with the third tied around his waist, leaving enough fabric to use as a makeshift leash. Then he briefly left the room, filled a tumbler full of water and poured it over Covington's face. He woke spluttering, searching the room wide-eyed until the reality of his situation hit home. "You've trussed me like a turkey," he growled, eyes glinting with hatred.

"That's the idea. Get to your feet."

Covington did not object and resignedly followed Lawrence from the room, limping cautiously behind as if he had not yet found his bearings. They exited through the front door into the cold, dark night. "No tricks," hissed Lawrence, raising his collar against the chill air.

Covington wavered for a moment, torn by a natural desire to disobey. But he was in no position to challenge with his arms out of commission behind him and a hellish headache from the punch. He swayed unsteadily. "Did you hear that?" he asked.

"I said no tricks." Lawrence yanked the waist rope and pulled Covington through the iron-railed gate onto the street.

"I wasn't. I heard..."

But Covington never finished his sentence. A crack shattered through the silent night, followed by the smell of cordite. Covington fell to the ground. Lawrence ducked down beside him at the sound of running feet. He waited until silence descended again before standing and glancing anxiously around. They were alone again.

With fumbling fingers, he pulled a tin from his jacket pocket and struck one match after the other before successfully lighting a candle stump. Then he moved Covington's recumbent body face up with his foot. Blood oozed from an angry red hole dead in the centre of Covington's forehead. Lawrence angrily kicked the iron railing. Someone had shut Covington up, and his secret had died with him.

Chapter Fifty-Two

FRIENDS IN HIGH PLACES

Thursday, December 2, 1909

Lawrence leaned his forehead against the cold steel bars of the holding cell in Tottenham Court Police Station and wondered how it had come to this. The good Samaritan bystander professing to help him after finding him by Covington's body in Fitzrovia had located the nearest constable and told him he had just apprehended a murderer. Lawrence found himself surrounded by half a dozen of His Majesty's finest before being hauled to the station where they took his possessions. They had marched him straight to a cell without a chance to explain, where he had languished for the last two hours. And all the time, Violet lay seriously injured in hospital and unaware of the risk Crossley posed as he travelled ever closer to London. Lawrence paced the cell again, teeth gritted, trying to work out what he should do, his low mood not helped by the loud snoring coming from the next cell. He seized the bars again, shouting for assistance as he had regularly done since his admittance. The usual silence followed. This time, he yelled again and did not stop. Lawrence's voice was hoarse, his throat sore and his temples pounding when the inspector arrived.

"Thank God," he said. "Now, will you listen to me? I can explain everything."

"Now's your chance. I'd have left you all night if it were up to me. But you have a visitor with influence over the gov'nor."

"Who?"

"Never you mind. Best foot forward now, and you can tell your likely story to the boss."

Lawrence followed, ignoring the cold metal against his shackled hands.

"In there."

The inspector opened the door and Lawrence entered.

"Let's get these things off you," said Sergeant Hawkins' welcome voice.

An hour later, with the dual approach of Hawkins and Inspector Wood together with E division's pragmatic chief inspector, Lawrence was making good progress. Hawkins could vouch that he was on officially known business; Wood was a confidant of D'Onston and tolerant of his acquaintances, and the chief inspector only wanted an early night and a good meal. He was open to Lawrence's explanation about Covington's death, if not fully understanding of it. But the tolerable atmosphere briefly stalled when they sent two young constables to pick up Clarke and returned empty-handed. He had admitted himself to a hospital, flatly denying he knew anything about the murders and had never met Leonard Covington in his life. The stab wound in his side was the result of a brawl with one of the homeless men at the back of his lodgings, and he denied ever speaking to Lawrence. The constables had left him in the hospital, intending to bring him back to the station after they'd patched him up.

But all was not lost. Lawrence could describe Clarke's room in detail; down to the unusual location of his alcohol supply, Frank Clarke could prevaricate, but he would have to tell the truth eventually. Though whether they would be able to charge him with anything more than procuring women for indecent purposes was a moot point. Poor, greedy Clarke was not a killer. Covington was. And someone had shot him dead. But despite Lawrence's conviction that Covington was responsible for the Camden murders, the chief inspector was doubtful. Though confident of securing a posthumous conviction against Leonard Covington for attacking Violet, he could make no further guarantees. He insisted Lawrence must not discuss the Camden murders openly and especially not with the press. For all his hard work, Lawrence feared his now solved case would remain forever open in the public eye.

The interview was coming to a close with promises of his imminent release when Lawrence remembered the remark about a visitor and asked the chief constable if he knew anything about it.

"I do. And not one visitor, but three. Sir Mark Brocklehurst has come to your rescue and luckily, I happen to know him. Brocklehurst speaks highly of you. I daresay you'd have had an overnight stay had he not stepped in."

"Mark Brocklehurst is a close friend. I'd be worried if he didn't hold me in high regard. But how did he know I was here?"

"No idea. Let's find out."

Lawrence followed as the chief constable strode briskly

to the front desk. "Hello. There's another one. Best you leave us, Mr Harpham before all your friends turn up."

Lawrence stared with relief at Lonni Carpenter, chatting animatedly with Ann Brocklehurst and her husband. But another familiar face sat away from the group, glowering rigidly behind them.

"Michael," exclaimed Lawrence. "What are you doing here?"

"Looking for my daughter," said Michael coldly.

Chapter Fifty-Three

FLEEING LONDON

Lawrence approached him. "Don't worry. Luna is safe."

"How could you take my child without telling me? I've been beside myself with worry."

"But Violet wrote to you."

"No, she didn't."

"I can assure you she did. I saw the letter."

"Well, I didn't receive it."

"Surely you spoke to your wife when you noticed Daisy was missing."

"Aurora took to her bed with a nervous attack. She's not well at all and keeps imagining irrational things. I thought Luna was with her. And when I realised she wasn't in the house, I asked Aurora. She refused point blank to tell me. All I could get from her was that Luna was safe and that you would be in touch. It's a disgrace. A man should not have to consult a so-called friend for details of his domestic affairs."

"And a wife should not live in fear," snapped Lawrence.

"My brother is dying. He is harmless."

"I haven't got time for this." Lawrence turned towards

the Brocklehursts. "Mark, thank you so much for your timely intervention."

"Your friend tipped me off." Mark Brocklehurst gestured to Lonni.

"And how did you know what happened?" asked Lawrence.

"I have contacts everywhere." Lonni winked.

"Did you know Felix Crossley is on his way back and expected in London at any moment?" asked Lawrence. "Violet and I must leave at once."

"I don't want to run into him either," said Michael.

Mark Brocklehurst pursed his lips. "Is Violet fit to travel?"

"Not in a car," said Lawrence. "She's tough and would never complain. But she's too badly injured, and I don't think the hospital will allow it."

"Give me a moment," said Brocklehurst. He strode to the police desk and spoke to the constable, who directed him to another room.

"What can I do?" asked Lonni.

"Nothing. You've been a good friend to us," said Lawrence. "Without you, I'd still be staring through iron bars. Take a break. Write the story, or as much of it as you can."

"You haven't told it yet."

Lawrence shook his head sadly. "And now I never will. They've sworn me to secrecy, not that the inspector believes my story. If it weren't for Mark, I'd still be inside."

"I'm under no such obligation."

"Wait until the dust settles, Lonni. Who knows. Perhaps this won't end up as another dusty, unsolved case. I guarantee there will be no more murders though."

"Good luck, Lawrence." Lonni extended his hand.

Lawrence watched as he left the station, momentarily distracted from his troubles until Michael spoke again.

"Where is Luna?"

"In Cheltenham. With Vera Ponsonby."

Michael sighed. "Thank God."

"I would never put Luna in harm's way."

"How did she get there?"

"Vera brought her here on Aurora's instructions."

"When all this is over, I must get Aurora the help she needs."

Lawrence shot him a glare and opened his mouth to reply. But Mark Brocklehurst returned from the back office, striding purposely towards them.

"I've called in a favour. A private ambulance is on the way to take Violet to Cheltenham General Hospital. It's all fixed up. Violet should probably hear it from you. You'd better head over there now. And I've asked them to let you travel home with her."

"I must pack up the room," said Lawrence. "But Violet should leave immediately."

"I'll go with her," said Ann. "I'm not working for a few days."

"Right. The car's outside. Let's get cracking."

Mark Brocklehurst's Bentley powered through the streets on its short journey. His chauffeur went through motions at the other end, but nobody had time to wait for the usual courtesies. The doors flew open. Mark and Ann approached the rear to meet the ambulance while Lawrence and Michael headed for Violet's ward.

"I can't understand why Violet didn't telephone me," said Michael, still visibly upset by their perceived betrayal.

"Probably because she thought your judgement was impaired," said Lawrence.

"This is about Francis, I suppose."

"Of course. Neither of us can believe you have taken him in after all the harm he has caused. Brotherly love is one thing, but Aurora is terrified. She has a right to feel safe in her home."

"But that's the point, Lawrence. "It isn't her home. Netherwood belongs to Francis."

Lawrence slowed his pace. "You mean, you have no choice in housing him?"

"Not much of one. He has the legal right to turn us out at any moment."

"Has he said as much?"

"Not exactly. And Francis has reformed, Lawrence, truly. But we have put so much of ourselves into Netherwood. It has become our home. And if we are kind to Francis and care for him in his final months, then Netherwood may become ours."

"I think Aurora would rather be penniless."

"That's easy to say. One cannot live on air. I must provide for my wife and daughter, and my current position comes without accommodation."

"I think you are making a mistake."

Michael sighed. "I'm doing the best I can under difficult circumstances."

"This is it," said Lawrence, approaching the ward door. "I'll only have a few moments with Violet."

Michael nodded. "I'll wait outside."

Lawrence emerged ten minutes later, looking a better colour than before he went in. Violet, sharp-eyed as ever, had noticed a small patch of blood on his shoulder where Lawrence had patched up the knife wound with a piece of Covington's smock. Strictly speaking, it needed stitches, but at Violet's insistence, a ward nurse cleaned and bandaged it while he told Violet of their plans. She reluctantly agreed to be moved by ambulance, only objecting at the thought of Lawrence remaining in London that little bit longer. Violet was confident the hotel could pack and transport their possessions, but Lawrence disagreed. It was a good use of half an hour, and Michael would probably help. Thus settled, he left the ward and found Michael pacing outside.

"Violet sends her love."

"Good. How is she?"

"Much better. Fit to travel. Says we should phone ahead and let Cora know we are en route."

"Good. I'm coming with you."

"Thank you. We can talk more on the train."

The two men strode down the hospital corridors, now more relaxed with each other. Lawrence pushed the foyer door open and headed past the desk before stopping suddenly at the sight of a bald man standing with his back to them. The man turned around as if he had eyes in the back of his head.

"You are quite the hero," said Felix Crossley, gazing at Lawrence through piercing eyes. Crossley was slimmer and more athletic than before. His tanned skin glowed, and his sharply pressed clothes bore no trace of the discomforts of travelling. Lawrence stood before him, lost for words.

"And how is your dear brother?" asked Crossley, turning to Michael.

"None of your business."

Crossley's eyes darkened. "You owe me a child," he whispered menacingly. "And I will collect my dues."

This time, Michael paled.

"I hear you killed my friend," said Crossley. "Now, which ward is your wife on?" His piercing eyes stared directly at Lawrence.

"Leave Violet alone."

"I will do as I please."

"How did you know we were here?"

"My dear Mr Harpham, I know everything. We have unfinished business, you, and I."

"No, we don't. I have nothing to say to you."

"You will in time. Now, either you lead me to Mrs Harpham, or I ask a nurse."

"Never. Stay away from her." Lawrence raised his hand, but Crossley fixed him with a stare.

"If you touch me, I will accuse you of assault, and they will eject you from the hospital, giving me a free opportunity to reach Mrs Harpham without impediment. If you are sensible, you will join me. I know exactly where to find her. I only asked you out of politeness."

Crossley smiled insincerely, then barged past them and headed down the corridor. Lawrence hastily followed with Michael in tow, walking the corridors as if in a nightmare and trying to work out what to do for the best. They arrived at the ward and Crossley strode confidently inside. "Where is Mrs Harpham?"

The ward sister recognised Lawrence and stared quizzically. He covertly put his finger to his lips, and she nodded imperceptibly.

"Mrs Harpham is acutely unwell. We have moved her to another hospital."

"Which one."

"Saint Bartholomew's."

Crossley glanced at Lawrence and grinned menacingly. "My car is waiting outside. I daresay I will beat you gentlemen to it."

Nodding at the sister, he left.

Lawrence threw his head back and sighed in relief. "Did she get away alright?" he asked.

The ward sister nodded. "A few moments ago. I don't like your friend's attitude."

"He's no friend of mine. And thank you for your discretion. I appreciate it."

"My pleasure. Is there anything else I can do to help?"

"Yes. Do you have access to a telephone?"

The ward sister nodded, and they crossed another wide corridor before reaching a small office containing two desks, a noticeboard, and a telephone. She left them there, and Lawrence took the instrument and tapped the handset. He spoke to the operator, and she put him through to the girl's school. He waited impatiently and was on the verge of giving up when he heard a familiar voice at the other end.

"Lawrence. Is that you?"

"Cora. Hello, yes, it is. No time to explain, but is Daisy well?"

"Very. We've enjoyed ourselves immensely. Is everything alright?"

"More or less. Violet is on her way back to Cheltenham in an ambulance."

"Goodness me. "Whatever happened?"

"I'll tell you another time. Please keep Daisy safe. I'll be back on the late train tonight. And do be careful. We've run into Crossley. He's back, and hellbent on vengeance."

"Oh, Lawrence. How dreadful. I'll keep Daisy at the school until you arrive."

"Thank you. Michael will be with me. He's coming to collect Luna."

"Luna? He can't?"

"Why?"

"She's already gone. Aurora picked her up only half an hour ago."

"She can't have. Aurora is ill in her room."

"What's going on?" Michael's brow knitted as he listened to Lawrence. He tried to snatch the phone, but Lawrence moved away, continuing the conversation in single-syllable words.

"I'll see you later," he said, terminating the call.

"What is it? Where is my daughter?" Michael's face paled at the sight of Lawrence's anxious expression.

"Michael. Aurora arrived in Cheltenham a short time ago. Vera handed Luna over, assuming she would return to Bury. But Aurora carried a large suitcase, which, in hindsight, seems unnecessary. I'm sorry, old man. But it looks like Aurora has left with your daughter. And who knows where they have gone?

Epilogue

24 December 1909

Walter Sickert turned the page and delivered the last paragraph of the eulogy he had hastily compiled the previous night. He squinted as he tried to pick out the final sentences while tumbling snowflakes turned the lines into rivers of blue ink. Wiping the wet page with his glove had been a mistake. Sighing, he folded the paper in two and ad-libbed the final words. "For all his faults, Leonard Covington was a fine artist, and I'm proud to call him my friend."

The vicar nodded solemnly while a nearby uniformed policeman shot a look of disdain towards the small group of artists. An elderly woman wearing a heavily netted veil sobbed loudly near the graveside of her boy. Otherwise, the funeral party was small. And for good reason. Leonard Covington would die the victim of an unknown attacker. His murderous part in the Croydon killings was buried forever for lack of hard evidence.

The minister stepped forward. "Would anyone like to say a few words?" Mrs Covington let out a strangled sob. Nobody stepped forward.

"Very well," he continued. "Dust to dust, ashes to ashes." The minister lowered himself on creaky knees, took a handful of earth and sprinkled it on the coffin. Mrs Covington followed, aided by a younger woman, Leonard's sister perhaps. Sickert, Gore and Lightfoot continued likewise, each taking their part in the ritual. Then the small funeral party moved to The White Lion on Egham High Street for an intimate wake.

Sickert passed a few moments with Mrs Covington and her husband, who joined her at the gathering, having been inexplicably absent from the funeral, while Gore and Lightfoot sat alone at a table. Ten minutes later, Sickert joined them.

"You're both very quiet," he said.

"We've just buried one of our own." Freddie Gore sighed and gazed into the distance.

"I know. Leonard was my friend too, and I am as sad as anyone that it has come to this, especially with Mr Harpham's bizarre accusations."

"You believed them. You accused us." Gore shook his head.

"I'm sorry. Harpham was extremely persuasive. He must have found Covington after he left my house and committed a violent attack. Leonard bore all the marks of an altercation according to the autopsy. How Harpham isn't serving a jail sentence, I will never know."

"He has friends in high places," muttered Gore.

"Undoubtedly. But they seem satisfied that he could not have fired a weapon or carried one on his person. But who else could have wished ill upon Leonard? It makes no sense."

"I doubt we will ever know," said Lightfoot, sipping wine unenthusiastically. He stared at the small spread laid on for the wake as if it was rotten.

"Bear up," said Walter, patting his shoulder kindly. "This seems to have taken a terrible toll on your health."

"I'm perfectly well," said Lightfoot unconvincingly.

"If you say so. You gentlemen can sit here all day, but I am ravenous and must eat. Won't you join me?"

Gore shook his head, and Lightfoot stared fixedly into the distance.

"Suit yourselves." Sickert headed off and helped himself to a large slice of game pie, eating while standing up in conversation with the barman.

"I don't know how much longer I can cope with his joviality," said Lightfoot, sipping morosely from his glass.

"Walter means no harm. You must get a grip, Maxwell. You're wearing your unhappiness like a cloak."

"Get a grip? How can I when Covington's mother is in the same room? I dare not speak to her for fear I will reveal my innermost thoughts."

"Do be quiet. Now is not the time."

"Why not? How could there be a more appropriate moment to discuss the manner of our friend's death than at his wake?"

"You'll have us on the end of a rope if you don't watch your mouth, Maxwell. We had no choice. You know it. If Leonard was arrested, he would have talked."

"I wish I had never met him." Maxwell Lightfoot squeezed the bridge of his nose, eyes downcast to the table, face filled with angst.

"Then you would not have produced such a fine piece

of work. Never have I seen more emotion in a pencil sketch."

"It is only a preliminary drawing."

"I know, but it will be a great masterpiece."

"Born from evil. Pure evil."

"But did you not gain inspiration as Leonard promised? You must remember how it was, standing in the room watching a life force ebbing away. Were we not enthralled? Did we not paint through the night trying to capture the scene?"

"I regret every moment of it. Twice, we danced with the devil. I am glad Covington worked alone last time. He would have carried on killing indefinitely, you know. Anything for another taste of his earlier success."

Gore nodded. "I agree. And that is why we had no choice but to kill him in the end. He would have given us away and spilt more blood. We did the right thing but, Maxwell, you must never mention it again, especially in front of Walter."

"Mention what?" Walter Sickert approached the table, licking his lips, a tankard in hand.

"Nothing. We were proposing a toast to Leonard."

Sickert nodded. "To Leonard, may he paint among the angels."

Gore and Lightfoot exchanged knowing glances, then raised their glasses. "To Leonard," they said.

Afterword

I based *The Camden Killer* on the true unsolved murders of Dora Kiernicki, Emily Dimmock, Esther Prager, and Lily Templeton, all killed in London between 1904 and 1909. No one was brought to justice for their deaths, though some have suggested that all four could have died by the same hand.

Walter Sickert had a widely known interest in Jack the Ripper and, according to some Ripperologists, was a serious suspect. Best-selling author Patricia Cornwell remains convinced of his guilt. But Walter Sickert also had an unhealthy fascination with the seedier side of Camden, producing several gloomy works during the early 1900s. One called *'Jack the Ripper's Bedroom'* showed Sickert's lodgings in Mornington Crescent. Another, entitled *'The Camden Town Murder – What shall we do for the rent,'* was painted directly after Emily Dimmock's death.

Spencer 'Freddy' Gore also moved to Mornington Crescent in 1909 and painted in various studios on Fitzroy Street, where other Camden Town Artists also worked.

Afterword

Interestingly, Fitzroy Street is only one block away from Whitfield Street, where Dora Kiernicki died. Gore also painted nudes of middle-aged women in a Camden Town setting but with a slightly brighter palette than Sickert's. Gore did not make old bones, dying of pneumonia in 1914.

Maxwell Gordon Lightfoot was the youngest of the group, born in 1886 in Liverpool. This talented artist studied at the Slade School of Fine Art before joining Sickert and Co. in Camden. His study of a girl created in graphite and watercolour partly inspired this book, which showed a young woman in a nightdress suffering extreme anguish. Lightfoot was no stranger to angst, falling in love with a promiscuous artist's model of whom his parents disapproved. The emotional stress was more than he could bear, and he committed suicide by cutting his throat with a razor.

Leonard Covington does not exist except in my imagination.

Next in the Lawrence Harpham series

When a tragedy compromises Lawrence and Violet's retirement, and with Crossley closing in, the couple must confront the grim reality that escape may no longer be possible.

Turn the page for a free preview…

Shadow Over Malvern: Chapter One

HUNTING AURORA

June 1, 1910

Lawrence Harpham gazed up at an imposing stone facade, its shadow looming as if to swallow him whole. The sun fought through dense cloud cover, casting the building in a grim half-light. Lawrence raised a hand to the sky, half-expecting rain.

"Weather is the least of our problems," Violet said pragmatically. "We won't care once they shut us inside."

They glanced towards the gloomy, forbidding walled entrance enclosing the heavy wooden door to the Semer Poor Law Institution.

"You don't have to do this," said Lawrence.

"I must. You won't get within twenty yards of the women's ward. I'm our best chance of finding Luna and Aurora."

"There are other ways," said Lawrence. "I hate the thought of subjecting you to the workhouse again."

Violet replied with steely determination. "If there's the

slightest chance that Aurora's inside, I'll do my bit. Michael would never forgive us if we ignored this lead."

"Even so." Lawrence sighed as he regarded his wife and soulmate dressed from head to toe in the sorry cast-off clothes he had recovered from a rag-and-bone man's cart. The worn threads barely hung together and emitted a stale smell with a hint of decay. Lawrence had fared better with his outfit, chosen from various disguises he had collected over the years, all moderately well laundered and ready for use. He had donned a fraying suit, applied a fake moustache, and blackened his face, looking like a tramp by the time he finished.

The prospect of entering the workhouse was no more than an inconvenience to Lawrence. But he hated the thought of Violet enduring the indignities she had faced growing up after her family hit hard times. He reached for her hand and squeezed it.

"I hope this is worth it," he said.

Violet adjusted her bonnet, its oversized brim casting her face into shadow. It was too big for her head, but if Aurora was inside, they might need to return wearing different disguises to secure her release. Violet must keep her face well-hidden for now.

"We'll learn something, whatever happens," she said. "If we don't see Aurora, we can cross this workhouse off our list. But if she's there... wouldn't that be a relief?"

"We can but hope," said Lawrence, trying to sound more optimistic than he felt.

They had searched long and hard for Aurora, chasing their tails to find a clue to her dramatic disappearance. Then, finally, they heard a whisper so nebulous that it was almost wishful thinking. It had come from Vera Ponsonby, who remembered a conversation with Aurora from the previous year. Already fearful of Francis Farrow's sinister presence, Aurora had discussed the prospect of disappearing into an institution like a prison and living in plain sight. Aurora had no criminal record, no reason to hide from the law, and was too decent and moral to commit a crime in the name of self-protection. But entering a workhouse was a different matter. It might act as a fortress against an outside world that had failed her. Their supposition was hardly sound logic, but it was all they had.

Vera Ponsonby had acted quickly, contacting various workhouse masters to enquire about January admissions. She had found four potential sightings of a woman seeking entry with a child the right age: two in East Anglia, one in Dorset and another in Staffordshire. Through the process of deduction and applying Aurora's concept of disappearing undisguised in a nearby location, Semer seemed the most likely. But they would only know by finding Aurora. And that required covert detective work and plenty of patience. Aurora, traumatised and on high alert after Felix Crossley's past attacks, was likely to bolt if she saw them. Lawrence knew workhouse inmates could leave whenever they chose, and the slightest mistake could foil their plans.

"Ready?" asked Lawrence, reaching for Violet's hand.

"Ready," she agreed. They strolled wordlessly towards the door, crunching across the stony pathway. Violet grimaced as her thin soles ground into sharp gravel, but she said nothing and proceeded stoically to the entrance. They knocked, and a small hatch opened, revealing a sullen, whiskered face.

"Name?" the man barked.

Lawrence wiped a fine spray of spittle from his face. "George and Jane Rayner."

"For admission?"

"Sadly, yes. A terrible shame it has come to this."

Violet tugged a warning on Lawrence's sleeve. "Too much talk," she muttered.

Lawrence checked himself. "We're down on our luck, guv," he replied, lowering his eyes.

With a dismissive grunt, the man opened the door.

"Get inside," he sneered. "And none of that holding hands nonsense. "Men's ward to the left, women's to the right. You'll wait in the receiving hall until the master is ready to see you."

The man pointed towards a hard wooden bench in a cold, unlit corner of the entrance hall. "And no talking," he continued before passing through a set of double doors. They heard a distant mumble, and he returned, clutching a bundle of clothes.

"Take these," he said, thrusting them at Lawrence. "Now come with me."

"What about my wife?"

"Someone will fetch her in a minute."

"But…"

"Are you coming or not? This isn't the bleeding Ritz."

Lawrence glanced at Violet. She smiled courageously, though he knew she would find their separation daunting. But he followed the man down a long corridor and into a ten-bedded ward that felt several degrees colder than outside. Lawrence perched on a bed while the man turned tail and left without further comment. Moments later, the far door opened, and another two men arrived, one carrying a notebook, the other with a black bag.

The taller, more assertive man barked a series of basic questions, which Lawrence answered convincingly. Seemingly satisfied, he lingered in the background while the other man removed a wooden splint from his black bag and

Shadow Over Malvern: Chapter One

advanced towards Lawrence. After an undignified health check, the medical man ushered Lawrence into the bathroom, where he changed into the rough workhouse garb.

Lawrence's resolve briefly faltered as he watched his clothes bundled into a ball, ready for fumigation. Now unrecognisable and feeling the effects of his lowly status, Lawrence considered Violet's quiet dignity and followed suit, walking meekly behind as the warders admitted him to the able-bodied men's ward. With no time to gather his thoughts, a burly warder immediately set him to work. Lawrence grasped two buckets thrust towards him, one empty and the other containing a weighty rope of dubious quality. He spent the next three hours teasing Oakum from a nail, the tarry fibres scratching welts into his skin. Relieved to be in for the short haul, Lawrence watched the cold, dead eyes of weary inmates performing tasks they carried out repeatedly during the daily grind, marvelling at their powers of endurance. He felt sick with guilt, knowing he was there by choice, but his fellow workers were not. Lawrence worked silently until supper time when he joined the exhausted inmates in the dining hall.

Supper was a calculated, solemn affair; each man allotted a place in a vast, orderly dining hall. Lawrence preferred symmetry to chaos but found the rigid dining arrangements unsettling and the number of men crammed together distressing. God forbid there was a fire. They would never escape.

His potato pie supper lacked flavour, and he recoiled when drinking from an insipid cup of tea tasting like dishwater. Lawrence glanced across the sea of hunched shoulders, silently shovelling food while the guards looked on like circling crows. The vastness of the place unnerved him, its rigidity and unnatural silence designed to break the spirit.

Shadow Over Malvern: Chapter One

By nightfall, Lawrence collapsed cross-legged by his bed, thoughts circling back to Violet, and he reflected on the next part of their plan.

Vera's research had uncovered a diagram that Violet carried with her. If the guards had not discovered it, she would know where to search within the labyrinthian walls for signs of Luna and Aurora. Lawrence had marked an alcove near the kitchen where they could meet to discuss her progress without prying eyes. But it was a mammoth task, and he wondered whether Violet would have time to check the women's wards before tomorrow. If not, they may need to stay another night.

Declining the offer of a card game, Lawrence settled for bed half an hour before the lights went out. Ignoring a minor scuffle between inmates, he fell into a deep sleep until the tolling bell rudely awakened him the following day.

Lawrence had been dreaming of his former home in Bury when the clanging bell put paid to visions of lustrous roses in his walled garden. He sat up with a start and remembered where he was. Still dressed, Lawrence rose and emptied his full bladder under the scrutiny of another inmate, intent on chatting through the most intimate of ablutions. The same man, introducing himself as Bryan, continued the one-sided conversation as they walked to the breakfast hall until the warder became so irritated by the chatter that he stationed himself immediately behind Lawrence's chair. After a depressing breakfast of tea and lumpy oatmeal, Lawrence was ready to put his plan in place, slipping from the column of men to head for the kitchen entrance.

Shadow Over Malvern: Chapter One

"And where do you think you're going?" boomed the warder, his hands on his hips.

"To spend a penny," said Lawrence.

"Oh no, you don't. You know the rules. You can wait until later. It's time for work. Now get on with it."

Lawrence sighed, internally debating whether to risk the warder's wrath. If Violet had completed surveillance of the women's wards, they could leave and walk away. But it would be devilishly difficult to extricate himself with a warder offside if she had not. Sighing, he followed the guard to the workroom, hoping that Violet would know what to do when he did not arrive, inwardly cursing that they had not made a contingency plan for such an eventuality. But neither had foreseen any difficulty getting to the kitchens for their rendezvous.

The morning workday ran from seven to midday, each hour feeling like a week as Lawrence picked and prodded the filthy tar-ridden rope. But he did a good job, and the warders grunted their satisfaction when he presented several buckets of teased-out fibres. His original plan had been to meet Violet after breakfast. Failing that after lunch seemed the most logical prospect. After hours of menial labour, the dinner break was welcome, with the inmates inclined to surge towards the dining room, eager to rest and fill their stomachs. With men moving quickly and in vast numbers, it might be easier to slip away unnoticed before rather than after the meal. Lawrence's thoughts vacillated during his walk between the ward and the dining room, and he finally acted when a stumbling inmate attracted the warder's attention. Within seconds, Lawrence had turned tail and slipped away.

Lawrence slunk towards the kitchen, feeling vulnerable in the silent corridors. As he neared the doors, he could hear the hustle and bustle of busy cooks and kitchen staff beyond. But for all the careful planning, the exposed corridor was a terrible place to meet, with nowhere to hide and no believable excuse for being there. Lawrence waited nervously momentarily, prepared to flee if the doors opened to expose a guard. But suddenly, from nowhere, a draught shivered around him, and he heard a low hiss before turning to see Violet beckoning through a doorway.

"Thank goodness you are here," he said. "I'm sorry about this morning."

"Wait a moment," said Violet. "Quick. Through here."

Lawrence slid through a half-open wooden door and wrenched it shut behind him.

"Good God," he said, peering into the windowless room. "What is this place?"

"A store cupboard, I presume," said Violet.

"But what's that scratching noise?"

"Try not to think about it."

Lawrence shuddered and held Violet close. "I'm sorry I missed you earlier," he said.

"Didn't you make it either?"

"No. Didn't you?"

"Sorry, I couldn't," said Violet. "I was busy keeping Luna in sight. I couldn't risk moving away until I was sure."

"And are you. Have you found her?"

"Oh yes. I'd recognise Luna anywhere, bless her little heart."

"But you didn't see Aurora?"

"Not then. But I first noticed Luna holding hands with a woman. She had her back to me and was too far away to see properly, but in hindsight, it must have been Aurora. She'd have left the workhouse in a heartbeat if they couldn't

Shadow Over Malvern: Chapter One

stay together. Aurora must work, but perhaps they spend the day apart and get together at night."

"I still can't believe Aurora would choose to come to this hellhole rather than take a cottage somewhere."

"How would she do that, Lawrence? Aurora has no income or resources without Michael. However hard her life is here, she has secured food and a roof over their heads at no expense."

Lawrence scratched his nose. "I couldn't do it," he replied. "One night is enough."

"But we're fortunate. I remember what it's like to have nothing. We must help Aurora if she lets us."

"Do you want to risk making contact?" asked Lawrence.

Violet paused and considered. "I can't. If Aurora trusted me, she wouldn't have left."

"True," said Lawrence. "But perhaps time and uncomfortable circumstances have changed her views."

"I don't think we can take that chance."

"I agree. Have you seen enough? Can we leave now?"

"Yes. If Luna is here, Aurora won't be far. We've done enough."

"Good. Because three's a crowd, and we appear to have a visitor."

Lawrence glanced at the ground, where a pair of red eyes glowed from a whiskery face. He took a tentative step towards the door, and the rat sprang.

Violet darted outside without a word, Lawrence following close behind. Lawrence slammed the door just in time to trap the rodent before bolting to the nearest exit.

Shadow Over Malvern: Chapter Two

UNDERCOVER

A quick bath and change of clothing later, and Lawrence and Violet returned to Semer.

"I don't feel right about this," Lawrence said as they approached the entrance for the second time.

"But you look more convincing now," Violet replied. "That hat gives you an air of authority."

"That's not the problem. Arriving together for two days running is too risky. Especially if our whiskered friend is manning the door."

"I see what you mean. Should I go ahead of you?"

"Why don't I?"

"I'd rather do it."

"But, Violet, although it pains me to say it, they're bound to take a man more seriously."

Violet scowled. "It would be a sorry state of affairs if that were true."

"I know. But we must put our opinions aside and do the right thing by Michael."

"I think you mean by Luna and Aurora."

Shadow Over Malvern: Chapter Two

"All three of them. Look, why don't I go first, tell the guard I am expecting my secretary, and you can arrive a few moments later. That way, he won't associate our arrival with the poor, bedraggled couple he saw yesterday."

"Secretary," said Violet stonily.

"Or any other occupation you prefer. What would you like?"

"If that's your attitude, call me anything you choose."

"Don't be like that."

"How should I behave? You may be part of the so-called superior gender, but you are sadly lacking in general knowledge. Women have been eligible for election to the Workhouse Board of Governors for many years. I've as much right to masquerade as an official as you have."

"Oh. Then I'm sorry. Let's assume an equal footing, shall we?"

"Just go, Lawrence. We're wasting time."

"Alright, old girl. See you on the other side."

Ten minutes later, they had independently sailed through the workhouse past the same bearded guard who had admitted them the previous day. This time, he was courteous, escorting them into the master's office where they now sat drinking tea. Violet's mood had improved, while Lawrence still felt the sting of her earlier rebuke. Though hungry, Lawrence couldn't bring himself to accept the offer of a biscuit, having firsthand knowledge of the poverty on the other side of the wall. His stomach growled in protest as the master helped himself to a handful of digestives.

"So, you're on the board of guardians?" asked the master.

"I am. And my companion is also recently elected."

"What happened to old Carruthers?"

"Still grinding along," said Lawrence, hoping his vague lie would convince the master.

"Good. Do give him my regards. I last saw Carruthers a good six months ago. Leaving it so long is unforgivable, but time is always pressing."

"Isn't it just," murmured Lawrence.

"Quite, Mr Gibbs. You did say Gibbs?"

"I did. And this is Miss Sara Craven, who occupies a financial position on the board."

"I see. Now, let's get down to the nitty-gritty. What's the nature of your visit?"

Lawrence hesitated, temporarily stymied. He had planned down to the tiniest physical detail, swapping the previous day's rags for smart clothing. He had also learned about the master's background and habits. But beyond that, Lawrence had not given much thought to extricating Aurora. Fortunately, Violet had.

"The relieving officer is concerned about the provenance of one of your inmates," she said.

"In what way?"

"He thinks she should be in a different union workhouse with an alternative means of funding."

"I'm sure he is not alone in his views. But he is harking back to the bad old days. We are a modern organisation now. Poor Law is a thing of the past. We don't resettle inmates and can bear their costs flexibly."

"Indeed. But an unwise allocation of resources may affect your future access to funds."

"I don't see how." The master pursed his lips and eyed Violet angrily. But she confidently returned his gaze.

"An adjustment would not necessarily be to the detriment of the Union Workhouse. Rather, to its benefit."

"You mean extra income. But why?"

Lawrence and Violet exchanged looks, both now floundering.

Lawrence broke the silence first. "We cannot give specifics."

"Then you don't know?"

"I mean, my lips are sealed." Lawrence nodded and raised his finger to his mouth. Then, for good measure, he extended his hand and reached out. The master returned his grip, his eyes widening at the familiar, secret handshake. "Well, well. As you wish," he said, nodding towards Lawrence.

"Good. Your cooperation would be most helpful."

"And how would you like me to resolve this matter?"

"With care," said Lawrence. We want to remove and relocate an inmate from your institution. Miss Craven knows the woman by sight but not by name. She is likely here under an alias, you understand?"

"I see."

"And we will require her child too."

"When do you intend to remove them from our premises?"

"Today if possible. We have arranged transportation. Please bring them to this office, saying nothing about our plans until they are safely inside. The mother may be unwilling to cooperate, but if you allow us a few private moments to talk with her, we will make things right and be on our way."

About the Author

Jacqueline Beard is a writer and genealogist living in Gloucestershire, with an East Anglian ancestry going back to the 1500s. She writes Victorian murder mysteries and is currently working on books in the Lawrence Harpham and the Constance Maxwell mystery series. Jacqueline's books are a rare mix of true crime and fiction inspired by old newspaper reports. When Jacqueline is not writing or researching "dead people," as her husband so charmingly puts it, she is walking in the glorious Cotswolds with her dog. Jacqueline enjoys technology and spends far too much time on her computer. She dislikes flying, dentists and balloons – especially red ones.